FATBOY AND THE DANCING LADIES

Praise for *Last Orders at Harrods* by Michael Holman

"One of my novels of the year."
Alexander McCall Smith

"Rather like Evelyn Waugh on acid meeting Alexander McCall Smith, veteran Africa journalist Michael Holman's book *Last Orders at Harrods* is an explosion of pure reading joy . . . For the sheer joy and vitality of this book *Last Orders at Harrods* gets my vote as book of the year thus far."
Cape Times, South Africa

"In this satirical feast, Holman hits his mark every time as he exposes the humbug and also humanity of life in modern Africa. With a Dickensian cast of characters in the troubled nation of Kuwisha, and a plot worthy of Waugh, this is a cracking fictional debut. Full of humour, home truths – and anger simmering beneath it all – *this is a book that must be read*."
Aidan Hartley, author of *Zanzibar Chest*

"Gripping, informative, satirical . . . a road map though the social, economic and political landscape of Kenya."
Sunday Standard, Nairobi

"Some devastatingly hilarious moments . . . a satire that should be required bedtime reading at Gleneagles."
Scotsman

"Michael Holman's new Africa novel is the fiction world's answer to Jeffery Sachs' *The End of Poverty*, combining cleverly drawn characters in the curious and poverty stricken nation of Kuwisha with a broad political narrative, exploring the causes of Africa's woes and questioning the wisdom of the West in its continual quest to bring Africa under control."
University of New South Wales, Australia

"This wickedly satirical novel is also a serious critique of Africa's troubled state."
The Guardian

"*Last Orders at Harrods* successfully gets under the skin of African society and politics in a way that is both insightful and amusing without being patronising. Mr Holman cleverly characterises both some of the continent's most notoriously corrupt leaders and some of the most resilient ordinary Africans for whom life is a daily dignified struggle; often by rolling several characters, situations and realities into one thoroughly enjoyable read!"

John Githongo, former permanent secretary, Kenya

"Michael Holman's beautifully realised comic first novel."

The Economist

"Michael Holman's excellent and witty debut novel . . . elevated by his skill at pitching entertaining characters into his tightly constructed, pleasurable plot."

Financial Times

"An immensely important book that fearlessly slaughters sacred cows, cuts through the rubbish and tells it as it is. The plot is educated farce, in the way that Tom Sharpe's novels are, but the message is deadly serious."

Geographic

"A corrupt dictator, menacing secret police, a bumbling British journalist – and the big-hearted bishop's widow who runs the Harrods International Bar (and Nightspot) on the edge of 'East Africa's biggest slum'. These are the spicy ingredients in this sharply written novel set in the fictional country of Kuwisha, lent a wolfish satire by its overtones of Evelyn Waugh's African romp *Scoop*. The author, a veteran Africa correspondent, reveals an intimate knowledge of the rogues, the chaotic chancers but also the innate enthusiasm of the continent. The hack here is Cecil Pearson, hunting for stories while pressing his rather amateurish charms upon a canny young aid worker named Lucy. She, meanwhile, is delighted by the thought of an outbreak of cholera, because of the work – and press attention – it will garner for her. Meanwhile, Harrods' owner, Charity, is being threatened by the London store demanding she change the bar's name. As a World Bank visit to the country turns into a riot, Pearson finds his naïve adherence to the truth in his reports is a distinct handicap. Jolly good fun."

Daily Mail

"The book is charming in its telling of Africa's unique foibles and nuances, in the style that Alexander McCall Smith has recently popularised, but behind the eccentric and ebullient characters there lies a far more steely gaze . . . here lies the book's real strength. It is a precariously difficult path to tread, the thin line between satire and polemic and Holman skirts the problem very effectively. His narrative is a confident one, the characters breathe life and the scenes are wonderfully coloured with detail in the manner that only a journalist could – here comparisons with someone like Jonathan Swift are perhaps not inappropriate."

South Africa Times

FATBOY AND
THE DANCING LADIES

An African Tale

Michael Holman

This edition first published in Great Britain in 2007 by
Polygon, an imprint of Birlinn Ltd

West Newington House
10 Newington Road
Edinburgh
EH9 1QS

www.birlinn.co.uk

ISBN 10: 1 904598 79 X
ISBN 13: 978 1 904598 79 4

British Library Cataloguing-in-Publication Data
A catalogue record for this book
is available on request from the British Library

Typeset by Hewer Text UK Ltd, Edinburgh
Printed and bound in Great Britain by Clays Ltd, Bungay, Suffolk

To my dear and courageous mother:
a long way from Gwelo

ACKNOWLEDGEMENTS

Heartfelt thanks to: Gabrielle Stubbs, who lovingly cares for me; Patrick and Patricia Orr, who provided a haven at Jinchini, (Jinchini.co.uk) on the Kenya coast, where Patrick Mwongela Munyao and Omari Masud'Dago made sure I had little else to do other than write; Chris and Janet Sherwell, whose hospitality in Guernsey helped me get over a hump; John Githongo and Mary Muthumbi, who represent the best of Kuwisha; Alan Cowell, whose courage is inspirational; Ann Grant, who continued to encourage me; as did JDF Jones, Quentin Peel, and Sandy McCall Smith; and Robyn Scott and Mungo Soggot; to Elina Tripoli, Dr Patricia Limousin and Professor Marwan Hariz, who between them renewed my battery and revived my morale. And I much appreciate the backing of Rye Barcott and the expertise of Salim Mohamed, president and manager respectively of the Nairobi children's association, Carolina for Kireba (cfk@unc.edu).

I am also grateful to Neville Moir for his patient support, and Nicky Wood for her sharp-eyed editing; to Lionel Barber, editor of the *Financial Times*, Robert Thomson, editor of *The Times*, and Patrick Smith, editor of *Africa Confidential*, for allowing me to draw on articles I originally published in their papers; to Peter Bale, former editor of Times OnLine, for urging me to get back on my soapbox; Marie Johansson for her insights into aid; and to Hutch at Hutch@pukkape.com, whose computer skills are legendary.

I hardly need say that the country of Kuwisha, and the characters that inhabit it, are products of my imagination. But the sect named after the Congolese preacher Simon Kimbangu, and described by Michela Wrong in her classic account of President Mobutu sese Seko's Zaire, *In the Footsteps of Mr Kurtz,* is a matter of fact and not fiction, as is the Kimbanguist belief that believers should never, ever be naked.

"Sometimes at midnight, in the great silence of the sleep-bound town, the doctor turned on his wireless before going to bed for the few hours' sleep he allowed himself. And from the ends of the earth across thousands of miles of land and sea, kindly, well-meaning speakers tried to voice their fellow-feeling, and indeed did so, but at the same time proved the utter incapacity of every man truly to share in suffering which he cannot see. 'Oran! Oran!' in vain the call rang over oceans, in vain Dr Rieux listened hopefully; always the tide of eloquence began to flow, bringing home still more the unbridgeable gulf that lay between Grand and the speaker. 'Oran, we're with you!' they called emotionally. But not, the doctor told himself, to love or to die together – and that's the only way. They're too remote."

Albert Camus, *The Plague*

PROLOGUE

The sounds of approaching dawn woke her. For a few minutes Charity Mupanga lay in the delicious warmth of her bed, and listened to Africa preparing to face a new day.

She could hear cousin Mercy, nurse at the only clinic in the slum called Kireba, stirring next door. The man with the hawking cough could only be Philimon Ogata, waiting patiently for the rattle of tin mugs which would signal the start of business at Harrods International Bar (and Nightspot). Soon his bad-tempered mongrel dog, banished from the bar's premises, would begin to bark. Across the still-dark valley drifted the chatter of *askaris* returning from their duties in the adjacent city, and exchanging ribald comments with the women setting out from hovels and shacks to hawk vegetables, or to clean homes and offices.

Kireba, East Africa's biggest slum, was rousing.

Closer to where Charity lay, on the other side of the wall, came the sound of running water, and whispered exchanges as kettles were filled from the tap by the clinic, and the clink of knives and spoons being set out for the first rounds of morning tea – only five *ngwee*, including a thick slice of Charity's excellent corn-bread.

The duty boys, Ntoto and Rutere, her little rats – though woe betide anyone else who used the term – were going about their business: Titus Odhiambo Ntoto, leader of the Mboya Boys, the slum's toughest gang, and his friend, Cyrus Rutere. Barely 14, they were the lucky ones in a growing army of feral children, orphaned by Aids, the plague that consumed the future. Thanks

I

to Charity, they could sleep unmolested, under the Harrods' bar counter, and enjoy one good meal a day – providing, of course, they did their chores.

The rasp of brush on nails as the boys prepared for hand inspection was followed by giggles. Then came a hiss from Ntoto: "Shish! She's sleeping . . ."

Charity rose, and dressed quickly, putting on her favourite green cardigan, with the worn elbows, for though it was mid-summer, there was an early morning chill in the air.

Before stepping outside, there was one daily ritual to perform. She took a dab of Vaseline from the jar kept on the bedside table and rubbed it into her skin, leaving her face smooth and gleaming, cheekbones accentuated. It was a face with character, handsome rather than beautiful, boasting strong white teeth and a ready smile.

Now she was ready.

Some thirty yards away the three shipping containers that made up Harrods, arranged as an E without the middle stroke, loomed like an elephant emerging from the morning mist. One container served as an eating room, the opposite one was a bar, with a counter made of old wooden railway sleepers which ran the length of the container; the third was the kitchen, where a gurgling second-hand fridge, connected by a cable to a power outlet in the clinic, kept the local Tusker beers cold, while the cooking was done on three gas stoves.

All three containers had windows cut away, and Charity could see a candle that flickered from within. A match flared, as the boys lit the gas stoves.

Thank goodness the foolish fuss about the name of her bar had been settled. She still found it outrageous that a London *duka* could own a name, wherever in the world it was used; and she still resented the fact that she had had to change it . . . now its official name was Tangwenya's International Bar (and Nightspot). May her late father, after whom the bar had been named, Harrods Mwai Gichuru Tangwenya, rest in peace.

The business undermined her belief in British justice. At least the lawyers no longer bothered her with foolish letters, with strange words like "pursuant" and "sub judice".

The last letter from them was especially unpleasant, she felt, even though it had been accompanied by a cheque for £200 "for the welfare of the orphaned boys".

She had asked her dear friend, Edward Furniver, manager of the Kireba savings bank, to explain some of the phrases.

"What does this mean, 'without prejudice'?"

She pointed to the offending phrase. "They think I am dead, yes?"

Furniver nodded.

"Killed by rioters? And that Harrods was destroyed, by looters?"

He nodded again.

"But I cannot find any sorry in this letter? Where is any sorry?"

Furniver had tried to calm her.

"I think that to say 'without prejudice' is as close as a lawyer gets without actually saying sorry . . ."

It was still a struggle to persuade her to keep the cheque, but she eventually agreed to spend half on drugs for the clinic, while half was to be invested by Furniver on behalf of the rats.

But Charity Mupanga had had the last word.

"For officials from London, we will call my bar Tangwenya's. For customers, they will always be welcome at Harrods."

Charity had crossed herself, smoothed down her blue and white apron, and disappeared into the kitchen . . .

It was getting lighter.

Ogata greeted her, coughed again, cleared his chest with a long rasp that shook his frame, and spat.

A few yards away from where he sat, patiently waiting for a

3

cup of good, sweet, milky Kuwisha tea, a smoky fire came to life in a hut made of plastic bags.

Clarence "Results" Mudenge, proprietor of the Klean Blood Klinic, was stirring. He too would join the queue for early tea and dough balls, the best value in town.

"Mo'ningi."

Mildred Kigali had promised to arrive early, and she was as good as her word.

The wife of Didymus, house steward to Furniver, could be irritating, particularly when she pretended to be deaf, and when she proselytised on behalf of the Church of the Blessed Lamb. But she was a good and loyal friend, and as active a 70-something as there was in Kuwisha.

"Morning, Mildred. Did you sleep well?"

Charity laid down the chewed, bristle-ended stick that served as a toothbrush.

Time for work! No loafing! There were mouths to feed, jobs to be done, and important matters to resolve

I

"Africa," said the Oldest Member, stretched out in his green leather armchair in front of the fireplace at the Thumaiga Club, favourite watering hole of the elite.

Dusk had fallen, and the sudden shift from bright sunshine to soft half-light, and then abrupt darkness, caught the last players on the golf course by surprise. The click of steel on ball gave way to conversation as the group entered the bar, nodding at the OM as they ordered their rounds.

"Africa," he said again, and sighed, his outstretched feet nudging the day's papers, dropped on the floor next to the chair.

The front pages had much the same headlines: "UK Aid Minister Backs Rhino Debt Link", declared one. "World Bank Pledges Rhino Aid", announced the other.

"Indeed," said Edward Furniver, wondering just what point his host was trying to make. He took a handful of roasted cashew nuts from the bowl on the drinks stand. Furniver was in no hurry to get back to his modest flat above the bank's office in Kireba. And while there were aspects of the Thumaiga Club he heartily disliked, there was something soothing about Kuwisha's leading social venue. Old values – dressing for dinner, signed chitties rather than cash, and a black ball for undesirable candidates for membership – were maintained with unbending enthusiasm by the successors to their colonial counterparts. Whatever their differences, they shared the same belief in rule through committees.

An evening at the club was like being in a protective cocoon, where mementoes of the past kept out the realities of the present.

He soaked up the atmosphere of down-at-heel gentility, where the sanctity of the Residents' Lounge was preserved by alert waiters, who courteously but firmly expelled visitors who dared to intrude. He loved to sink into the leather armchairs, flick through an old copy of *Country Life*, and wonder who had gone to the trouble of collecting what seemed to be the complete works of Dornford Yates. The last entry in the notebook attached with a piece of string to a stub of a pencil was dated a decade earlier: "Residents Only", said a note on the dusty cover. "Two books maximum".

"How about one for the road?"

The OM's voice boomed around the bar, now nearly empty, the golfers having departed. Boniface Rugiru, the long-serving bar steward, took the orders for another round.

Rugiru was a member of the "too late" generation, for whom independence had come just a few years too late. He missed out on a place at one of the hitherto segregated state schools that had opened their doors to black students; and without a secondary school certificate he had no chance of getting a job in a civil service that was open to black citizens of Kuwisha.

Instead he ended up behind the bar at the Thumaiga, a chief bar steward at the height of his profession, and earning a pittance. But if he was bitter, he didn't show it. Instead he radiated a quiet confidence – a big man with an easy smile, proud of the seven children he had brought up to respect their elders and to fear God.

"And more cashew nuts, if you please, Mr Rugiru," the OM called out. "As I was saying . . . Plenty of activity. Too many gimmicks, not enough progress," said the OM.

He gestured at the newspapers:

"Trouser talk, my boy, that's all it is. These chaps turning up for this World Bank conference – all bloody trouser talk. Save the bloody rhino one week, gender issues in semi-arid regions the

6

next. When that doesn't work, the silly buggers hug a tree and plant a street boy," he rumbled on.

Did the former district commissioner have a point, Furniver wondered?

Forty years after independence, Kuwisha was poorer than ever. Millions and millions of dollars in assistance from donors seemed to have made little discernible difference. Surely the OM was right – things should be better?

"It's all a bit like the wheeze that chap Potemkin pulled."

Edward must have still looked puzzled, and the OM continued: "You know, the soldier chap who fooled his wotchacallit, empress, Catherine, Russia, couple hundred years ago. Gave her the impression that she was in charge of a better show than was actually the case."

History was not the strong point of Edward Furniver, ex-London investment banker turned micro-lender to the masses of Kuwisha's biggest slum. But he dimly recalled reading that in General Grigori Potemkin's time, Russian villagers were instructed to erect elaborate façades portraying thriving settlements. They concealed the brutal realities, and misled the empress about conditions under her rule, leaving her convinced that her affairs were in far better shape than was actually the case. The OM drained his gin and tonic, and again summoned Boniface, who was polishing glasses behind the mahogany bar counter. He said something in Swahili that made them both chuckle.

"These days we fool the old ladies who run the WorldFeed bookshops and rattle the collecting cans. Get them believing that poor bloody Africa is better off for their help. Not so. In fact, it's the victim – of the very people who claim to be its friends."

"Steady on," said Furniver, although somewhat nervously. Disagreeing with the OM could bring out the mean streak in the old settler. "Steady on. May have been true a few years ago, but things have been picking up. World is taking notice, and there

7

is more aid money promised. Growth rates up. And there's debt relief . . . and China wants its raw materials, oil, copper, coffee . . . Geldof, Bono and so on . . ."

Edward Furniver tailed off.

The OM brushed his intervention aside, flapping a dismissive, liver-spotted wrinkled hand.

"Fact is, you and I know that Kuwisha is deep in the poo. Africa ditto. Writing was on the wall long before Aids appeared. God knows who to blame . . . foreigners, slave trade, colonialism, Cold War, didn't help. The indigenous have got a lot to answer for . . . and the poor sods have been cursed with bloody awful leaders."

If it were possible to take an angry sip of a gin and tonic, the OM took one, and as he swallowed he made a face, as if he had downed a mouthful of bitter medicine. He wiped his narrow moustache, a carefully trimmed mix of ginger and grey, and reached out for the nuts.

"Not just that they were unable to run the traditional in a brewery. Not their fault they couldn't. Weren't trained. But come independence, the blighters drank the place dry, so to speak, and borrowed from banks, which were all too happy to lend. And instead of spending the money on a decent brewery or whatever, they put it under their mattress. Not in Africa – in their new homes in London, or Paris or New York . . ."

The OM marked the end of what for him was a speech by sucking his teeth, and with his tongue, adjusted his dentures, making a soft clicking sound.

"Of course, the Foreign Office Johnnies didn't help, giving 'em independence too soon. Frankly, we all share the blame. Now we plan to send more billions in aid, to little effect, ends up in bank accounts abroad."

He reached into his jacket, and extracted a packet of Sportsman cigarettes, along with a box of matches. After four unsuccessful attempts, he got a stick to light.

The OM took a long draw.

"Have to justify this help, so we all pretend aid works. WorldFeed and their pals pretend it works, otherwise their collection boxes would be empty. The local politicians pretend it works, or their overseas bank accounts would run dry. Visiting politicians pretend it works, otherwise they would have to explain to their voters back home why so much has been wasted.

"And of course there are the tossers who come to Africa at the taxpayers' expense."

In the OM's pecking order of villains, a tosser was about the worst there was, reviled beyond a "loafer", and far worse than a "so-and-so".

"See the ads, every week, in *The Economist*. Take the latest one . . ."

He picked up a copy of the magazine from the rack next to his chair, and flicked through the appointment pages.

"Got it! Listen to this: Climate Change Adaptation Support Programme for Action: Research and Capacity Development in Africa – CCASPARCDA."

A piece of cashew nut had stuck under his dentures; he removed the plate, gave it a wipe with his handkerchief, replaced it and continued.

"As a general rule, old boy, the longer the acronym of an Africa do-gooder, the bigger the waste of rations. And what will these chaps in CC etc. do?" He tapped the offending page with a nicotine-stained forefinger.

The OM read out the job description: "The successful candidate will have an entrepreneurial approach to the identification, design and management of research for development; providing intellectual leadership . . . a demonstrated track record in working effectively within multidisciplinary teams . . . What the hell does all that mean?"

The Oldest Member tossed another cashew into his mouth, and looked at Furniver with sharp pale blue eyes.

"Flogger had the right idea," he said wistfully. "Ever hear from him?"

The OM had got it into his head that Furniver was related to "Flogger" Morland, a district commissioner notorious for his iron rule during the colonial era, when he ran an area of Kuwisha nearly the size of Texas. Furniver had given up trying to convince the OM that Morland was no relation; indeed, he had never heard of the man. He said nothing, and shrugged his shoulders.

"Pity," said the OM. "When you next write, give him my best."

The evening was ending.

Furniver went to relieve himself while his host signed for their drinks.

He took advantage of the full-length mirror in the Gents, and on his way out paused to inspect his reflection. He sucked in his stomach, pulled his shoulders back, and straightened up. Charity was right. His posture was terrible. He vowed to take more exercise.

Re-emerging into the lobby a few minutes later, he nearly bumped into Boniface, busy polishing the brass door-handle of the Gents. The steward looked embarrassed, and mumbled a response to Furniver's greeting. Looking back a few days later, Furniver realised that he should have spotted that something was amiss. Club chores were allocated with iron precision. Never would a bar steward perform any task not directly connected with dispensing drinks.

The OM joined him in the lobby, and sniffed loudly.

"Has someone been using a bloody aftershave?" He sniffed again: "Pongs to high heaven! Give you a lift home? By the way, gather you and that bar owner, Charity Mupanga, good friends, hmm? Splendid woman! Word of advice, old boy. Marula berries make the thingy wotsit – old Batonka proverb. Or to put it crudely, the wise man counts his buttons when the crow feeds, as they say in Nyali. Get my drift?"

The two men walked through the arched club entrance into the African night, and Furniver used his expensive high-tech key-ring torch, "visible from a mile away" the makers claimed, to light the way.

He changed the subject.

"About this Potemkin business . . ." he said as he got into his host's Mercedes.

The OM's reply was drowned out by the roar of the night flight to London as it passed overhead.

In the undercarriage of the plane, a young stowaway started to shiver . . .

2

"Fatboy!"

The sun was still burning the dew off the grass when the call from Lovemore Mboga emerged from within State House, seat of government in the East African state of Kuwisha.

"Fatboy!"

Ferdinand Mhango Mlambo, the disgraced kitchen *toto*, stirred, his head full of dreams, still in the thrall of the last of his store of Mtoko Gold, the best *bhang* the country grew.

"Faatboy!"

The mocking summons left the colonnaded, colonial mansion, white as a wedding cake, once the residence of the British governor, drifted across the ninth green of the State House golf course, between the strutting peacocks, and beyond. It slid like a snake, through the flowerbeds, around the purple bougainvillaea and red hibiscus, sidling along the unkempt rows of cabbage and gone-to-seed lettuce, in what was once a well-maintained kitchen garden.

Finally the call, sustained in its journey by a brisk breeze, crossed the overgrown path which led to a long-abandoned boathouse on the banks of a green, weed-infested dam that once was the home of the Kuwisha Sailing Club. It slipped through a gap in the sheets of corrugated iron and old plastic bags with which, in happier days, the boy had constructed his den, and burrowed into his ears.

"Faaatboy!"

Mlambo squeezed his fingers deeper into his ears.

They failed to stop the insult from reaching its destination, deep inside the soul of Ferdinand Mlambo. Given the chance, there it would thrive and grow fat, like a tapeworm in a cow.

No-one, least of all Mlambo, would dispute the fact that he was a big boy. He had always been big for his age, even before becoming the senior kitchen *toto* soon after he turned 13, when the privilege of office entitled him to feed on unlimited scraps from the State House kitchen.

He was large, certainly, with a massive *butumba* that served as a counterweight to his substantial belly, both resting on thick thighs, which made him such a formidable figure on the football pitch. Indeed, his eligibility for the Mboya Boys Under-15 football team had been regularly challenged by opponents, sceptical that someone of his girth and height could qualify. And of course there had been some boys who dared to call him *mafuta*, or "lard guts". That was stopped easily enough, for when he won the fights that ensued he sat on his opponent's head, until he heard a muffled cry for mercy.

But to suggest that Mlambo was fat was simply not true . . . well built, certainly, stout possibly, even a little overweight. But fat? Never!

His limbs twitched, as if kicking phantom footballs. Mlambo reluctantly began to surface into the reality of his new life.

His offence had been unforgivable. He accepted that. He should never have agreed to conceal a tape recorder in the life president's study on behalf of that English journalist, who hoped it would provide a recording of a compromising exchange between President Nduka and the opposition leader. Loyalty to the president had to be absolute.

It was no defence, he realised, to explain that the leader of the Mboya Boys' street gang, who was also the captain of your football team, had threatened to tell the dreaded *mungiki* thugs that you were uncircumcised. And what those *mungiki* did with a rusty nail . . . Mlambo's testicles shrivelled at the mere thought of it.

"Faatboy! . . . Faaatboy!"

Once more came the summons, with that sneering, contemptuous tone for which Lovemore Mboga, the State House chief steward, was renowned.

Ferdinand Mlambo tried to ignore his tormentor. Stretched out on an old mattress, bartered in return for favours to the deputy housekeeper, he pulled a stained grey blanket around his ears and thought about his dear departed grandmother. How he missed the warm untroubled nights, spent curled up under the huge table in the State House kitchen, deep in a nest of old newspapers, like a large dormouse.

Now he lay restless in his garden shed, alone and vulnerable to the evil spirits that prowled the night, making noises that could quite easily be mistaken for the sound of the wind whistling through the cracks and crevices in his makeshift sanctuary.

"Let him Fatboy me. I will not answer."

Mlambo still felt light-headed from the night before, when he had over-indulged, and had smoked too much Mtoko Gold. Indeed, he had smoked so much that he was finding it hard to distinguish fact from fantasy.

There was one way to find out.

He felt under the mattress, scrabbling for the trophies he was almost certain he had carried home from the monthly meeting of the Kireba Christian Ladies' Sewing Circle. For a few seconds, he was filled with doubt. Could he have imagined the events at Harrods International Bar (and Nightspot)?

Suddenly his fingers encountered something long and thin, like a bicycle spoke but with a filed, pointed end.

"Ouch! Ayna!"

He sucked his thumb, sat bolt upright, and lifted the corner of the mattress, revealing two grey knitting needles.

Mlambo's eyes widened, and his stomach tightened.

Needles? Knitting needles, number nine size?

If the needles were there, then . . . he had not been dreaming!

His terrifying encounter with a *tokolosh*, that mischievous and malicious creature, southern Africa's fabled equivalent of an Irish leprechaun, ever-present yet seldom spotted, was no creation of the *bhang* he had been smoking. He, Ferdinand Mlambo, had seen it, with its hideous face, bathed in a curious blue light. Indeed, he had heard it give out a blood-curdling moan as it advanced on his hiding place, next to Harrods, where a meeting of the Kireba Ladies' Sewing Circle had been in full swing.

The events of the day before, surely the worst day in his fourteen-year life, were all coming back to him . . .

The calling ceased. Perhaps Mboga had simply been rubbing salt into the wound. Perhaps it was a reminder that Mlambo was obliged to attend the weekly State House staff meeting that Friday. Whatever lay behind the taunt, Ferdinand Mlambo embraced his bitterness, like a broody hen nursing an egg, reliving that grim morning twenty-four hours before, when he had been summoned to Mboga's pantry.

It was there, in that cool, dimly-lit room, with the unexplained aroma of vanilla, shelves running from ceiling to floor, big enough to accommodate a desk which was part of the original State House furniture going back to the 1930s, when it began life as the residence of the British governor, that he heard his punishment.

From behind the desk, Lovemore Mboga, sporting the ruling party's flaming torch emblem in the lapel of his green jacket, informed the boy of his fate with all the solemnity of a judge in the colonial era delivering sentence on a "cheeky" native who had dared challenge the European administration.

Mboga himself had come up with the ingenious and cruel punishment he set out with unseemly relish.

The steward began quietly.

"Don't worry, Mlambo. I am not going to sack you," he said.

15

Mlambo had looked up in astonishment.

"Sacking is too good for you. Instead, you are demoted. You are now a small boy."

Mlambo winced.

To be demoted to a non-job, a job with no status, at the very bottom of the ladder, was punishment indeed. He would be subject to the beck and call of people whom he considered nonentities, sent out to buy lunch for the State House telephonists, to collect a chicken for the messenger . . . even to buy cigarettes for the pantry boy, a lad he despised. It would be an endless cycle of daily humiliation.

He had no option but to accept the blow. If he stayed, his life was hell; but if he left, the life on the streets that awaited him was at least as bad. As Mlambo tried to explain to Mboga, it was his fear of *mungiki*, Kuwisha's fast-growing street gang of nihilistic thugs, which had overcome his loyalty to the president.

He would have done better to stay silent, for the steward immediately turned this confession to advantage.

"Perhaps I should change my mind . . ." Mboga mused, "maybe give you to *mungiki* as a present . . ."

He appeared to consider his proposal, lips pursed, and looking over and beyond the boy at the end of his desk.

"Perhaps, perhaps . . . Remember, boy, those *mungiki*, they are everywhere."

Then Mboga got down to business.

"Your friend Mupanga . . ."

Mlambo stiffened.

Charity Mupanga was one of the few people outside his family who had shown him any kindness.

"She is a troublemaker, a dissident, even," Mboga continued.

Mlambo wanted to protest, but fear had frozen his tongue.

It was true that Charity Mupanga was no supporter of President Nduka. She made little secret of her contempt for the man whom many believed had contrived the death of her husband David, Kuwisha's much loved bishop, some four years earlier. And as the deputy president of the Mboya Boys United Football Club, as well as running the best bar and eating house in Kireba, while providing a refuge for the city's growing army of street children, she was a person to reckon with.

But to call her a dissident was going too far. Frightened though he was, Mlambo tried to speak in Charity Mupanga's defence.

"Shut your face," snapped Mboga. "She is holding dark corner meetings every month. You know this. Every month."

He looked suspiciously at the boy.

"They call it the Christian Ladies' Sewing Circle."

Mboga then spelt out his demand: Mlambo was to become an informer, that creature which had been encouraged during the colonial era and flourished after independence. Reporting back on Charity and her friends was to be the boy's first task.

As Mboga detailed the new duty, setting out everything he would expect, from information about the meetings of the Sewing Circle to Charity's relationship with that Englishman Furniver, Mlambo felt himself swaying on his feet, close to fainting.

But the worst was yet to come, a final turn of the screw, devised and applied by Mboga himself, a man whose influence went well beyond that of a State House steward, powerful job though it was. According to the gossip, he was almost certainly a senior member of Kuwisha's Central Intelligence Organisation.

Mboga stood up.

"Ferdinand Mlambo, I call you by that name for the last time. I am giving you a new name. Your old name is finished. I have caught it already."

His hand reached behind Mlambo's left ear as he spoke, as if plucking something out of the air.

"Your old name is now dead, finished," he said with relish. "It is ready to travel with me, now."

He thrust his clenched fist into a small cardboard box which had been sitting on his desk, and withdrew his hand while closing the top, as if an insect or a small bird was now trapped inside. Mlambo watched, horrified and wide-eyed, as Mboga wrapped the box, about the size of two packets of Sportsman cigarettes, in a copy of the previous day's paper, and carefully bound it with twine.

"I will bury it near my home," said Mboga, "and my dogs will piss on it, so the name of Ferdinand Mlambo, which is already dead, will rot."

The boy was dumbstruck.

To subject Ferdinand Mhango Mlambo, great-grandson of the famous Mzilikazi Mlambo of Zimbabwe, who had fought for his country's liberation during the first *chimurenga* in the 1890s, to such inhuman treatment went well beyond the bounds of decency.

Then the full implications of losing his name sank in. Without a complete and proper name, would his late grandmother be able to find him? And would his earlier ancestors, including his great-grandfather, be available for advice and counselling? A shiver of terror went through the boy's frame, and his insides turned to jelly.

Mboga looked with contempt at the quivering youth, standing at attention before him.

"Now, repeat your new name. It is Fatboy. You are now called Fatboy, only."

Mboga was relentless.

"Repeat after me: 'I am a piece of nothing. I am Fatboy,' " said Mboga. "Fatboy, just Fatboy. Fatboy! Forever!"

The chief steward sneered.

"I will see you Friday morning, ten sharp, at the staff meeting. I expect many people. We will meet on the lawn. And I will announce that Ferdinand Mlambo is finished. Only Fatboy is left . . . and you can give your report on that Mupanga woman. Now go! Go, go! You dog shit! Go!"

Mlambo had fled from Lovemore Mboga, his bare feet feeling the cool polished corridors of State House for the last time, past the vases with the aroma of fresh cut flowers, through the kitchen where the presidential tea-tray was stored. No longer would he be entrusted with the task of preparing the mid-morning glass of hot water and honey for the Ngwazi, the Life President, the Cock that Conquered all the Hens, Dr Josiah Nduka.

It was the worst day in his young life. He had lost more than his name. He had been deprived of his identity, his very sense of being. He, the former State House senior kitchen *toto*, Ferdinand Mlambo, had been reduced to a single word, offensive beyond measure.

Fatboy.

Ferdinand Mlambo's dismissal as kitchen *toto* at State House, albeit the senior kitchen *toto*, might not seem a matter of great import. Yet only an ignorant outsider could come to this conclusion.

To have a job, any job, enjoying a monthly income, was rare in a country where only a comparative handful out of half a million school leavers who came onto the market each year ended up with work and regular pay. To be the senior State House kitchen *toto* was more than a job. It offered status, clout and influence.

Indeed, it could be said that Mlambo was the most influential and powerful 14-year-old, soon to be 15, in the land.

He was not merely on the staff of the president. He was part of the president, and he enjoyed making the most of this privileged position.

When, for example, at any one of the many police check-points on roads leading out of the city, he was asked his name, and just what job he did, he would reply with the spurious modesty that he had cultivated, combining timing and tone to perfection.

"My name?"

He would pause, looking at his feet, and rub a toe in the ochre earth of Kuwisha, for all the world like a shy, illiterate up-country oaf.

"Er . . . Mlambo, Ferdinand Mlambo . . ."

"And what do you do, boy? Are you a loafer? Or are you useless?"

Mlambo would wait for the laughter that accompanied such jibes to die down. Then would come his reply, said so quietly that the words were barely audible: "Kitchen *toto*."

Then after a further pause, he would casually add another word, like an afterthought, almost mumbling, so sometimes the listener would not quite catch what he had said.

"What? What?"

"Senior . . . kitchen *toto*."

And in case there was any doubt, he would utter two final, magic words: "Senior kitchen *toto* . . . State House."

The sharp intake of breath that invariably followed, a mix of fear and envy, was a response that gave Mlambo much pleasure. It acknowledged that this was a youngster with prospects, a boy who could do favours, a boy who could be useful – not just part of the minister, but part of the president!

To work at State House in any capacity at all was remarkable. Indeed, there was a living to be earned by simply knowing someone at State House, ensuring that in return for a few *ngwee*, a letter to an official would be delivered, or a message would reach its destination. Even the kitchen *toto*'s humble duties, which ranged from shining the silver for State House banquets, to acting as the president's food taster, and serving as the supplier of *bhang* to the State House staff could be turned to advantage.

Now this influence and power had gone, as worthless as ashes.

For he was just Fatboy – and unless he, Ferdinand Mlambo, did something about it, he would be Fatboy forever.

★

Perhaps it was the salty taste of his blood as he sucked his punctured thumb that set him thinking; possibly it was the influence of the knitting needles themselves, no longer mere needles but instruments of revenge; or the benevolent intervention of the spirit of his grandmother, who, contrary to his initial fears, soon managed to contact her favourite grandson that played a part; not to mention the fact that Mlambo was a cunning young man . . .

But whatever it was, something had triggered a chain of thought in the boy's head. And the thought turned into a plan. And if the plan were to be put into practice, Ferdinand Mhango Mlambo, senior kitchen *toto* (retired) would recover his name and ensure the public humiliation of Lovemore Mboga, chief steward at State House.

All he needed was a little help from his friends.

3

The first pink traces of dawn over Kireba turned into the glowing orange ball that would in a few minutes become the wondrous African sun. The proud owner and proprietor of Kuwisha's top meeting place took stock of her world, and gave thanks to her Maker.

Charity put aside all the excited talk about the event that had caused such a tumult the night before. She no more believed in the existence of a *tokolosh* than an Irish woman believed in leprechauns. It could wait.

There were more important matters on her mind, and it was that special time of the day when she tried to put aside trivia, and counted her blessings.

It seemed right that she should begin with a silent prayer for her special friendship with Furniver, the retired investment banker from England, who had been running the Kireba savings cooperative for some four years. It was a friendship that, provided her suspicions could be laid to rest, seemed set to become a loving, lasting companionship that would see them spending their autumn years on Charity's coffee-growing *shamba*, a two-hour drive from the city.

It had been Edward's idea to lay the brick patio under her feet. Not for the first time, he had had to scrape something particularly unpleasant off his shoes in the wake of one of Kuwisha's magnificent rainstorms, which made even the shortest of journeys from his modest flat above the bank's office more than usually hazardous. For nearly four years he had lived in the flat, which he had helped build – the only brick building in the slum, apart from the small clinic.

At first she had been against the patio. The bar was doing well, but bricks cost money. So what if there was mud?

"You live in Kuwisha, in Kireba. There is always mud in Kireba, English," she had said, calling him by the nickname she used when she was feeling particularly fond of the man who was insinuating himself into her life, slowly and surely filling the gap left by the death of her husband in a car accident.

It had been Edward who backed her loan application for money to buy the containers that were to make up Harrods; and it had been Edward who supported her in the battle with the Anglican hierarchy, who had bitterly opposed her plans for the bar.

"You are the widow of a bishop," the chairman of the Anglican management board had remonstrated. "How can you run a drinking house?"

"It will be a place for eating good food, and meeting, and talking, and teaching street children," Charity had replied, and stalked out of the study in his comfortable home. She hadn't been back since.

Charity looked at Furniver sternly.

"In Kuwisha, when it rains, there is always mud. That is life," she concluded sternly.

"Mud I can take," Furniver retorted, "but not what they do to it in Kireba."

She tried another tack.

Both of them would have to be on hand to supervise the work; this would mean sacrificing one of their precious weekends at her *shamba*, high in the hills beyond the city, Charity pointed out.

Furniver was undeterred.

He had called for volunteers from the Kireba football club, the Mboya Boys. With their help – at a rate negotiated by the team captain, Titus Ntoto, of one sugared dough ball per boy, per four-hour shift, and freshly-cooked by Charity – the patio had been finished in two days.

The sun was now emerging. In a few minutes she would have to put water on the gas ring for the first of the day's rounds of soup: pumpkin and groundnut soup, with a dash of Worcester sauce. So tasty!

The wound from the loss some four years earlier of her dear David, Bishop of Central Kuwisha, was healing. There was still a scar on her soul, but the raw pain had eased. And Harrods was not only making enough money to supplement her tiny pension from the Church; it was evolving into what Charity had always envisaged, notwithstanding the doubts and disapproval of many of David's fellow clerics.

Harrods had become part community centre, part crèche, part refuge for the city's street children who could earn a dish of nourishing food in return for doing basic chores.

Soon it would be time to start work – but not before she also gave thanks for the fact that she had a warm home to go to, or at least a room that she rented from cousin Mercy, staff nurse at the only clinic that served the densely packed slum of half a million souls. What was more, she slept on a proper mattress, free of bed lice, on a bed frame with each leg standing in a tin of water, which kept cockroaches and other *goggas* at bay. She also had clean clothes on her back, and she had wholesome food in her belly. Above all she had dear friends around her.

Charity massaged her calves in preparation for the day ahead. Running a bar as busy as Harrods was tough. At the end of the day, her feet ached, and there was the odd twinge in her back. But at 40-something she was in remarkably good shape. To enjoy good health was to have drawn a winning ticket in the lottery of life.

She sat down at one of the bar's white plastic tables, a stop-gap until the wooden replacements she had ordered from Philimon Ogata, the nearby coffin-maker, were ready. Ogata, who had recently lost his wife to Aids, was not short of business, but he had a favour to return. For weeks after Agatha Ogata had died, Philimon had eaten regularly at Harrods, and making the new tables was his way of saying "thank you" for Charity's support.

She offered a brief prayer for the soul of Agatha, and gave thanks for the fact that the two of them had reconciled before the argumentative lady had taken the hand of Jesus, as Philimon had put it. And only then did Charity allow herself to return to her worries about Edward Furniver.

Even to harbour the tiniest suspicion, rather than confront him, made her feel uncomfortable. What was it that David had said?

"Embrace the sinner and denounce the sin."

That worked when she dealt with an Mboya Boy who sneaked a suck of condensed milk from a freshly opened tin, or who stole sugar from the storeroom next to the bar. It was not so easy when the sin and the sinner were in parasitical embrace, and the sin had captured the very soul.

Furniver would not be the first European to succumb to the combination of African sun and cheap drink. Before too long, thirst for liquor became insatiable, and the beer at sundown was less a social occasion and more a vital daily ritual. Then it became compulsive. All too often the drinker turned to violence, taking out frustration on his wife – just ask Didymus Kigali, who had seen many a white madam in distress!

A pattern to Furniver's consumption was emerging. Brief absences during the day, usually to the toilet, were becoming more frequent, and he would return, smelling slightly of *changa*, and looking a bit unkempt.

The last report from Boniface Rugiru was especially disturbing. Furniver having a drink with that old settler at the Thumaiga Club was acceptable – that was in the open, and men enjoyed buying each other a beer, or a glass of gin. But when drinking it became furtive, or secretive, then one should get worried . . . and if Boniface was right, Furniver had been drinking in the Gents!

Customers were starting to drop in. One had the Kuwisha *Independent* newspaper, and was looking for other readers who would be willing to share the price.

Charity noticed that it had a column by one of her favourite journalists.

"Is your man a drinker?" it began, but there was no time to read it now. More customers were arriving, and their time was precious.

One old-timer cleared his lungs with a long, deep cough and was about to spit the result onto the patio floor, but caught Charity's disapproving eye. He decided against it and instead propelled the gob of phlegm over the purple bougainvillaea hedge that she had planted in honour of Samora Machel, the founding president of Mozambique.

"Grow flowers," Samora had urged his people. "Just because we are poor, it does not mean we do not enjoy beauty."

A couple of Mboya Boys waved as they passed by, carrying plastic bags dripping with the juice of rotten fruit, collected before dawn that morning, on their daily rummage through the refuse dump outside the city's central market. She knew full well that the fruit – mangoes, pineapples, bananas – would become part of that fierce, raw alcoholic brew called *changa*. She knew that. But the wave from the boys, who usually treated all adults as enemies, lifted her spirits and gave her hope. Suddenly she remembered.

Avocados. She was out of avocados, and avocado soup was on the menu that night. With a thick slice of bread included in the price, it was a bargain. Demand would be high.

"Boy!" she called. "Duty boy! Urgent for duty boy . . ."

It was going to be another busy day.

"Yes indeed, life is good," said Charity Mupanga, "life is OK."

4

The contrast between the clear, blue and sunny December sky above Kuwisha and the freezing, grey and grimy blanket that enveloped London could hardly have been more striking.

In the gleaming steel and glass building on the banks of the Thames, morning news conference at Britain's biggest-selling tabloid, the *Clarion*, had been interrupted by the arrival of an exclusive set of photographs, bought that very morning from a Heathrow mortuary attendant.

The body, the third in two weeks to have been found on the main approach to Heathrow, had apparently fallen to earth when the undercarriage of an incoming flight from East Africa had opened.

Thanks to a hand-made postcard found in a pouch strapped to his midriff, it was possible to learn something about the boy. On the one side was a picture of a mango, cut from a local magazine and glued to a piece of cardboard cut from a cereal packet; on the other, in large capital letters, was written: "FROM YOUR FREND".

The card was addressed to: "Mr Titus and Mr Cyrus, Harrods International Bar (and Nightspot), Kuwisha."

"That's enough to go on," said the editor, impatient to get to the nub of the story. There were more pressing concerns. The first was whether the picture of the corpse, estimated age between 12 and 15, should be run on page one or on page three, where it could replace the usual picture of a near-naked girl.

Meanwhile discussion was stimulated by a question from the pictures editor.

"Could we have a reconstruction, you know, not with the body itself, obviously, but a stand-in, you know . . . where the body was found, or curled up in the undercarriage?"

It was, the editor conceded, a very good idea. There might be one problem, however.

"Do we have his clothes?"

The editor's personal assistant was sent to check on the availability of the clothes the dead boy had been wearing, and reported back.

"He wants another £100 for the kit. Says the boy was wearing an Arsenal shirt. About ten years old, but he said it would clean up nicely. Worth a few bob. Collector's item."

If there was one thing the editor could not abide, it was a source that became greedy.

"He can sod off . . . bloody body-snatcher."

For a few minutes conference debated the merits of dressing a stand-in in a pair of tattered shorts and an Arsenal football club shirt, but integrity won the day.

"What if we were to dress him in the wrong strip?" asked a young man in his early thirties who was leaning against the office door, looking down the blouse of a woman in front of him. "Fans would be sure to spot it," he continued. "We'd be a bloody laughing stock!"

It was an intervention typical of the paper's up-and-coming columnist who had recently been given his own thirteen-part TV series. Geoffrey Japer knew his football.

His point was taken and the idea abandoned.

Conference then considered whether it would be in good taste to run the picture at all in the week ahead. Christmas, after all, was approaching.

Traditionalists spoke up in favour of using the page-three girl, Phoebe, prompting an angry response from the news editor.

"Punters," he observed, "do not want tits with their turkey."

"Nor," retorted Geoffrey, who enjoyed picking fights, "do they want a stiff with their stuffing."

After further debate, a compromise was reached.

A photo of the body, covered by a sheet except for the head, would be run on the front page. There would be a warning to readers of a delicate disposition that more photos were to be seen on inside pages. Phoebe would continue to occupy her usual position on page three, but dressed in the traditional attire of an African maiden.

A debate got under way over just what constituted "traditional attire". It was resolved by the foreign editor, who, after all, had been on a beach holiday to Gambia.

"They wear bugger all," he said authoritatively. "Poor sods cannot afford it. Just a little grass thingy over their fannies."

A file photo of Phoebe, scantily clad, was passed round conference.

"Not enough there to line the hutch of a hamster," said the pictures editor approvingly.

Geoffrey Japer could not resist it: "In fact, barely enough to cover her hamster."

Various ways in which Phoebe would be displayed to the readers were considered, including dressed as Santa Claus, and surrounded by gifts to the children of Kireba which the *Clarion* and its readers could donate.

"We could call the campaign Toys for African Tots," said the women's editor. "Phoebe could help, dishing out the prezzies. Next to one of those sweet rhinos we've been reading about. All being poached, poor things. Our readers can adopt one."

She looked across the room.

"And send him." She nodded in Japer's direction. "With Phoebe. They can visit the rhino place I read about in *The Guardian* last week. And that should produce some decent pics: 'Phoebe gets the horn for Geoffrey'. Wonderful."

For a moment the editor was tempted to agree. He began biting his nails as he was wont to do when the pressure of his office bore down on him.

Japer certainly should go. Who better than the cynical, caustic columnist and up-and-coming controversial TV celebrity, to cover a story of Christmas compassion? But Phoebe . . . ? She was needed in London for page-three duties. Then he had an idea.

"We'll keep Phoebe here. But let's cover her in stamps, and each stamp will be worth £500. And for every £500 contributed by the readers to the fund, Phoebe will remove a stamp. We'll have a competition. The winner has to guess how many days it takes until all but the last two stamps are left. By then she will be down to her nipples . . ."

"What's the prize?" someone at the back of the room asked.

"If you cannot work that out, you shouldn't be working here," the editor snapped. "The lucky winner gets the chance to peel 'em off."

It did not take long for conference to agree that the *Clarion* would use part of the money contributed by readers to sponsor a rhino; and the balance would be donated to Britain's annual charity appeal, run by NoseAid, whose twenty-four-hour, nationally televised "fundfest" featuring the UK's best-loved TV newsreaders, was due to take place soon.

Since the organisers had already decided that children would be the focus, and conservation of the world's wild life would be one of the themes, the timing of the *Clarion* story could not have been better.

And by a happy coincidence of concerns, Kuwisha was an ideal beneficiary: it had an abundance of street children, and a diminishing number of rhinos.

Just before conference broke up, the editor made a final inspired suggestion. The *Clarion* would sponsor the visit of a Kuwisha street boy to London, where he could appear live on the

NoseAid fundfest, accompanied by Japer. Both would be wearing a *Clarion* T-shirt, emblazoned with whatever slogan the subs came up with.

"Save a rhino, help a child!" seemed a winner, until it was pointed out by the chief sub that it could as well be: "Help a child, save a rhino!"

"Whatever," said the editor. "You sort it."

The wheels of a mighty newspaper rolled into action, and the next day's *Clarion* displayed the flair for which it was famous.

On the front page, above the red masthead, appeared the slogan: "The paper with a heart as big as Africa".

Below this ran a front-page editorial on the subject of African children who lost their lives in doomed efforts to reach Europe, which gave the campaign a substance and a gravitas that might otherwise have been lacking.

The tragedy of the street children of East Africa was made sadder, the *Clarion* noted, by the fact that the body had gone unclaimed; and not even was there a name for the lad, the "unknown victim", as the paper dubbed him. The boy would be buried under a gravestone thus marked, readers were advised, after a service in St Bride's, the journalists' church off Fleet Street. But in the midst of the pain and sorrow, the editorial concluded, there was one source of comfort for distressed readers: "With your support, the *Clarion* can promise that this child – Africa's child, our child – will not have died in vain."

5

"When in doubt, dust."

This advice, passed on to Didymus Kigali by his father, who had been in domestic service before him, had proved sound and sensible.

It certainly served him well. Kigali soon discovered that brandishing his yellow duster, with its faint whiff of Brasso that remained no matter how thoroughly he washed it, brought some important benefits.

For a start, if you were polishing the brass fittings on the windows, your employer was unlikely to accuse you of being a "loafer", or even worse, a "lazy loafer", which was as serious an accusation as could be levelled at a house steward in Kuwisha.

It was not a guarantee against an accusation of being "cheeky". But that was "politics", and Kigali steered clear of politics.

What was more, dusting was an activity that induced a sense of order in the universe. "All is well when you dust well," and once again his father's observation had proven true over the years, passing the test of time.

And finally it seemed to make you invisible to the settlers who employed you, something Kigali was at a loss to explain. But many were the times he had been a witness to, or within earshot of, a row between madam and master, both apparently oblivious to the presence of a black man as they traded insults or exchanged blows.

To these three reasons for dusting, all evidence of his late father's wisdom, Kigali had added a fourth – albeit with some diffidence, for he was far from certain that his father would have approved.

Dusting and polishing gave him the chance to reflect on Life, and compose his weekly Admonition, or sermon, as other churches called it. Indeed his maiden Admonition, which had been widely praised by his fellow elders, had been composed while dusting the books that occupied one complete wall in Furniver's flat.

The theme had been a controversial one. Members of the sect had been increasingly subject to taunts, particularly from the youth who were loyal to traditional faiths. They scoffed at the absence of any material manifestations of the Lamb's presence, much to the anger of militants in the sect who were becoming increasingly hard to restrain in the face of provocative chants.

"No church, never naked, No home, nothing sacred", ran the latest sally.

After much dusting and a great deal of deliberation, Didymus Kigali chose his maiden Admonition to speak out.

Standing on a termite mound, surrounded by tens of thousands of Lambs, Kigali gently mocked the materialism of other faiths.

"They ask where are our churches? Where are the big houses for our leaders? Where are our altars?"

"Admonish," some in the huge open-air congregation in the city park called out.

"Admonish!" The call was taken up as the spirit of the people responded to Kigali's theme.

"They must look around."

"Admonish!" they cried.

"The very world, created for His people by our Blessed Lord, is the meeting place of the followers of the Lamb."

"Admonish!"

"The hills around us are our altar, the trees are our canopies, and our home is in the hearts of our people!"

As one, the congregation raised the index finger of their left hand and thrust their fingers towards the blue sky:

"Admonished! Admonished! Admonished!"

It had been a triumph, and Kigali's only regret was that his father had not been alive to attend his subsequent induction as an elder. The old man, who had witnessed the arrival of the white settlers with their bibles and bullets, had died a staunch animist.

The next day, as he polished Furniver's life-size bronze cast of a lion's paw print, Kigali pondered the question he regularly asked himself: would his father have taken up the faith of the Church of the Blessed Lamb? It seemed unlikely. But of one thing Kigali was sure: his father would have been proud of him.

Noises from the bathroom indicated that Furniver was going about his daily ablutions. Any minute now he would emerge, trailing that curious smell the steward had recently started noticing, like a bad aftershave. Kigali was starting to fear the worst. He renewed his polishing with especial vigour. His yellow duster snapped and cracked as he turned the brass to gleaming gold, but his heart was not in it, and his mind failed to resolve his predicament.

Kigali greeted Edward Furniver's entry into the flat's kitchen by gently clearing his throat, just one of a repertoire of conversational coughs that was quite remarkable in its range.

It included the rumble of the alarm cough, the persistency of the drawing attention cough, the murmur of interrogative cough, the reassuringly affirmative cough, and the obedient obsequious cough. Add variations of tone and pitch, and the result was a mini vocabulary, but one in which the context was all-important.

Didymus Kigali did not cough in a vacuum, however. Edward Furniver, founder, manager and sole employee of the Kireba Co-operative Savings Bank, played his part.

Just as Kigali used his coughs, Furniver used ums, ers, pauses, rise and fall, and tone, well as a number of all-purpose basic words including *thingy*, and *wotsit*.

Kigali's opening cough had brought a response from Furniver, who politely produced a modest rumble in his throat.

Early morning pleasantries over, Kigali coughed again, indicating that he was all ears for whatever Furniver wished to raise.

"Mr, er, Mr Kigali, um," Edward Furniver began.

He could no more call his elderly, grey-haired steward Didymus than Kigali could call Furniver anything other than "sir".

"Suh," said Kigali.

He gave Furniver time to gather his thoughts, and while he waited reviewed the admirable qualities of his employer. Edward Furniver, Didymus Kigali had no doubt, was a good man. And this was not because of what Furniver had said to Charity, who had passed on an expurgated version to Mildred, who had in turn told her husband.

"Put my foot down on this one," Furniver had insisted soon after his arrival in Kireba. "It's one thing to have a chap old enough to be my dad working for me, who wears an all-white kit that makes him look like a bloody elderly cricketer in shorts, and who keeps count of my underpants. But I'm not letting him live under a couple of plastic bags or two, stretched over a few sticks!"

Mildred had not been particularly happy at the move to the new house, for it meant a longer walk to Harrods every day, but changed her mind when its corrugated tin roof held up without a single leak during the storms that had left much of the slum under a foot of water.

In the opinion of Kigali, Furniver had a further virtue.

"Never has he spoken about having talks behind the *kia*," Kigali told Mildred. "Never!"

He shook his grizzled, peppercorn head.

"Never."

He continued to rub the brass lever on the kitchen window. Then he stopped. Furniver was trying to communicate. Kigali resumed rubbing and dusting while his employer marshalled his thoughts.

"We need to, um, clear the, er, air. Indeed. Air. Um. Clear.

"Clear, the, um, air," Furniver repeated in an attempt to be helpful.

Kigali thought furiously.

Air . . . clear . . . insects . . . spray?

"We already have air clear, suh," preceding his response with an uncertain cough. Mosquitoes were a menace and Kigali sprayed Doom, the "Fast-kill all insect killer", every day at dusk. He had checked the night before, and there were at least three unused cans of Doom in the kitchen cupboard.

Nevertheless, Kigali gave another cough, deferential, yes, but nonetheless the tone indicated that the subject was not closed should Furniver wish to pursue it.

Furniver provided a conciliatory "um" in return, and tried again: "No, um, no, Mr Kigali . . ." Surely he was making himself plain?

Kigali coughed, encouragingly.

Furniver took the initiative.

"The, er, the, um, Vaseline thingy."

That was easy, thought Kigali, mistakenly.

"In the bathroom cupboard, suh."

Too easy. Kigali rebuked himself as the penny dropped.

He could have kicked himself for failing to recognise Furniver's concern.

"For *jipu*, suh," he quickly added.

Surely the poor man didn't have another one.

There had been an embarrassing misunderstanding when he had encountered Furniver, naked, inspecting an excruciatingly itchy bump in the cleft of his posterior. It was the result of an egg, laid by a fly known as a *jipu*, in a pair of underpants hung in the sun to dry, which had burrowed into Furniver's pink flesh.

Years of experience had taught Kuwisha settlers and their servants that the best way to deal with the menace of the *jipu* was to ensure that one's steward, or "boy" as they were known in pre-independence days, ironed one's underwear with a very hot iron – and failure to do this was, understandably, a sackable offence.

But if by ill-chance, or neglect, a *jipu* egg survived this pre-emptive hot iron, there was only one course of action: a dollop of Vaseline petroleum jelly smeared over the itchy bump soon overwhelmed the maggot and forced it to emerge for air.

It was while Furniver was preparing to tackle his affliction that Kigali had entered his employer's bedroom with a cup of tea. To say he was shocked by what he saw does not do justice to the steward's trauma.

"Even baboons," a distraught Kigali had told his wife Mildred, "even baboons, I have never seen doing that thing with finger – and Vaseline."

Ever since that unfortunate episode, happily resolved when Charity took Furniver to Cousin Mercy's clinic to have the *jipu* seen to, Kigali had watched Furniver's underpants like a hawk circling the veld.

Kigali coughed again. Not so much a cough as a gentle conciliatory clearing of the throat.

"Quite. My fault. Hot iron. Chap at the club warned me. Didn't check. *Jipu*, er."

Furniver had completed his confession.

There was no more to say, really.

Mr Kigali coughed appreciatively in turn, and both men averted their eyes.

The matter was closed.

But Furniver's decency did nothing to help Kigali resolve the other delicate matter that disturbed him so deeply. Indeed it made it all the more difficult. The more he thought about it, the more he was inclined to blame Charity. A wise madam never asked her steward to report on her man's drinking habits.

His father's words came back to him: "Do not take sides, Didymus, never. No-one can say who will win in a battle between madam and master. One thing I tell you – the house boy who interferes will always lose. That is for sure."

6

"What a little prick!"

Geoffrey Japer tossed the newspaper aside and stretched out in his business class seat on the BA flight to Kuwisha. It was the third time Japer had read the critical review of his latest TV series in *The Guardian*.

The snide comments left him all the more determined to make a success of the project that he had taken on. Normally Japer would have dismissed out of hand a request from the *Clarion*, NoseAid or anyone else for that matter, that he fly to Kuwisha to make a short documentary on the country's growing army of street kids and dwindling number of rhinos.

He did not care about the fate of rhinos in Kuwisha, nor was he bothered about the country's children or about children in general, for that matter. What was more, he would have been hard-pressed to locate Kuwisha on a map of Africa. Nor, to be frank, did he feel it was his role in life to raise money for the country's street kids who, it seemed from the briefing notes prepared for him by NoseAid, were roaming the streets in their hundreds, molesting tourists.

Finally, he was baffled by the slogan devised by the *Clarion*, which he could never get right.

Was it: *Save a rhino, help a child.*

Or was it: *Help a rhino, save a child.*

Or: *Save a child! Help a rhino!*

Or even: *Help a child save a rhino!*

And there was no guarantee that the project would be successful. His agent had been promised that the documentary would be shown at peak time on NoseNight, the annual televised fund-raising event; but it could as well disappear into the viewing graveyard after midnight.

Japer looked down at his briefing papers, given to him before he left London. Across the front of the folder was written a "mission statement": "Africa's children are its most precious asset. And the continent's wild life is one of the children's most important inheritances. If we can help, we must."

But the link between the fate of Kuwisha's street children, the plight of the country's rhino, and a NoseAid campaign to write off external debt, was no clearer.

He read on. The rhino-debt relief proposal, first made in a World Bank study, was now gaining credibility, it seemed, and was expected to be endorsed at a bank conference due to take place while Japer was in Kuwisha.

He put aside a paper on the subject and looked at the timetable that Lucy Gomball, resident director of WorldFeed, had e-mailed from Kuwisha before he set off for Heathrow: *11.00 Outspan Hotel: Guest appearance by UN children's ambassador Geoffrey Japer. In support of rhino/debt campaign.*

The stewardess began patrolling the aisle, handing out immigration cards and checking that passengers had fastened their seatbelts in advance of the landing, now some thirty minutes away.

Japer filled in the card, taking much satisfaction from answering the question about occupation. "NoseAid International Ambassador", he carefully and proudly printed.

A certificate to that effect, signed by the BBC's deputy director of programmes, had been presented to him when he checked in at Heathrow, "in recognition of (his) dedication to children in need, endangered animals and the environment".

He folded it into the pages of his passport, set aside his notes, and turned to his copy of the *Rugged Guide to Kuwisha*. Before stuffing the book into his overnight case, he finished the section on the Masaai. It didn't take long for him to grasp the gist of it: they were tall chaps who bobbed up and down in what was described as a dance, drank fresh blood from their cattle, and the young warrior men were called *moran*.

He must have dozed off, because when he next looked out of the cabin window, Africa's Rift Valley was well behind and the sprawling suburbs of the capital of Kuwisha lay below.

There were no tarred or paved roads in the crowded shanty town that Japer's plane flew over, only a muddy path that ran along-side the railway line that began its journey inland from the East African port of Mombasa and ended in neighbouring Uganda. The line served two purposes: cut into the side of the hill, it demarcated one boundary of an area smaller than New York's Central Park; and the railway itself provided pedestrian access to ramshackle shacks and shelters.

On one side of the track, the formal city began, with brick-built shops, albeit tatty and run-down, and with cars and roads, potholed though the latter were; less than a mile away were the fenced grounds of State House.

On the other side was a weed-encrusted dam, marking the western boundary, which used to be the home of the long defunct Sailing Club. Work had just begun on a motorway, slicing the slum down the middle, exposing a line of red earth like the first sweep of a surgeon's scalpel.

This controversial project, the brainchild of the city's mayor, Willifred Guchu, awaited the award of the final contracts for a scheme that, if aid donors were to be believed, would provide low-cost housing for the people of Kireba. Critics of Guchu, however, a long-time supporter of President Nduka, believed otherwise: the flats would surely be allocated to supporters of Nduka, and sold off for party funds.

*

Meanwhile Kireba's residents endured a daily struggle for space, jobs, and survival, eking out a precarious living.

On both banks of the winding path known as "Uhuru Avenue", so called in ironic tribute to the post-independence freedom that was proving illusory, hard-working people plied their trades. Gleaming, gutted fish were laid out on sheets of newspaper, as were green peppers, eggs, maize cobs, piles of salt, and small mounds of rice; chickens tethered by their feet, pecked in the mud; goats bleated; tomatoes and small oranges were set out next to piles of beans; onions were cut into quarters for those who could not afford to buy a whole one; all were on display, at keen prices.

The manifestations of law and order hovered carefully, cautiously on the outskirts. The police station where the officers of the state counted their daily takings in bribes and protection money, and the magistrates' court where those who did not pay up were disciplined, were located as close as they dared venture. And dotted around them were the offices of non-governmental organisations and their allies: from USAID to Christian Aid, from DANIDA to UKAID, from Oxfam to ComicAid and WorldFeed, walled outposts of international assistance.

This was Kireba.

To call this squalid slum the "home" of Titus Ntoto, Cyrus Rutere and the other street children who made up the Mboya Boys United Football Club might be misleading, for the word conjures up cosy images of some sort of family, some sort of security. Ntoto and his friends in the soccer club enjoyed none of this. But they knew no other place, let alone somewhere they could, in the conventional sense, call home; so whether as a point of reference, or as a geographical location, the boys – just like the other residents of Kireba – had a curious, perverse loyalty to the slum.

Yet what most people regarded as no more than a festering muddy compound with a collection of hovels was to other eyes a piece of real estate that made the city's property developers drool.

The prospect of a middle-class takeover concentrated the minds of the NGOs; who could blame them for seeking an alliance with the World Bank and UN development agencies, with which they could put their principles into practice, and build affordable homes, with water-borne sewerage, and taps with clean running water, and a school and a clinic?

And so sociologists and specialists, consultants and advisers, nearly all from overseas, the home of expertise, were in Kireba every day, clipboards in hand and briefcases at the ready, PhDs on display, sucking ideas from the locals, and their fees from aid budgets, and warning that without an injection of new buildings, the city centre would surely die.

And was not a rejuvenated Kireba the best place for recovery to start?

And who better than WorldFeed to lead the way, with the generous backing of the international development agencies, the World Bank at the helm?

Life in Kuwisha had, over the four decades since independence, settled into a rhythm that owed more to the generosity of Man than the blessings of Nature. The latter tended to be capricious in timing, and erratic in delivery, particularly when it came to rain. Man was far more dependable, and unlike Nature, was open to flattery, vulnerable to cajoling and to appeals to a sense of fairness and decency, as well as susceptible to exploitation of a sense of guilt.

The rains, on the other hand, were unpredictable, unreliable, and often inadequate. More than one third of Kuwisha was arid, unproductive land, and there were no mineral assets of any significance.

Poor though it was, the population had doubled in twenty-five years. And as it increased, so the people spread across the land to areas where, had it not been for the generosity of the donors, life would have been impossible. Organisations like WorldFeed ensured that while people might go hungry in bad years, they would not starve to death; and in order to ensure that the food aid would reach its destination, WorldFeed officials played important roles in Kuwisha's railway system. Indeed, were it not for this assistance, it was probable that the railways would not have worked at all.

It was seen as a measure of the government's determination that it regularly forecast food self-sufficiency by the end of each five-year national development plan, drawn up with the backroom advice of foreign experts and consultants.

In an uncertain world, at least the people could depend on the reassuring presence of the many international agencies based in the country, on the annual largesse of the aid donors, and the generosity of the body which brought them together every couple of years: the Consultative Group, chaired by the World Bank.

With the regularity of clockwork, in a cycle as ordered as the seasons themselves, the bank and the rest of the international donor community assessed the benefit of their presence since independence, four decades during which donors and government had joined forces in what was proving a long and sometimes frustrating battle against poverty.

Some cynics and sceptics claimed that while the odd battle was won, the war was being lost. Forty years after independence from Britain, they argued, echoing the Oldest Member, more people than ever were poorer – nearly two in every three struggling to survive on less than two dollars a day, according to official figures from the Ministry of Development.

This materialistic appraisal, this crude yardstick of progress, was dismissed as Afro-pessimism at its worst. Any differences between the two, between lenders and borrowers, donors and recipients, were set aside. True, they had sharply contrasted views on the merits of conditionality, or the advisability of programme aid, and harsh words passed between them on the pros and cons of project aid, and the virtues of budgetary support; but they diverged on the strategy of bypassing state institutions altogether in an effort to avoid the corruption that had become endemic.

Yet for all these differences, both givers and receivers agreed on one thing – nothing should be allowed to stand in the way of continuing efforts to ease the plight of the poor.

This year, however, the bank's consultative conference would break new ground. A plenary on the subject of the language of international assistance would be opened by its president, Hardwick Hardwicke.

Even for a man with a reputation for being controversial, the title of his address was the talk of the donor community: "Aid: the enemy of development". As delegates gathered in the lobby of the Outspan Hotel, one question was uppermost in the minds of them all: was the head of the world's biggest development agency really going to attack the very lifeblood of their business?

7

"Duty boy! Urgent!"

The cry from Charity rang out.

There was a rustling from under the bar counter of Harrods.

Two teenage boys emerged, the one short, the other taller, both skinny, and both clad in T-shirt and shorts, so worn and stained that the original colours had been driven out and replaced by drab khaki.

Their early-morning shift all but over, they had retreated to their den for a sniff of glue. The boys rubbed their bloodshot eyes.

Charity could tell from their dilated pupils that they had started their day by inhaling from the plastic bottle each had dangling from a string round their necks.

"Breakfast?" they asked anxiously.

She nodded. No matter how often they ate at Harrods, each time they were fed seemed both a surprise and a relief to them.

Titus Ntoto and Cyrus Rutere looked cautiously around them, like bush buck at a watering hole, alert for enemies. Only then, satisfied it was safe, did they emerge from behind the counter.

Neither boy knew the precise date of their birth, but their parents had told them they had been born during the great drought that had afflicted Kuwisha some fourteen years earlier, and which had forced their families to abandon their parched patches of land, too small to sustain them even when the rains were good.

Like thousands and thousands of others who fled the barren land, the two families headed for Kireba – Ntoto's from the west, Rutere's from the north.

The respite was short-lived.

In the riots that followed the influx of destitute competitors for Kireba's scarce resources, whether water, or shelter, or jobs, both sets of parents had fled, and Ntoto and Rutere were separated from their families in the bloody confusion. Thrown together, the boys had forged a friendship over the years that transcended their ethnic differences.

But nature and nurture had created two boys who could hardly have been more different in appearance. Ntoto was easily the taller of the two, with spindly legs and narrow chest; while Rutere, the runt of his family's litter, was short , with a distended belly.

Rutere led the way to the kitchen.

Usually the boys would fire questions at Charity, after wolfing down a bowl of maize porridge, and if they were lucky, a sweet dough ball which she had discarded as too stale for paying customers.

Today they were quiet. She resisted the temptation to enquire, even though it was clear that something was up. For the past few weeks, usually after football practice, members of the Mboya Boys had sat at the table set aside for them at Harrods, chattering as loudly as birds at dawn, but falling silent if she or any other adult came within earshot.

And always present, always at the centre of attention, had been Bright Khumalo, the leading scorer for the Under-15 team that looked a certainty to win the Lardner Burke cup, a trophy presented to the league by a philanthropic settler.

One morning about two weeks ago, she had been asked, with a studied casualness, by Ntoto, about how one became a professional footballer in England. She had not a clue, and told him so: "Stop this dreaming business, Ntoto, otherwise you will become a loafer."

During the evening of that day there had been a lot of laughter and much drinking of *changa* by the boys, and a group, which included Ntoto, Rutere and Bright Khumalo, had set off for town. Charity had lain awake that night, fearful that they would get into trouble with the police, or would come off second best in the goading of security guards that had become a popular sport.

Only when she heard the voices of Ntoto and Rutere on their return, well after midnight, and the clink of empty bottles as they moved the crates that protected the entrance to their den under the bar counter, was she able to relax, and fall asleep.

But she had not laid eyes on Bright since then.

"He is on safari," was all Ntoto said when she had asked, and a mask of indifference came over his face. She knew from past experience that further questioning would get her nowhere.

Charity took a sip from her mug of tea, and called out to Ntoto and Rutere, who were about to set off on their daily journey to the post office.

"Avocados. Collect from Mr Ogata's cousin, at the market. And when you have been to the post office," she continued, "go to Central Bank. There is a letter for me from the governor."

To Charity's surprise, the boys, usually keen on city-centre outings, had bridled.

"Say the magic word," said Rutere.

"Please, will you go to the bank," said Charity.

Rutere seemed to be satisfied, having turned the tables on Charity, who was a stickler for courtesies.

But Ntoto pressed home the advantage.

"Two dough balls," demanded Ntoto.

"It's worth one dough ball,' said Charity.

Ntoto stood his ground.

"Two."

"One," repeated Charity, who was starting to get irritated.

"One dough ball is for normal service, with delivery tomorrow. Two dough balls is airmail service, with delivery today. Guaranteed. No halfway bargaining."

"That Ntoto," she concluded, after telling the story to Furniver over breakfast at Harrods, "he is intelligent."

Furniver had no doubt about that: the boy was certainly sharp, cunning, devious, manipulative and not without a certain charm. What he also suspected – although he was reluctant to put his suspicion too bluntly to Charity for fear of upsetting her – was that Ntoto also had the qualities of what locals called a *tsotsi*. In other words, the boy had a streak of the ruthless in him.

While he, Furniver, had little knowledge of the deep and treacherous waters of township politics, he suspected that Ntoto had what it took to fill the vacant slot of the Kireba ward area boy – effectively the township's gang boss. And if past events were any guide, the next stage in Ntoto's career would either be death in the traditional car crash, or he could well become the local MP.

"The boy does have a certain rat-like cunning," Furniver began.

He regretted the word "rat" as soon as it left his mouth, and braced himself for the explosion that followed.

Charity gave a furious click of frustration and irritation.

"Rats? What's this business of rats, Furniver?"

Only when Charity was especially angry did the syllables of his Christian name become elided to what sounded like "Funva".

"Rats are for dreams, and sometimes for eating," she continued. "I am talking about a boy, called Titus Ntoto. And you are saying he is a rat? Shame for you! That boy, he is going to be an area boy! An area boy! And all you can say is he is like a rat!"

Before Furniver could point out that Charity herself called the boys "rats", albeit affectionately, she disappeared into the Harrods kitchen, which was out of bounds to adult males.

It was outbursts like this that tested their relationship, but as always, Furniver was sustained by his resilient belief: life would undoubtedly be better, in every way, with Charity Mupanga by his side.

8

Just how, or when, a pair of ordinary knitting needles began to assume a symbolic significance at the Kireba Christian Ladies' Sewing Circle, no-one could quite recall. It may well have begun when the needles, a gift from the Diplomatic Wives Association, were brought out to open the meeting, and paraded round the room with mock gravity, like the mace in Kuwisha's parliament.

The circle itself had been set up by Charity not long after she opened Harrods. Launched in the bad old days of one-party rule in Kuwisha, the purpose was simple. Women needed a place where they could exchange thoughts without the inhibiting presence of their men folk.

If men felt excluded from the democratic process in a one-party state, women were doubly excluded in what was a male chauvinist society. The ladies of Kireba wanted a venue where they could discuss everything from domestic violence to the cost of living and the pain of economic reforms, but without attracting attention, either from their men or the state. So Charity had sought a name for the group which in itself would provide a pretext for women to gather regularly at the bar and discuss the issues of the day, but discourage husbands who felt nothing but disdain for what they called "women work".

Some of the members did indeed sew, or knit, but a pair of the needles had become little more than props, kept at the back of the bar in a wooden box made by Philimon Ogata; and while fingers nimbly engaged thread and wool, their minds were on conversation about current affairs, or discussion of the weaknesses of men in general.

On circle evenings the women pulled up the benches to form a square, and during winter there was a charcoal brazier in the centre, on which those who wanted could roast cobs of tender young maize. Beer was not available, partly out of deference to Mildred Kigali who, like her husband Didymus, was an ardent teetotaller. The main reason, however, was that the absence of alcohol made it a particularly unattractive environment for the men of Kireba.

But even if alcoholic drinks had been on sale, few of the women could afford it, even at the keen prices set by Charity. Instead the ladies began their sessions fortified by mugs of strong tea, sweetened with dollops of condensed milk, or a glass of fresh fruit juice accompanied by a few bowls of fried and salted potato skins, all laid on by Charity at cost.

Everyone was happy: husbands were satisfied that they knew where their wives were and what they were doing, and after a few initial checks, the Special Branch stopped monitoring the circle, and left it to get on with matters, discouraged by the reference to sewing, and the absence of alcohol.

And if there was any doubt about the boring, esoteric nature of the subject supposedly for discussion, it was there for all to read, posted outside the bar. This month's topic was pinned to Harrods' notice-board.

Laboriously set out in hand, Mildred Kigali had used a blue ballpoint pen for the text and a red pen for the underlining. The result was indeed impressive:

Christian Ladies' Sewing Circle (Kireba branch)
NEXT MEETING
FRIDAY at 7
"INFLATION: THE CURSE OF A NATION"

Speaker: William Otamu, Governor, Bank of Kuwisha
ALL WELLCOME

NB Subscriptions will be collected at door
STRICT
NO PAYMENT NO ADMISSION
BY ORDER
MILDRED KIGALI
CHAIRWOMAN

It was the first time a man had been invited to address the circle, and Mildred had sought an explanation.

"It was Furniver's suggestion. But Otamu is a very boring speaker. No man will come to listen to him, especially if there is no beer, and if he has to pay, and there are so many women," Charity replied.

And so when Otamu was summoned to Washington for emergency talks with the IMF, Furniver immediately did the decent thing.

"Look here, my dear, I know a fair bit about inflation and the velocity of money," he reassured her. "I don't even need to prepare notes, I can rattle it off at a moment's notice. But just to be on the safe side, I will go to my office right now, and tap something out. What time is kick-off?"

"Fine," said Charity. "Seven exact."

Odd, thought Furniver. It seemed to him that she had been more relieved than disappointed when he had told her that the governor had pulled out. And she was less than appreciative when Furniver had insisted on standing in.

Odd, damned odd.

All of this did nothing to ease his mind on the subject of the Lambs. He would have to raise his concerns with Charity . . . and the sooner the better.

9

Mildred Kigali put down the cloth she was using to wipe the early morning dew off the table-tops at Harrods, and pulled up her long green skirt a couple of discreet inches, revealing smart white tennis shoes at the end of lean, muscled legs. She flexed her knees, and did a couple of tentative dance steps, shifting and swaying from foot to foot.

For a few glorious moments last night she had felt like a teenager again. Not that she would like to be a teenager in this day and age. But as she had led the assembled ladies in an impromptu conga, weaving its way through the bar, knitting needle in each hand, their sharp tips covered with two small paw-paws, the impulse of youth had coursed through her veins.

Indeed, such had been the impact of her performance, she had been asked to repeat it at the next meeting . . . well, not asked exactly, but when she had suggested she might do it again, no-one had objected.

Her moves became more confident and she drifted into nostalgia, remembering the first time she had spotted Didymus Kigali, the handsome young man who was to become her husband. She began to sing – or at least, she made a sound that was mainly a low pitched hum, with the occasional word emerging.

Like Charity, Mildred Kigali had risen especially early, for there was much work to do. Usually the clearing up after the monthly meeting of the Christian Ladies' Sewing Circle was done by a handful of volunteers at the end of the meeting itself. But the appearance of the *tokolosh* had meant that the session had ended in disarray and the ladies who usually lent a hand had scattered.

Perhaps her young friend Charity, so sceptical about the existence of a creature that could assume whatever shape that their need required, though more often than not they took the form of a goat or a donkey, would now think again. After all, it had been spotted by Edward Furniver, a European!

Mildred continued to shuffle and sing. Soon she was back at her childhood home, in the village where she had been born, soon after the great floods of 1925. One memory stood out above all others. On a sultry hot morning, soon after the start of World War Two, she had seen her father for the last time.

She would never forget the day the men of her village, volunteers all, had gathered to board the trucks that would take them to the training depots, where they would prepare to fight for Britain.

Her father had led them, led a singing column that waved goodbye to wives and children left behind. Amongst those children was a boy who looked straight ahead, and saluted the departing men, holding his hand in place until the trucks had moved out of sight, down the track that led to the tarred road and the city that lay beyond.

Mildred had moved closer to the boy, and he had been surprised by this forward behaviour.

Mildred, still in her teens, plucked up her courage.

"What is your name?"

"Didymus Kigali."

It had been a long time ago.

So long ago that the wild animals had roamed free. Today her home village was a town, and the animals had all but disappeared, hunted for their flesh, for their tusks, or for sport. Mildred seldom visited her birthplace. The hut in which she had been brought up had gone, along with the village mango trees, and she found that going back was painful and disturbing.

But she had never forgotten the song of the villagers on that day, the song she sang at Harrods that morning, as the sun's early rays began to take the chill off the morning air.

Mildred Kigali started her chores.

She began, as always, by wiping away the chalked contents of the blackboard menu, propped up on an easel, which was also used during the weekly literacy classes. A list of wholesome dishes had been set out below the hand-painted sign at the top: "Good Food, Best Prices!"

The menu had started with pumpkin and corn soup, then there were "bitings" of thick potato skins, fried in chicken fat and lightly salted; and goat stew and cabbage; also the ever popular *ugali* and beans ("groundnut relish, or gravy, extra"); and the bill of fare ended with Charity's famous dough balls ("sugar extra") and "frut juice" – mango, passion fruit or orange.

For a few seconds Mildred Kigali was confused. Something was amiss. Was it spelled frute juce? Or frut juice? Neither seemed quite right. Those Mboya Boys! They were in charge of chalking up the menu each day. Despite Charity's efforts to teach the street children the three Rs, there was at least one spelling mistake in the menu each day. "Frut juice" indeed. Sometimes she suspected that the spelling mistake was not a mistake at all, but a deliberate error, just to get a rise out of an old lady.

Mildred grunted. Someone had scrawled "Nduka is a thief" at the bottom of the board, and because she shared the sentiments about President Josiah Nduka, it was the last of the marks she rubbed off. But it was not proper, a president should be respected . . . even if you did not agree with all the things he did.

"Eh-heh," said a voice in her head: "What if he has lost the right to your respect because he chops, because he is corrupt?"

Mildred Kigali had reached an age when certain things distressed her. In particular, people no longer understood the difference between right and wrong. Her old friend Charity should be tougher and stricter with the Mboya Boys. Instead she spoilt them.

"It is a slipping slope," Mildred had warned, more than once.

Mildred also felt duty bound to keep a close eye on Charity Mupanga's relationship with the English man in charge of Kireba's community bank. She did not disapprove of the budding friendship between the two. But it was well known that all men were driven by base needs, interested only in what Mildred called "steamies", the invariable outcome of "hanky-hanky".

If only Charity and Furniver would acknowledge their share of the sins of mankind and seek redemption through the Church of the Blessed Lamb. As for Charity's late husband, the Anglican bishop of Central Kuwisha, surely he should have an influence that extended beyond the grave?

Not that being an Anglican bishop meant anything these days. She had followed the debate about homosexual marriages on the BBC World Service, broadcast in FM from the radio that sat on the top shelf, behind the bar. She shook her head indignantly. Marrying one man to another man! Whatever next? Man and goat? It was, she felt, the sort of moral aberration that had confirmed the decision of Didymus Kigali to leave the Anglican Church several years earlier. The couple now sought everlasting life in the capacious but stern bosom of the Church of the Blessed Lamb, Kuwisha's fastest growing sect, which defended old values and warned of the eternal damnation that awaited those who denied the Light of the Lord.

"Mildred!"

There was a tone of urgency in the call that came from Charity, who had arrived a few minutes earlier, still rubbing her eyes and yawning.

"Mildred!"

"Coming, coming . . ."

10

"I suppose," said Cecil Pearson, Kuwisha-based Africa correspondent of the London *Financial News*, standing in front of
Punabantu's desk as if before the headmaster, "I suppose you are
going to deport me."

"Why on earth would we deport you? Why would we do that?"

The press secretary to President Nduka seemed genuinely taken
aback.

"Investigate your tax returns, yes. Check your foreign exchange dealings, certainly. We might even ask your steward
and your gardener whether you contribute on their behalf to
the national security fund, as every employer is obliged to do."

As Puna almost certainly knew, there was not a journalist in
town who had not broken all these laws.

"But deport you?"

He shook his head.

"Why should we do you a favour? Before you know it, you
would be an 'award winning journalist' – that's the phrase, isn't
it, 'award winning'?"

He shuddered. "And then you'd be giving lectures in London,
addressing Amnesty . . . no telling where it would end."

Matters had moved with extraordinary speed.

A couple of days earlier, Pearson had been on the BA flight to
London, awaiting take-off, relishing the prospect of disclosing the
contents of a secretly tape recorded session between the leader of
the opposition and President Nduka, in the president's office.

Minutes before the cabin doors were shut, Pearson had
been marched off the plane by a senior Central Intelligence

Organisation official, and both men had sat in the airport office as the tape was replayed.

Quite how it was that, instead of hearing President Nduka attempt to bribe the country's opposition leader, they listened to Edward Furniver reading a story to his god-children. Pearson could not understand.

But even the notorious CIO needed more than circumstantial evidence to put a British journalist on trial for what could well be his life. And after two nights in a filthy prison cell the Africa correspondent for the London *Financial News* had been driven to State House, where he found himself standing in the office of Jonathan Punabantu.

Punabantu looked positively agitated.

"Deport you?" he asked again.

He shook his head. "Of course not. In fact, you're welcome to stay for a few days. Probably get another interview with the Old Man. He's very keen on this debt-for-rhino swap. You know about it? Top of the donor agenda . . . the meeting starts today."

Pearson had heard rumours that such a swap was in the offing. Here was Puna, all but confirming it. The journalist in him took over, and he began composing an intro to a news story, in his head: "Africa's threatened rhino population will benefit from an unprecedented debt relief deal between Kuwisha and its external creditors."

Not a bad lead, he thought. The next paragraph all but wrote itself:

"Underwritten by the World Bank and backed by the international aid agency WorldFeed, the scheme links an increase in the country's depleted game stock to the write-off of external debt. If the pilot programme in Kuwisha proves successful, it will be offered to all of Africa's highly indebted poorest countries."

Not bad at all. Certainly a story worth staying on for for an extra few days, before returning to London for a stint on the *Financial*

News foreign desk. His time in Africa had spoiled him. Try as he may, he could not get excited by editing stories on vehicle emission control regulations issued by Brussels, or the latest flat-bed knitting machine directive from the Ministry of Industry.

Was there a catch in the offer, wondered Pearson. The mood in the presidential press secretary's office at State House certainly remained a bit frosty.

Punabantu studied the nervous young man.

Pearson, blood caked around the head wound where a rioting student's stone had hit him three nights ago, started to feel dizzy. The room began to tilt, and Pearson concentrated his gaze on a Christmas tree, complete with angels, which occupied a corner of the office.

"Be sure, Mr Cecil Pearson, we know your tricks. You have been lucky, very, very lucky. The tape you were listening to when security picked you up on the plane was the wrong one.

"But" – Jonathan Punabantu wagged his finger vigorously – "now we know you. This time, we watch you. Maybe, you are a spy, someone Joshua Nkomo, you know, the big man who fought Ian Smith of Rhodesia, used to call 'a journalist plus'?"

Pearson said nothing.

"I hope you have been well treated?"

Looking back over the events of the past couple of days, Pearson had to concede that no-one had actually laid a finger on him. But he had been more frightened than he cared to admit. In fact the experience had been ghastly. And when the Central Intelligence officers had come to question him, they made some nasty threats.

He described some of the more upsetting suggestions to Puna.

The press secretary made noises of sympathy.

"Dreadful, quite dreadful. The things they can do with a plastic bag and buckets of water. Will you be making a formal complaint, then?"

Pearson shook his head.

For the next couple of minutes Punabantu leafed through a file, which Pearson assumed was his.

Every now and then, the man smiled, or clicked his tongue and looked up disapprovingly at Pearson, who was still standing in front of the desk. At last, he said: "Sit down, sit down. You really are a lucky man . . ."

Pearson lowered himself into one of the office green leather armchairs, bought in the 1950s from London's Reform Club by the British colonial governor of Kuwisha.

Punabantu put the file to one side.

"So, Pearson. You didn't take the president's advice."

Puna could only be referring to the interview with President Nduka granted not long before his airport arrest.

"What advice was that?"

"To keep your nose out of Kuwisha's business."

"He invited me to come back, for God's sake. Said I could write my book here. Even said I would be welcome. In fact, suggested I shouldn't leave . . . instead of behaving like a typical expat, going home after a three-year contract is up . . ."

The words tumbled out, and to his dismay, Pearson felt close to tears.

Puna shrugged.

"Pearson," he said, "you are too clever" – the word "clever" was seldom used in a complimentary sense in Kuwisha. It was redolent of contempt, leavened only by grudging respect for sheer cunning.

"When you asked me at the end of your audience with HE whether he was talking about domestic politics, I said he was."

Pearson nodded.

"Yes, of course I remember. So what?"

"So you were warned, but still went ahead."

Puna stood, came round his desk and dropped into an armchair opposite the journalist.

"It was a warning to all dissidents, foreign and local. He spoke about lions that attack bravely from the front, yes?"

Pearson nodded.

"And leopards that are more dangerous because they are snakes and attack from behind . . . yes?"

For a moment Pearson was baffled . . . lions, leopards, now snakes. Then he realised that the press secretary was talking about sneaks.

Puna wasn't finished.

"Well, Mr Cecil Pearson, whose father so admired Cecil John Rhodes, are you like a leopard? Or perhaps the president was too kind. I myself think that you and your kind are like vultures. Not killing, but watching, always watching."

The press secretary stood up, sucked in his paunch, stuck his head forward, elongated his neck, and flapped his arms. For a moment he had become one of the scavenging birds that descended on the city each day.

He resumed his seat.

There was a knock on the door, and a steward came in with a tray which he set down on the table between them, and then backed out, deferentially.

"Help yourself . . . scones made in the State House kitchen," said Puna.

On the tray was a pot of tea kept hot by a cosy with a print of Anne Hathaway's cottage, two teacups and saucers, slices of lemon, a bowl of sugar and a jug of milk, with the flies kept at bay by a beaded muslin cover. In the middle, protected by this array of crockery, stood a silver cake holder piled high with scones, while a bowl alongside had strawberry jam and butter.

Pearson could not help noticing that the butter, individually wrapped in foil, was from Denmark and the jam, sealed in little tubs, was from Holland.

"Yes," said Puna, following his guest's gaze, "we have many

cows and grow strawberries on the Nyali plateau. But you know why we import these things, Pearson, my friend?"

The journalist nodded.

WorldFeed, the Oxford-based development agency, had lectured him often enough. Taxes on goods processed in Africa, such as coffee, imposed by Western governments, made it difficult for locals to compete.

Spare me, he thought, but braced himself for a homily. It wasn't forthcoming. Instead: "One lump or two?"

"One lump, please."

"Scone? You realise, Pearson, that you have finished that kitchen *toto* once called Mlambo?"

Suddenly Pearson felt physically ill. Surely they hadn't killed the boy?

"And not only Mlambo. You finished many people who were depending on that ex-*toto*."

Pearson lacked the energy to respond and the cut on his head continued to throb.

"More tea? I gather the ex-*toto* has at least seven brothers and sisters; his parents had their siblings as well. They all depended on him."

Puna sat back in his chair.

"We in Africa believe in power sharing. This is why Mobutu lasted so long in Zaire. He shared the benefits of power."

He laughed. "What does this have to do with Mlambo?"

Puna answered his own question.

"Being close to people with power can be very useful, very profitable, like having power itself. Now the poor boy is finished, and many, many people who lived off him, like ticks on a dog's back, will find life harder. Don't meddle, Mr Pearson, if you don't understand."

"But Mlambo's not dead?"

Once again Puna looked shocked.

"Why would we kill him? There are worse punishments for people who abuse the president's trust . . ."

The comments fanned a spark of rebellion in Pearson's soul. He wanted to say that corruption and bad government affected a million Mlambos; that Kuwisha's politicians did more harm than good, and a lot more harm than any Western journalist . . . but he lacked the energy.

Puna stood up.

There were still some scones left on the tray. Puna wrapped one in a paper napkin, and offered it to Pearson.

"Take it," he ordered. "A present for your Lucy."

They left the office, and together walked to the main entrance of State House, where two ancient stuffed lions guarded a pair of elephant's tusks, taken from a beast shot by "Flogger" Morland's father, M.Q. 'Tubby' Morland, in 1936 according to the engraved brass plaque.

As they exited the building, the heat of the day almost overwhelmed Pearson, and his eyes took a few seconds to adapt to the sun. He stumbled, and would have fallen but for Puna's steadying hand.

Much to Pearson's surprise the press secretary stayed with him until they reached the gate. Proximity to power, he thought. In a country where symbolism counted, was it Punabantu's way of indicating that he was being forgiven?

"Get someone to take a look at that cut. And please, Pearson, write your article about debt and rhino. Stick to what you know and to what your people really care about. No more politics. Greetings to Rucy," smiled Puna, deliberately transposing the L and the R, in the way that was characteristic among most residents of Kuwisha.

"You should marry that woman, she is very tough. I phoned before you came, to tell her you will be waiting for her."

I I

A battered brown Jeep with 'WorldFeed' stencilled in white letters on the door panels drew up just before the sentry box outside the red-brick main entrance to State House. The driver ignored the soldiers on duty, and sounded the car horn. Pearson emerged from the guard house, looking sheepish. As always, the sight of the fair-haired, blue-jeaned figure of Lucy Gomball made his heart beat faster.

"Tit!" she said, and kissed his cheek. "Get in, I'm driving. And you can't stay with me. Sorry!"

The soldier, who had been obliged to move aside smartly or risk being run over, acknowledged Lucy's apology with a snappy salute.

"Isn't he sweet? The house is absolutely chocka. Protect the Pastoralists and Save the bloody Nomads. Just out from Oxford. I can't stand them, and they can't stand each other. Booked you at the Milimani. Told the paper you're OK. Cecil who, they asked . . . Joke. Message from the foreign desk. Need a new photo for your by-line. And ring the Outspan, ask for accreditation. Puna told me you could stay for the donors' do, by the way. Pooh! You need a bath!"

Pearson didn't respond immediately.

A *matatu* driver, his passengers so tightly packed that arms and heads poked through the open windows, like straws from a bale, was on the point of pulling out. He thought again, moving closer to the road verge rather than risk a clash with a woman who drove as creatively as any of his fellow *matatu* drivers.

Lucy and Cecil flew past the taxi van, with its slogan, hand-painted in green and yellow, "Death Leads to Everlasting Life", and with charms and tokens dangling from the driver's mirror, including a long-expired air freshener in the shape of a fir tree.

Lucy took her hand off the horn, and waved.

The driver waved back, grinning broadly.

His *matatu* boy, collector of fares, crammer-in of passengers, hung from the side-step of the van, shouting out the name of the next stop, negotiating passenger prices and propositioning pretty girls in between exchanging badinage with rivals and cursing drivers who had the temerity to exercise their right of way. He too caught Lucy's eye, and smiled.

How did she do it, Pearson wondered. Any other civilian, male or female, black or white, pretty or plain, young or old, that came between a *matatu* driver and his destination did so at their peril. Any hint of doubt about directions, or any display of indecision about when to turn, and they would be greeted at best by a prolonged blast on a powerful horn, followed by a longer blast of scorn and invective – and at worst, forced off the road.

In the tough competitive world of *matatus*, time was money; and if aggressive driving and a powerful horn saved enough minutes, enough to allow an extra journey in the day, well, why not? The extra cash would not be declared to the owner of the *matatu*, as likely as not a fat-cat politician or official from the ruling party.

There was a price to pay for the risks taken – an accident rate as high as anywhere in the world, but even that brutal reality could be cushioned.

There was always religion to fall back on.

"Love the Lord and cheat Death," otherwise known as the Kireba Express, "First class service, economy fare", roared on its noisy, fume-ridden journey through the city to the slum, the driver exchanging hoots and waves with Lucy when she turned down the road that led to the Hotel Milimani.

"Bloody cheat. Three all. I'll get him next time!"

And Lucy flashed Pearson a conspiratorial smile that melted his heart, at about the same moment he realised that she had been racing the *matatu*.

"S'pose you're pleased with yourself . . ."

"I feel such an arse," said Pearson.

"Perhaps that's because you *are* an arse."

"At least I don't race with *matatus*. Bloody dangerous."

"Prig!"

She thumped his thigh. "By the way, you know the new toilet designed in Zimbabwe? The type that Charity has been asking WorldFeed to finance?"

Pearson nodded.

Charity's campaign to instal the cheap and ingenious design which trapped flies and thus saved lives in Kireba had been unremitting.

"Well, we have the go-ahead for six. First goes in tomorrow. Charity thinks it's Christmas!"

The journey from State House to the Hotel Milimani took them past the Uhuru Park with its monument to Kuwisha's founding president – built to resemble a flaming torch, his party symbol – and into the city centre.

The traffic was dreadful.

Alongside modern four-wheel drives ran ancient cars and old buses which belched clouds of acrid exhaust fumes; the fact that they were still on the road a tribute to the ingenuity and skill of the self-trained mechanics who worked from open air garages, rudimentary tools set out on oily canvas sheets spread out under the jacaranda trees planted during the colonial era.

The number of old bangers was carefully monitored by the police. The more there were on the road, the more the number of fines that could be levied at the numerous check points in and around the city – the proceeds going into police pockets, of course.

Lucy swerved to avoid a pothole.

"Puna said I could stay to cover the donor meeting. The rhino-debt swap seems on."

"I know. Just said. He told me."

"What do you think?"

He well knew that Lucy did not share his enthusiasm for budget deficits, exchange rates and World Bank development programmes, subjects that made him go weak at the knees. But external debt, surely that did interest her?

"Will they really let me stay to cover the meeting?"

Lucy shrugged.

"Don't see why not – though don't see why they should."

"The *FN* is the only paper that has followed the story." Pearson ran his forefinger along the grizzled snout of Shango, Lucy's dog, who wagged his tail.

Lucy prodded the animal, stretched out under the passenger seat, with a pink toe. "He's only pleased to see you because you dish out dog biscuits."

"He's a dog," said Pearson, as if this explained everything.

"Why on earth do you want to stay? Nothing will change."

"The donors' meeting," said Pearson wistfully. "It will coin-cide with NoseAid and that rhino project. The IMF and the bank will be there. They're bound to discuss debt relief. Save-a-Child is sending someone out to lobby for a complete write-off."

"So are we," said Lucy. "Some deal with the *Clarion*."

She pursed her lips and flicked back a strand of fine blonde hair that had escaped the faded blue sweatband around her forehead.

"Nothing will change," she said again. "You underestimate Nduka. Always have. And overestimate the editorials you write. The *FN* pretends that they make a difference; the donors pretend to get cross, and lay down the law; and Kuwisha pretends to put things right. Everybody happy. 'Cept the bloody *wananchi*, the *povo*, the people, the masses . . . whatever you call them."

There was relish in her voice, but Pearson either failed to notice it or ignored it. Instead he said again, but quietly, more reflectively: "I *am* an arse . . ."

He flicked through the local newspapers Lucy had brought with her.

The stories they carried said as much about Kuwisha as effectively as anything he filed.

There were examples of corruption; the environment was deteriorating; coffee production was falling; and the government seemed to place the interests of its Western allies above its own.

Fish eagles had been found dead on Naiva Lake, having eaten fish poisoned by pesticides used by the flourishing horticultural ventures on the edge of the lake, which were running down the water table.

Meanwhile British soldiers, on a training exercise in Kuwisha and who had allegedly been involved in the theft of a car, had been released without explanation; and US marines arrested during a bar room brawl at Kuwisha's main port had been allowed to rejoin their ship.

Parliament had begun another long break, but not before awarding members a further salary rise which left them the best paid legislators in the world.

Pearson finished reading the headlines to Lucy.

"It's a mess. But I can't help caring. I've really got Africa in my blood," said Pearson. Although he was in the jeep, and out of the sun, he recovered his floppy cotton hat from the jaws of Shango, wiped off the dog's saliva, and put it on.

"Don't say it!" he warned Lucy.

"Say what?"

"That I look like a condom when I wear this hat."

"You said it," said Lucy, and sniggered.

"I love Africa, I really do."

"Rot. If you have anything African in your blood, it's bilharzia. And you are not in love – you're just infatuated."

Pearson appeared not to have heard.

"Thanks for your help in getting me out," said Pearson. "Puna told me to marry you, by the way."

Lucy just grimaced.

She parked the car next to the Milimani, and the exchange continued as they climbed the stairs to the third floor of the hotel, where Pearson would be staying until there was a spare bed at Lucy's home in Borrowdale, one of the city's suburbs favoured by aid workers and diplomats.

The Milimani sat hunched on a hill, not far from State House, in slow, idiosyncratic decline, a 1960s concrete block, brooding and scarred like a retired boxer remembering old glories, lost in the past.

Over the three years he had been based in Kuwisha, Pearson had got to know the place, adapting to its ways, and tolerating its eccentricities.

He had learnt how to jiggle the key to get into his room – always 339 – thanks, he suspected, to the Central Intelligence Organisation. He had mastered the manipulation of the handle required to flush the toilet. He had come to terms with the mysteries of the hot water system. He now hardly noticed the stains on the green-grey carpet; he no longer speculated about their origins.

True, he had failed to track down the source of a curious smell from one of the cupboards, and some late night noises had been alarming. And he had yet to discover if those wires that trailed by his door were live, or how the television worked.

Nevertheless, he felt at home in Room 339. It had not always been thus.

At first Pearson had needed to overcome his distaste at the state of the room's carpets, and cope with a journey that made him squeamish.

Bed to bathroom was but a few early-morning barefoot steps, but it was not just the variety of stains on the threadbare carpet that deterred him. It was its topsoil ingredients, trodden in by many guests over many years: a mulch of skin flakes and toenail cuttings, gravy from countless take-aways, cigarette ash, crumbs and crisps, a veritable compost in which exotic varieties of athlete's foot and other fungi surely flourished.

But the hotel was cheap, and the staff were friendly. Once up-market, the Milimani now catered for a different clientele. There were still back-packers from Europe, but most of the guests were from Kuwisha, or business travellers from Sudan or Somali, who had come with families, and rented long-stay apartments.

Of course, the Outspan, up-market, venerable and redolent with nostalgia, was still his favourite hotel in Kuwisha; no doubt about that, but if you didn't book well in advance, you wouldn't get a room.

"Lift!" Lucy said bitterly. "Never bloody works."

She was showing signs of the expatriates' notorious three-year fever, switching from deepest pessimism to boundless optimism, and through to angry cynicism. When these emotions were contained in the same breath, when scepticism and hope followed hard on each other's heels, like a dog chasing its own tail, it was time to leave. Soon she would start talking back at ministers when she heard them on radio or TV.

"There is something about Africa you just don't get in Europe," said Pearson wistfully.

"Intestinal worms, jiggers, river blindness, malaria . . ." Lucy responded, and snorted.

"I love Kuwisha. I love Africa," said Pearson again.

"Balls!" said Lucy. "I told you. You're infatuated. Not in love. You're just in love with the white man's lifestyle. Not really, really in love. Love involves pain. You haven't felt pain."

Pearson ploughed on.

"Such friendly people . . ."

"Now you sound like a diplomat. You'll be calling them 'impressive' next."

Their words were buried beneath the rumble of the lift, as it came creaking and wheezing back to life. And while they moved together, climbing stair after stair, their conversation seemed to pull them apart, as they talked about the same subject but to different audiences long-converted.

Snatches of their exchanges carried through the air, distinguished by tone and pitch as well as content – sometimes aggressive sometimes defensive. Verbal punch was followed by counter-punch, attack by defence, sally and retreat, each going over familiar ground that led them to different destinations.

"Wonderful music . . ."

"Leadership dreadful . . ."

"They're dying of Aids . . ."

"Traumatised by their past . . ."

"Badly led . . ."

And so it went on.

"Aid is wasted . . . donors are duped . . . the collapse of the state . . . blame WorldFeed . . ."

"You really do sound like an apologist, and a Scandinavian one at that," said Lucy.

Below the belt, thought Pearson, but he stayed silent.

They reached the door to his room.

Overhead, the day flight from Kuwisha to London cut through the blue sky, still gaining height.

The sound of children frolicking in the hotel's outdoor swimming pool carried upwards, and a hawk, wheeling in the blue sky, high above the garden, was eyeing the skinny cats that prowled the grounds.

"That rhino and debt relief scheme," said Pearson, "it could just work . . ."

"Oh for fuck's sake . . ."

"Really no need to be like that, Lucy, it's not such a bad idea."

Lucy looked at him coldly.

"Saving the rhino could be the basis of world peace for all I know. But at the moment, I don't give a fig. They have given us the wrong bloody room key."

Lucy stormed off in search of the right key, and returned in an even worse mood. Her office had rung to change the time of her briefing for a WorldFeed ambassador called Geoffrey Japer, due to arrive that morning.

"See you at Harrods. Thank you again. I thought of you," said Pearson.

"And I thought of you."

Pearson was still recovering from Lucy's unexpectedly warm reply as he waved her good-bye from the balcony of his room.

The sounds of the city rose towards him. The local church choir, in fine voice as ever, was practising for the Christmas service. Their hymns drifted through the morning air, up to where he stood. Inspired, Pearson took out a notebook from his jacket and jotted down what would become the opening sentence of the novel he was working on: "Africa sings like the rest of the world breathes."

Beyond the jacaranda trees that surrounded the swimming pool he could see rain clouds building up, and a hush settled over the grounds. Pearson relished the prospect of real rain – not the grey, miserable precipitation of Europe. In Africa the elements seemed to be orchestrated by an Almighty conductor who marshalled wind, thunder and shafts of lightning, bringing them together in a glorious release of plump drops of water that hit Kuwisha's dry earth like tiny grenades which exploded in puffs of dust. Seconds later, pedestrians scurried for cover as gutters became streams, and streams turned into ochre-foamed torrents.

Now this was rain, thought Pearson, this was Africa.

Cecil adjusted his trousers. He had reached an awkward age: old enough to notice that his waistline was expanding, and young enough to do something about it.

This was not the only sign that the watershed birthday marking thirty-five years was fast approaching. He was discovering that he agreed more often than not with his dad. For a start he no longer resented the fact that his father had named him after Cecil John Rhodes. And he was starting to share his father's view that professionals were ruining football. What was more, his taste in clothes was becoming as conservative to the point of eccentricity. The shirts Pearson wore were hand-made by Turnbull & Asser in London's Jermyn Street, always in the same shade of blue; and his socks were always pink, in tribute to his hero, the late Joe Slovo, South African guerrilla chief and leader of its communist party.

And ten minutes later the wondrous display was over, and the sky was blue again.

12

"Phauw!"

Charity's nose wrinkled as she detected a familiar sour-sweet fragrance that hung like a spider's web, gossamer-fine, in the bar's rudimentary kitchen. It was the subtle perfume of *bhang* that lay beneath the stale odour of cigarettes left behind by customers who had dared to ignore the hand-lettered "No Smoking" sign. Could the culprit be Willard Luthuli, the cheeky youth who sold wooden giraffes to tourists? Luthuli smoked more *bhang* than was good for him; on the other hand, he had been nowhere near the bar.

She sniffed again.

"Mildred!"

She had long suspected that her elderly friend was going deaf, but she would not have put it past Mildred to pretend. All too often it seemed that Mildred heard what she wanted to hear, and screened out the rest.

"Mildred!"

This time the call was more urgent. Mildred Kigali gave a table a final wipe, and hurried over.

Charity beckoned from within the bar, where the sweet aroma was strongest. The two ladies, the one buxom and in her mid-forties, wearing a blue and white striped apron, and the other wiry, lean and elderly, head covered in a red scarf, together sniffed the air, judiciously and deliberately.

The older of the two nodded in confirmation: there was indeed no doubt in her mind, none whatsoever. The smell was unmistakable. Someone had been smoking *bhang*. While it couldn't be ruled out, it was most unlikely that one of the circle members had sneaked off for a quiet draw. Anyone who attended the monthly meeting was self-evidently of independent mind and would smoke *bhang* openly.

"Could it be an Mboya Boy?" asked Mildred.

"There were no Mboya Boys on duty last night," said Charity, a trifle sharply.

She did not want to provoke Mildred into one of her fulminations against the gang – none of whom, as Mildred never tired of pointing out, was a Lamb.

And if there had been a duty Mboya, why should they act against their own interests, even when they were in a drug-induced stupor from sniffing glue? They were cheeky enough, that was for sure. But why? Why would they risk losing the chance to have a square meal in return for helping out with chores at the bar?

It did not make sense.

And while she did not support moves to legalise the drug, she felt that Kuwisha had far more serious and pressing problems than the use of the plant that grew like a weed between the coffee bushes and tea bushes, and together with tourism made up Kuwisha's struggling economy.

The serious area of difference between the two ladies was alcohol, over which there was much debate. Mildred would ban it if she could; Charity felt there was no harm if consumed in moderation.

Mildred must have been reading her thoughts, for she gave a disapproving "Tsk." People no longer understood the difference between right and wrong. Her old friend Charity should be tougher and stricter with the Mboya Boys. Instead she spoilt the rascals, especially Ntoto and Rutere.

Mildred's views on discipline and today's youth were passionately felt and forcefully expressed: hard work and a sound thrashing were good for them. And should there be any hint of rebellion – which she had seen on the faces of the Mboya Boys, oh yes, there was cheek in their eyes, and as far as Mildred Kigali was concerned, eyes were windows into the soul – it should be quelled.

And Mildred had no doubt, no doubt whatsoever, about the course that should be followed. It was time they joined the Lambs.

She wondered if Charity would lead the way. My, my, what a great day that would be! What a catch for the Lambs, to have the wife of the late bishop, Bishop David Mupanga, no less, join their ranks.

And Kigali himself, he could baptise her. And then surely the street children of Kuwisha would follow, like the children that followed the piper. Furniver, also, would follow, Mildred was sure. Men were men, all over the world.

Her reverie was interrupted.

"Mildred!"

Charity had just noticed that something was missing.

"The needles! Where are the needles, Mildred?"

13

"I don't mind telling you," said Furniver, "I was absolutely terrified."

The mid-morning sun was beating down, and the crown of his head, where his hair was thinning, was starting to turn pink.

He, too, had risen early, and after a couple of hours' work on his bank's annual review, had made his way along the muddy path that led from his flat to Harrods, wrinkling his nose as his footsteps released an array of disgusting smells from the accumulated filth that lay below. It was time to lay a path, but it would cost a fortune in dough balls.

"Good morning, my dear."

Charity gave him a small kiss on the cheek in return. She was never demonstrative in her affection, but Furniver had no doubt: something was up. There was definitely a hint of disapproval in her attitude, but for the life of him, he could not put his finger on what might have caused it. Unless it was those Lambs putting pressure on her to join them.

Furniver settled into his favourite wicker chair, near the thriving purple bougainvillaea, and took a sip of coffee, made from beans grown on Charity's *shamba*, and roasted and ground within the past hour.

Charity beckoned to Mildred, who was keeping a close eye on the kitchen, where Titus Ntoto and Cyrus Rutere were washing dishes ahead of the next sitting for breakfast. "Come, Mildred, come join us. It is time to talk about last night."

Furniver had just started his account of the previous evening when Lucy Gomball, looking particularly attractive in jeans and

T-shirt – "all tits and teeth" as a frustrated *Telegraph* correspondent had once put it – emerged from behind the bar.

"Hi guys! Pearson's been let out, just collected him. He'll join us later."

Charity let out a hoot of delight.

"Dough balls on the house!"

"Puna rang with the news, and said he can stay on to cover the donors' do," continued Lucy.

"Can somebody lend me my taxi fare? Left the house without a cent."

Furniver handed her the money. Lucy was back inside a minute, face screwed up in disgust.

"God knows what I stepped in," she said, picking up a pencil-long stick lying on the table, and scraping something off the sole of her trainer. "Sis!" she said, and flicked the stick away. "So what's up?"

"That," said Charity coldly, "was my toothbrush."

Lucy turned red with embarrassment.

"Oh shit, I'm so sorry, Charity."

Charity gave Lucy's hand a forgiving squeeze.

"So where is Pearson?" asked Furniver.

"Just dropped him at the Milimani. He'll join us as soon as he can."

Furniver took advantage of Lucy's arrival to pop into the Zimbabwe-designed toilet, briefcase in hand, and he emerged a couple of minutes later, looking dishevelled. He felt Charity's eyes on him, and he blushed.

"Jolly fine toilet, no flies. Jolly good. Just um, checking."

Amidst further expressions of relief about Pearson's release, Charity turned to Furniver.

"Start again, so Lucy can also know."

In a sentence or two, Furniver brought Lucy up to date about the events of the night before, and continued.

"So there I was. I had been taking a turn round the bar, reading the notes for that talk on inflation I was due to give the circle. Just about to knock on the door and this thing, this creature, like a dwarf, hiding among the beer crates, suddenly starts screaming its head off. Right in front of me. Gave me a hell of a fright. Dropped my torch. Told it was a bloody tolothingy . . ."

He looked around for help.

"*Tokolosh*," said Charity Mupanga.

"That's it, *tokolosh*. Heard it scream: '*Tokolosh*! *Tokolosh*!' Terrifying! Sort of goblin, you say? Bit like a leprechaun, maybe. Hangs around at night, doing mischief. As in Ireland."

He took another sip of coffee.

"Then the door flies open. Just there."

Furniver pointed to the entrance to the bar.

"All hell breaks loose. Bizarre! Half the women who come out ask me where the damn thing is. The rest keep going, screaming blue murder. I had no idea what was happening, dropped my notes of what would have been a pretty decent talk, got trampled in the rush . . ."

He paused. And then he shook his head.

"Don't believe in spirits, but frankly cannot explain what happened. Call it a *tokolosh* or whatever, there certainly was something there. No doubt. Scared the pants off me. Got to admit it."

"What do you think, Lucy?"

Lucy Gomball, securing her blonde hair in a pony tail, decided that she would keep her head below the parapet. Her head said one thing, and her heart said another.

On the one hand she was certain that a *tokolosh* was a figment of the beholder's imagination; on the other, she had little doubt that many in Kuwisha firmly believed in the existence of the creature. And if people believe in something strongly enough, perhaps it did exist, after a fashion, in their heads?

It was Charity, however, who was openly doubtful.

"Why should a *tokolosh* shout '*Tokolosh*!'"

Mildred, who by common consent had been the heroine of the evening, displaying a coolness that was a credit to her advanced years, and whose account was eagerly awaited, gave her a pitying look.

"These *tokolosh*, they are clever. When it saw Furniver, it was afraid of being caught. So it shouted, and made confusion. People ran out of the meeting, and the *tokolosh* was able to escape."

The two women agreed on one thing: what was remarkable was not so much the presence of a *tokolosh*. They were common enough, and the old generation took care to close windows and doors at night to stop the creature from entering, often in the guise of a goat or a pig or, more usually, a donkey. But neither could recall ever hearing of a *tokolosh* behaving in this extraordinary way.

The table fell silent.

"Too bad about the talk, really sorry," said Furniver. "Dropped my notes, got mud all over them, but I remember the joke. Rather good. Want to hear it?"

Mistaking the silence at the table for consent, Furniver began.

"A minister from Kuwisha visited his counterpart in Nigeria, and admired the Mercs and the huge home. 'How did you manage to get all this?' the minister asked. His host gestured through the window at the new hospital that was going up. 'See that? Ten per cent commission.' A few months later the roles were reversed, and the Nigerian minister was the guest . . . And the house in Kuwisha was even bigger, with more cars . . .

"He pointed out the window. 'See that hospital?' The Nigerian looked and looked and said: 'Hospital? I can't see any hospital.' And the Kuwisha man said: '100 per cent commission.'"

★

79

"Next we must hear Mildred," said Charity, and gave Furniver an affectionate pat on the top of his head.

Phauw! There it was again! The scent that Boniface Rugiru had detected at the Thumaiga Club was surely the whiff of local gin. Sooner rather than later she would have to tackle him.

Just then Lucy's mobile rang.

"I'm on my way," she told the caller. "The office. Reminding me that this NoseAid chap is arriving this morning. Would you be a sweetheart, Ed, and collect him from the airport?"

"WorldFeed should send a car," said Furniver. "After all, NoseAid gives you a fortune every year – you should be meeting him."

Lucy pouted.

"If you can't go, I'll have to send a driver. I haven't finished the briefing paper, and he's off to the rhino place later this morning."

Furniver looked at Charity.

"I don't waste my time with loafers," said Charity firmly.

"I say, Charity, bit harsh surely . . ."

"Please, Ed," Lucy wheedled.

Furniver sighed, and was rewarded with a kiss from Lucy.

"What about the rest of my story?"

"We can hear you and Mildred after lunch," promised Charity, and the group broke up.

Furniver looked at his watch. He would have to leave soon if he was to get to the airport in time to meet the flight, such was the state of the city's traffic. He could make it, provided he kept short the meeting he had promised to a chap from UKAID, Mullivant, Dr Adrian Mullivant, who had asked him to spare an hour to talk about the Co-operative Bank's work in Kireba. These days the airport journey, which used to take twenty minutes or so, could take very much longer. Most visitors saw the city's horrendous traffic jams as a sign of a booming economy.

Furniver had his doubts.

The jams were the result of a declining, corrupt state, he told his colleagues at the Kuwisha Economic Society. Roads were deteriorating, and huge potholes were common; ageing cars were kept on the road, their frequent breakdowns holding up traffic; the town council was corrupt and incompetent; and broken traffic lights went unmended. Only the four-wheel drives could be certain of completing their journey, and every self-respecting politician and aid worker, journalist and consultant had one of the petrol-guzzling beasts.

Furniver returned to the flat, hoping that Mullivant would not be late, while Charity headed for the kitchen and summoned the duty boys who were kicking around a football made of plastic bags and string.

"Ntoto! Rutere!"

The lads, plastic glue bottles bouncing at the end of string tied around their necks, ignored her.

She called again, sharper this time.

Still no reply.

Then she realised her mistake. What were the names of those football people the boys so admired?

"Beckham! Rooney! No loafing. Kitchen duty."

There were chicken necks to prepare, dough balls to fry, not to mention fresh bitings, avocado soup to get ready, beans that needed soaking . . . and if young Rutere had forgotten to restock the fridge with sodas and Tusker beers he was in deep trouble.

Back in his office, Furniver frowned at the notes he had made. He hated compiling the annual report. Paperwork was a waste of time, but it had to be done.

He had made a useful start earlier that day.

"Long snakes, short ladders," was the headline. He was tempted to add "and dizzy worms" but decided against it. It was probably a mixed metaphor. Pity. But somewhere he would work in the story about the US ambassador to Zaire, who had been asked about the significance of the president's latest cabinet reshuffle.

"What do you get when you shake up a can of worms? Dizzy worms."

About summed it up, thought Furniver. He settled to his task: "Long snakes, short ladders: A review of the year in Africa . . ."

Only every now and then did Edward Furniver allow himself to think about the continent's plight and each time he did, regretted it. Once a year, however, he was obliged to submit a report to the London-based fund that supported the bank, in which he had to put the operations in Kuwisha in a wider context.

From his desk in the spare bedroom that served as an office, Furniver looked over the sprawling slum teeming with life, full of energy as its hard-working residents went about their business, and looked at what he had written.

"Looking back on the past twelve months has left us little the wiser about the continent's prospects. Often it has seemed as if unseen hands were playing snakes and ladders across Africa.

"News from this part of the world has been as unpredictable as a throw of the dice. Snakes marked famine or flood, corruption or coup, Aids or civil war, writhe across the board, alongside ladders marked cease-fire and peace deal, debt relief and multi-party elections, foreign investment and trade deals."

Furniver sucked his teeth. This was good stuff!

"Or is it on the verge of recovery, undergoing a transformation as profound as any in its history as it comes to terms with a traumatic past, enjoys the benefits of debt rescheduling and write-off, and gets to grips with the economic and technological revolutions that are reshaping the global community?

"In the continent's struggle for revival there is no single, simple front line, no single battle, and no homogeneous Africa with an all-embracing culture or a collective identity. It is not possible in a region with more than a thousand languages and as many ethnic groups, all living on a land mass that could accommodate China and Europe, India and the United States, with room to spare for Argentina and New Zealand.

"Over the past four decades the continent has undergone a political and economic revolution, with the lives of its peoples changing more radically in the last forty years than in the previous four centuries. Colonial powers have withdrawn, white rule has ended, and apartheid has crumbled. One-party states have given way to multi-party politics, and state-controlled economics have succumbed to the market; as the Cold War ended, African presidents lost the patronage of Moscow and Washington, and donors demanded 'good governance' from mismanaged regimes they had previously tolerated or encouraged. From Cape Town to Cairo, the mood has altered dramatically as Africa enters a new era . . ."

Furniver paused, and studied the words on the screen of his laptop.

"New era . . ."

He liked those words. They had a good ring to them, though he was far from clear as to what they meant.

14

Ferdinand Mlambo sat on the edge of his mattress, kept an eye trained on the State House kitchen garden in case anyone tried to sneak up, and tried to cheer himself up by singing a popular Kireba ditty.

He had a fine voice, even by the standards of a country where a good singing voice was taken for granted.

> "Together, together again,
> United, united by pain . . ."

It was a brave effort, but it didn't work.

For a few minutes he sat, snivelling. Then he decided. There was only one thing to do, one place to go.

The boy pulled on his only pair of shorts, cleared his nostrils, blowing first one side then the other, and fastidiously cleaned his fingers on the grass. He then brushed his teeth with the bristles of a well-chewed twig, hawked and spat, wiped his face with the back of his hand, and set off along the overgrown path to Kireba via the old boathouse.

He had made up his mind and there was no time to lose.

He had betrayed President Nduka. He would not betray Charity Mupanga, never! But whatever he did, he needed to talk to Ntoto and Rutere.

As he trotted on his way, sounds of Kuwisha swept over the urban landscape like a returning tide. From east of his lair came the murmur of traffic, a choir whose voices merged to form a single sound, from the rumbling bass of the huge lorries carrying steel containers through Kuwisha to its landlocked neighbours, to the endlessly honking *matatus* and the sharp noise of the buzzing motorbikes.

All these sounds seemed to be subsumed by the hum of the many Range Rovers and Land Rovers, jeeps and Mitsubishis with which Kuwisha was blessed, travelling each day like animals to a watering hole, their bewildering range of acronyms emblazoned on their frames as they moved slowly through the morning traffic, hooting their frustration while signalling their importance.

Within the air-conditioned interior of their vehicles, usually on the back seats, sat the men and women who did so much to help the frail economy of Kuwisha tick over.

They were rich targets for the street vendors, who were making the most of the opportunity, as alert to a flicker of curiosity or interest as an auctioneer on a slow day at market; as assiduous and as persuasive in their patter as life-assurance salesmen, as they good-humouredly touted their wares.

From the west, just half a mile from Mlambo's den – if one of the sleek black crows that nested in the eucalyptus trees were to make the journey – came a different sound. Kireba produced an industrious buzz: a mix of hammer on anvil as old tins were turned into mugs and paraffin lamps; and the tinkling bells of the bicyclists hawking vegetables; and the rhythmic thump of hammer delivered by Philimon Ogata as he shaped the planks of wood that became coffins.

On fire with resentment and burning with humiliation, Mlambo took the short cut from State House to Kireba, along the overgrown path which passed his den, and on to the State House boundary fence. He checked there was no-one in sight, before slipping through the hole he had made for the purpose.

In the old days, the fence had run along the edge of a dam, which was fed by a small stream that flowed through the patch of land that came to be called Kireba. Some of the older residents recalled the time when the dam was home to the Sailing Club, and they had fished in its waters. But as is the way with old people, they had succumbed to false memory, and claimed that they had swum in the stream, bare-arsed with white boys. Anyone who believed that it had ever been possible to swim in the foul-smelling black rivulet of filth that ran through Kireba must be making it up; and as for swimming with young *mzungu* . . .

Whatever the truth of these claims, these days the dam was barely a dam. Rather it was a weed-encrusted eyesore, gradually silting up, and anyone who was careless could sink knee deep into the surrounding mud. Perhaps the security officers had decided that in this way Nature had protected State House from intruders, and the fence did not need to be reinforced. More likely, the contractor responsible for fencing the perimeter of the grounds had claimed for work that was never done.

Mlambo secured the section of the fence behind him, paused in the bushes for perhaps a minute, and again checked that the coast was clear. The rocks he had put down to serve as stepping stones across stretches that were especially muddy had sunk out of sight, but Mlambo had no difficulty finding them, having taken the precaution of marking them with sticks, that made the route easy for him to follow.

Within a few minutes he was passing by Ogata's place, and he made a point of keeping his distance. One could never be too careful.

Mlambo was not entirely sure why he had always gravitated to Harrods. Once when he was senior kitchen *toto*, he had braved the night, climbed a tree near his State House lair, and looked out into the huge dark saucer that was Kireba, pin-pricked by cooking fires.

He had tried to pick out Harrods.

It had been easier than one might imagine, because Harrods

had electricity, thanks to the cable that ran from the clinic. And at night, its lights gleamed like a beacon of hope.

And once or twice, during the day, he had arrived early for football practice, and had lurked behind a nearby makeshift toilet. From there he could hear Charity's slightly husky voice, encouraging, rebuking, and cajoling. But above all – though Mlambo himself would not have put it like this – underlying her every call and tone was a constant sense of concern.

Charity cared passionately about the future of her street children, whose lives seemed destined to end in their teens, struck down by the plague that was visited on the world, and, it seemed, on Africa in particular.

Her nightmare in which rats, with the faces of young humans, ate the seed corn from Kuwisha's granary, continued to afflict her; and showing the little rats that she cared about them was the only response she could devise.

And as Mlambo listened to her rebukes, head cocked, he was reminded of his childhood, the years he was looked after by his grandmother.

"Where is the grater, Rutere? If I find you using it . . ."

That Rutere boy, he was often in trouble, but he always had a good excuse, thought Mlambo.

"If you don't wash your hands and scrape the carrots, young Cyrus Rutere, you will lose breakfast rights."

"Ntoto, where is the clean water?"

Sometimes the boys answered back, sometimes they were downright cheeky, and Charity's patience ran out. The sound of rapid Swahili, followed by the smack of hand on flesh, and wails from the boys carried to the toilet from where he watched, and Mlambo winced in sympathy.

But he noted that the wails were howls of outrage at the indignity of being smacked by a woman, and not cries of real pain.

★

87

Willard Luthuli, Sportsman cigarette dangling from his lip, chipped away and created his long-necked elegant giraffes for which tourists had an insatiable appetite. Mlambo took care to avoid him, for he was a notorious gossip, not to be trusted.

Concealed behind a shack, he listened to the tuneless whistling that came from the Klean Blood Klinic, where proprietor Clarence "Results" Mudenge, Registered Doctor, sat on a three-legged stool.

For a moment Mlambo thought of seeking his help.

Surely amongst his many *mutis* was one that could assist him?

It would be unfair to suggest that Mr Mudenge was a conman, if only because it was a term that did not do justice to his many skills – part psychologist, part traditional herbalist. His friends agreed: Mudenge was a man who could sell desert sand to a Kalahari bushman.

He was especially persuasive when potential customers asked why he, Mudenge, whose head was as bald as an egg, had not taken advantage of his own product, the best-selling all natural hair restoring lotion he prepared on the spot.

It was a question which every would-be client asked, and a lesser man might have grown so tired of it that his patent hair restorer would have been abandoned. At the very least, Mudenge would have been pardoned had he responded to the question with a degree of asperity, or if, just every now and then, a note of irritation came through.

Far from it.

Mudenge treated each questioner with fresh respect, praising their acute observation, their profound insight.

It had been his own experience of hair loss, he would explain, that had driven his research into this distressing condition called "baldness". Alas, he had made mistakes when he treated his own hair loss with the lotions and potions he had assembled. These experiments had taken their toll. But the fewer the hairs on his head, the more he was determined to find a solution, and the greater his resolve.

While he was talking, Clarence Mudenge would take the questioner by the arm and guide them into the privacy of his "office".

There, when the visitors' eyes got accustomed to the gloom of his plastic and tin-sheet shack, they could see hundreds of boxes, from floor to ceiling, marked with strange words that Mudenge offered to translate.

Every now and then Mudenge would pull out a box, and shake it with a frown on his face, or hold it to his ear, and listen intently.

He would invite his patient to listen for himself, and express astonishment if the patient could hear nothing. If the customer had not been convinced, Mudenge would use his ventriloquist's gift, and engage in rapid conversation with one of the boxes.

Then, with lowered voice, Clarence Mudenge dealt with the caller's concerns, using words and phrases that came from a medical dictionary an Mboya Boy had stolen from a visiting doctor from England some years earlier.

But the medical terms alone would have been of little use had it not been for the fact that Mudenge had a shrewd, intuitive insight into how people functioned, what made them happy or unhappy, and how their moods were at the heart of many of the problems for which they sought his help.

Even Charity was impressed.

Sometimes she would pause in her duties at Harrods and watch "Results" at work.

"You are a spiderman," she once accused him.

"You invite these people inside, Mudenge, and then you are a spider and they are flies, or like fish, slowly, slowly pulled in."

It was the first and only time Charity had seen Mudenge get cross.

"I do no harm," he said, thumping the old school desk at which he sat. "Everything I use is clean. The *changa*, even, I brew myself, and use only a few drops."

It was true. If the potions and powders he provided did no good, there was no evidence they did any harm.

And many was the patient who felt better after taking a dose of the Klean Blood Klinic's best-selling tonic. A few drops, taken three times a day, of Mudenge's secret concoction: a squeeze of lemon, a fragment of vanilla, a teaspoon of clove oil, well shaken.

"Take for three weeks – DO NOT OVERDOSE" ordered the instructions on every bottle.

And there was his guarantee: "Results," said Mudenge, "or your money back."

Had Ogata not spotted Mlambo, and called out, beckoning, "Come, Mlambo, come!" the boy might well have sought Mudenge's help, for it was well known that he made powerful *muti*.

Instead he moved on. When Philimon Ogata called, it was best to respond without delay. A man so closely associated with death should never be crossed.

If Mudenge was one of nature's mediators, Ogata was a natural businessman, with an eye for opportunity, head cocked to one side as he assessed the potential of a project.

Both men dressed with care – Ogata wearing an all-black concoction he considered appropriate to his job, while Mudenge, squat and tubby, looked like a favourite uncle.

15

Business was booming at the Pass Port to Heaven Coffin Parlour. But for reasons which no-one could understand, not even the parlour's owner, Philimon Buchema Ogata, there were fewer demands on his time between eight o'clock and ten o'clock in the morning. And the busiest part of the day was between four o'clock and five o'clock. That day was no exception, and Ogata was using the morning lull to study the obituaries page in the *Kuwisha Times*.

As Mlambo drew closer to Ogata's place, he could hear a strange sound – a roll-call of the recently departed, recited by Ogata himself, while he marked with a pencil stub the best lines from the funeral announcements.

Every now and then, Ogata, a tall and thin man in his mid-forties, with an extraordinary bass voice, read an extract in a way that made the hairs on the back of Mlambo's neck bristle.

"Edward Tambo: Now your journey is ended, heaven awaits. Oliver Mukuzi: No more tears, no more fear, Only trumpets, loud and clear."

He repeated the sentiments with relish: "No more tears, no more fear, Only trumpets, loud and clear. Faith Gumede . . . Free at last, in the Almighty's hands . . . Baby Grace, Called to Jesus . . . You see, Mlambo," Ogata broke off, startling the boy, "all the departed are either living in America, or have relatives in America . . ."

Could he break into the US market, Ogata wondered, and if so, should he take on an extra worker?

On the one hand, the personal service that Ogata provided was at the heart of his success, and anything that reduced this might well drive customers away. To be measured for an Ogata coffin, Furniver had observed, was as important an experience as getting the tailor at Turnbull and Asser, in London's Jermyn Street, to run up half a dozen of their hand-made Sea Island cotton shirts. In both cases, the clients expected personal attention.

On the other hand, although business was especially good, profit margins were narrow in what was a very competitive business. Ogata had scandalised some people when he first put his slogan into effect: "Try at home – before going Home". The invitation to people to choose their coffin, and sleep in it for a night before making a final decision on purchase, not only got his business talked about; it had become a great success.

Mlambo shuffled closer, listening and watching, fascinated as Ogata continued with his litany. Every now and then the coffin-maker expressed respect for the dead, and condolences for the living.

And as Philimon Ogata made clear to his customers, in Kuwisha people did not die. Dogs died, yes; but people were not dogs. At worst they passed on. And as far as Ogata was concerned, very, very few of his customers did something so simple, as mundane as to "pass on".

His customers deserved far better an introduction to the Life that was to come. So never did they die. Instead they were "Promoted to Glory", or "Risen to the Lord". That was only right and proper for these hard-working people who had been such devout servants of the Maker.

Ogata beckoned Mlambo to move closer, to cross the black stream of effluent that divided them.

"Lost a bit of weight, I see. Lose a bit more – it will be good for you. Score more goals."

He wiped the sweat off his brow, and added: "But not too much! I don't want you to become a customer yet."

Ogata laughed.

The joke, such as it was, may have been in bad taste, but Mlambo was grateful for the humanity of the exchange. He had little doubt that news of his humiliation would have reached Kireba, and he appreciated the fact that Ogata had not called him Fatboy.

He came closer.

"Sit, boy, sit!" Ogata patted a bench alongside him.

Mlambo sat down, and then realising it was an upturned coffin, leapt up as if he had lowered his bottom onto the embers of a fire.

Kireba's leading coffin-maker continued to read from the obituary pages: "And the dead were living, and the living were as dead, save those who had honoured the Lord; and so it will be on Judgment Day, when tears will cease, and joy will conquer pain. Revelation 9(vii)."

Ogata marked the passage in his battered Bible, marked "Gift of the Gideons".

"Joy will conquer pain . . . now that," he said appreciatively, "is good. I like that. Very much."

Mlambo crossed himself. Just in case.

"There is good business in the USA," Ogata returned to his theme.

"Every notice," he explained, his pencil tapping the paper, repeatedly making his point, "has family in USA. Sons, brothers, sisters."

He looked at Mlambo, who was now peering over Ogata's shoulder. Should he confide in the boy? Why not?

"One day, I will make coffins for Kenyans in the USA. Plenty needed. Good business."

Like most residents of Kireba, Ogata was an ambitious man.

He coughed, spat, and lit a cigarette.

"Mlambo, if you want to learn this business, you become my apprentice . . ."

Mlambo must have looked doubtful.

"And you get a free coffin," promised Ogata.

"Guarantee?"

"Guarantee. Ask your gran," replied Ogata.

Mlambo nodded.

She had been buried in an Ogata coffin. He had little doubt that had his gran had any complaints about the service provided, she would have let him know.

Just then a thin and wasted woman who looked 50 but was probably half that age appeared, and Ogata got up to greet her.

Mlambo joined in the greetings, and then left Ogata to his potential customer. He reflected, as he often did, on the wisdom of his old grandmother.

"Power and success do strange things to people," she would say to anyone who would listen. And since she looked after Mlambo until he was nearly six, at which age he was judged ready to herd the family goats, he heard her say it more often than most.

"Power!" she would say to him as they sat round the lunchtime fire. "It affects the memory. People with power forget old friends. They lose their manners. They are rude to ordinary folk.

"But strangest of all, when they get power, they grow bigger; when they lose power, they go smaller."

She would pull her old blanket around her narrow shoulders, clear her throat and expectorate, punctuating her words of wisdom with a gob of phlegm, directing it at an unfortunate lizard, and laughing if it found its mark.

The eyes of a lizard, Mlambo had noticed, and the eyes of his gran, had much in common. Both had a rheumy film over them, and both seemed to have 360-degree vision. She had laughed and laughed when a much younger Mlambo had asked whether she and the lizards were related – but she had not denied it.

"Listen to me, young man. What I tell you about power is true. True! I have seen it myself. When my sister's daughter got a place in school, the girl thought she was very clever. And sure enough, she looked bigger. When she had to marry the boy who made her pregnant and left school, sure enough, she looked smaller. Even though she was with child.

"You, Mlambo, are big now, because you are the boy in charge of goats. This makes you bigger. But if you lose a goat, you will lose your job, and then you will get smaller. So be careful, young Mlambo. Look after your goats!"

Could it be that his gran's warning about the loss of power was already coming true? Could it be that he, Ferdinand Mlambo, was becoming smaller? Perhaps he had Aids. The thought that he might be yet another victim of the ghastly plague made him feel sick in his stomach.

But it also encouraged him, and helped him as he drew up the plan for revenge – the plan that had begun when he pricked his thumb on the sharp end of one of the knitting needles.

As he later explained to Ntoto and Rutere: "It grew in my head, like a paw-paw grows from a pip."

But first, he would seek the boys' help. As he approached Harrods, he felt himself getting smaller, his shoulders sagging, his arms hanging limply at his side, and his feet dragging.

By the time he arrived at Harrods he had convinced himself that his gran's warning was literally true.

16

The city's main post office had yet to open. It was too early to collect the letter from the governor of the Central Bank that Charity had asked them to bring back, and the avocados would be picked up on the way back to Harrods, so Titus Ntoto and Cyrus Rutere squatted on the kerb, content to watch the traffic go by.

It had been fifteen days since they had cheered on Bright Khumalo from the airport's perimeter fence, waving as their friend climbed into the undercarriage of the London-bound flight, just as the plane had turned and paused before rumbling down the runway.

"Perhaps Bright has lost the postcard," said Rutere, "and he cannot send a new one, because he does not want people to know that he is irriterate . . ."

Ntoto merely grunted.

Taking an occasional sniff from their glue bottles, they slouched in the shade cast by an advertising board on Uhuru Avenue, the city's main thoroughfare, and ever-watchful for policemen, security guards and other enemies, waited for the post office to open. Rutere took the opportunity to quiz his friend.

"So, Ntoto," said Rutere.

Titus Ntoto sat, heavy-lidded eyes keeping watch for prowling *askaris* for whom thrashing street boys was a welcome break from their boring routine.

Rutere ran his finger round the rim of his nose, an unconscious gesture that helped him concentrate.

"Have we decided – we are not going to be bang-bang boys?"

Ntoto shook his head. He had told Cyrus that if ever he became a bang-bang boy, Rutere would be his choice of partner. But he had no intention of taking a dead-end job. The life of a bang-bang boy was not for him.

"A geography boy?" asked Rutere.

It could be lucrative; and it could see you through your life, because age was no barrier to a geography boy. But you had to keep learning.

"I will think," said Ntoto, but very soon shook his head.

A geography boy might be glamorous, but the job was hard work – the equivalent of learning the "knowledge" before qualifying as a London black cab driver. Hence the not infrequent sight on a city street corner of a group of boys huddled round the page of an atlas torn from an in-flight magazine, and asking each other questions.

Providing the correct answer to tough questions – such as "What is the capital of Finland?" – was only part of the skill required if you were to be a first-rate geography boy. You had to be able to judge the character of your "mark", and to be able to make a reasonable guess at their country of origin – or surreptitiously read the address label on their knapsack. Above all, you had to have a thick skin, for nine out of every ten foreigners approached would respond with crude language. A few would even cuff the boy who approached them.

But the successful one out of ten could make it all worthwhile. For some reason Norwegians were the best. If you could start up a conversation with a visitor from say, Oslo, you were unlikely to go away empty-handed – provided of course you got the patter right.

And provided you delivered it with conviction.

"Phauw! From Norway! My brother is a student in Oslo. He likes it very much. Do you like Kuwisha?"

If such a question got an answer, it was a sign that the visitor was sniffing the bait; if they answered a second question, they were hooked. And by the third question, the exchange had become a conversation, at the end of which any street boy worth his salt would have "borrowed" one hundred *ngwee*.

The most demanding of the street-children jobs was that of a collection boy. "Very risky, but good money," said Rutere, watching Ntoto for his reaction. Chief requirements were an angelic appearance, a good knowledge of the scriptures and a Fagin-like skill in pick-pocketing, or in this case, stealing from the church collection basket.

But if one were caught it was curtains. The righteous wrath of a congregation that discovered that there was a sinner in their midst, and that the cherubic altar boy was stealing their hard earned mites, was fearsome, and their reaction had an ecumenical certainty. Culprits had been lynched in the past. Those collection boys who went undetected, however, could go on to lead a congregation, and have a whole flock to fleece.

The two friends continued to explore their options.

Customs boy? This involved greeting a tourist on the street and claiming that their "father" had been on immigration duty and had helped the visitor through customs; and was followed up by a request for a loan that would be repaid when they returned through the airport. "Just ask for Chiluba, senior officer, security."

Again, Ntoto just shook his head.

"Whatever you decide," declared Rutere. "You are my friend."

The two boys spat on the palm of their right hands, did a high five, spat again, this time on the other's hand, rubbed it in the dust, and punched their hearts.

"I have decided, Rutere. I will become the Kireba area boy."

Cyrus was not surprised. Word on the street had long been that Ntoto was in the running to become area boy for Kireba, the equivalent of a ward boss.

It was a tough job that called for a tough individual, equally capable of inciting a riot, imposing discipline or creating mayhem, conscripting residents to serve as rent-a-crowd mobs, ready to demonstrate at short notice, home or away. And it was the job of the area boy, working closely with the local member of parliament, to supply these mobs on demand, for a few *ngwee* per head.

The job required ruthlessness, courage and perseverance, and street cunning, all qualities which Ntoto had. But it was also dangerous. Rutere was about to ask questions when the post office double door swung open. The woman behind the counter raised her head.

There was mail for Harrods, about half a dozen items, and Ntoto handed over the usual fee – the equivalent of the postage on the envelopes. The woman held out her hand for more.

"Service charge has gone up."

"Will you credit me?" Ntoto asked.

She pointed to a hand-printed sign, taped above her desk: "No credit today – try tomorrow!"

Alongside was a picture of Jesus, with a typewritten homily: "God is my Light."

Ntoto tried to read the newspaper on her desk upside down.

"No free reading."

She studied him through bloodshot eyes. "Go!"

Ntoto emerged empty-handed – though the woman had allowed him to check that there was no postcard.

"Perhaps it was stolen," said Cyrus Rutere, more worried, it seemed, than Ntoto, who rummaged through a pile of rotting fruit outside the market. Rutere squatted on his haunches, letting the red dust of Kuwisha trickle through his fingers and make a pattern that spelt the initials of the Mboya Boys' missing centre-forward.

Titus Ntoto handed Rutere a banana, overripe to the point of being black, and the boys took it in turns to suck out the sweet contents. Now sitting cross-legged on the kerb alongside his friend, Ntoto gave a non-committal grunt, and kept his eye on the *askari* guarding the entrance to the Asian shop across the busy city road.

"Perhaps."

"Why did the post lady want more money?"

"The price has inflated," said Ntoto.

"What do you mean, Ntoto? Inflated?"

"The lady says it is the fault of the *matatus*. The cost of her journey has risen from 20 *ngwee* to 30 *ngwee* in two months only."

"Everything is costing more," said Rutere.

One chore remained. They had yet to collect Charity's note from the Central Bank governor, and this could not be delayed – after all, they had promised airmail delivery.

They made their way along the dusty streets, keeping a sharp eye open for *askaris*. The boys were like chameleons. The colour of their ragged clothes, grey and brown, became an urban camouflage; their skinny brown and dusty legs merged with drab pavements; the grey of their torn shorts was the colour of the rubbish heaped on street corners; all the time their demeanour was apologetic and as submissive as a scavenging wild dog and just as attentive to danger.

They blended into a fading city. The skyscrapers of the 1960s, evidence that Africa was resurgent, the faces of commercial optimism that went hand in hand with political liberation, had become dull, featureless office blocks now, lining Uhuru Avenue, the potholed thoroughfare which ran through the heart of the city.

In its cracked pavements, every few yards a paving stone had been lifted, revealing a jumbled junction of telephone wires, or an intersection of pipes, or simply a hole, dug for a long abandoned purpose, starting to fill with detritus.

There was no rubbish like Kuwisha's rubbish. It had been sifted and assessed countless times by countless hands, a super-efficient form of recycling, driven by poverty and not by green principles. By the time it was eventually carted away by the barrow men, it had been reduced to a dry sludge of no conceivable value at all.

On the pavements the street sellers set up their booths and displayed their wares in front of buildings once totems of progress and modernity. Now they were landmarks of an *ancien régime* that was dead or dying.

The boys' destination, the Central Bank of Kuwisha, was soon to move back into slightly refurbished headquarters from its temporary home at the posts and telecommunications building.

This last redoubt of an old order was vainly attempting to keep state control of information as effective as a fortress on the Maginot Line. On Uhuru Avenue banks that had been built like castles, and grubby state-owned hotels, seemed like whales cast up on a beach, stranded by the departing tide.

Mobile phones and internet cafés, deregulation and privatisation had overtaken these monuments from the past. But within them, the workers defended their interests from behind a series of barricades: messengers, tea-makers, small boys, clerks, secretaries and security staff, all protected by filing cabinets with drawers missing, broken typewriters and three-legged tables marked Property of GoK. These were the weapons of the poor bloody infantry, frontline troops in the state's battle against change.

Any visitor who wanted to get access had first to get past the security guard, behind a desk whose top was stained with the patina of ages, and who insisted on the visitor's name being entered in a grubby exercise book. Then, after waiting for a lift that didn't work, such a visitor climbed flights of stairs, passing landings stinking of urine, until the outer sanctum of the permanent secretary, or the minister, or the chief executive of the state-owned industry was reached.

In the ante-room to the inner sanctum, where a blast of tepid air from the noisy air conditioner made the drab curtains sway, the governor's secretary moved with the speed of a sleep-walker under water as she looked for Charity's letter.

At first she claimed that there was no letter; then maintained that it was in the governor's office, which was locked. Only when Ntoto spotted the envelope on her desk, partially concealed by a telephone directory, did she surrender it.

The boys began the long trudge back to Kireba.

17

Dr Adrian Mullivant, a much-travelled expert and consultant for UKAID, knocked on the steel door of Furniver's office and was shown into the upstairs flat by Didymus Kigali.

Mullivant, in his mid-forties, had a head of black hair thick enough and healthy enough to make Furniver jealous. And he was inseparable from a pair of dark glasses, which as often as not sat atop his head.

He had flown in the day before from Darfur, he told Furniver. Respected throughout the aid community, his degree in development studies from the University of Sussex had been followed by a gap year spent in Sudan, working as the information officer for a voluntary aid agency. A couple of years later, he applied for a place at London's School of Oriental and African Studies, where he completed a well-regarded PhD. This was followed by a two-year spell with WorldFeed, working in the Central America section as a researcher.

As Mullivant acknowledged, it was a splendid job, but he left for a simple reason: "I missed Africa – wanted to stay in development and make a contribution to the place, and I wanted to be my own boss," he told Furniver, who nodded sympathetically.

The two men were sitting in the living room of the flat, waiting for Kigali to bring in the coffee. For a moment, Furniver wondered if he should show Mullivant the draft of his annual review, but already the man was starting to irritate him.

He persevered.

"What's brought you here?"

"In town for the aid conference, to present a paper on gender and savings. Read yours, by the way."

Furniver knew he should never have circulated that address he had presented to the Kuwisha Economic Society; and he regretted the title, which made him appear flippant: "Women on Top: The Money beneath the Mattress".

"And to launch my book," added Mullivant.

He brought out his briefcase.

"Thought you might enjoy reading this."

Mullivant signed a copy of his book, *Sowing the Seed, Reaping the Fruit*, and presented it to Furniver.

"It's on sale at the conference – 10 per cent discount."

He pointed to a footnote on page 24 which cited the "pioneering work in this field by Edward Furniver", and sat back expectantly.

"Very, er, kind of you," said Furniver.

"Don't mention it."

"You still working for the UN Development Programme's small business unit?"

"Not exactly," said Mullivant. "On attachment to the Ford Foundation, and working closely with UKAID."

"Ah, yes."

"Now doing work on the informal sector. Right up UNDP's street, so I'll go back to them."

"Jolly good."

There was a pause.

The silence was about to become embarrassing, when Kigali brought in coffee. Furniver moved a model car fashioned out of wire, and made by a former street boy, to make room on the table.

"Point about my line of business is that it is not really about banking at all. Often all that's needed is the money to buy a pair of pliers," he said.

"Mind if I take notes?"

"Go ahead."

With a fluency that came to him when he was talking about his work, Furniver outlined the principles on which the bank operated. "Trouble is, if you are a street kid, or left school early, no prospect of a job, you cannot afford a decent meal, let alone the price of a pair of decent pliers. You can't get a loan from a commercial bank. Can't get past the front door in fact. Don't really blame the banks."

"Presumably because the ratio of loan to return is too low, and their high risk profile?"

Furniver blinked.

"Not to mention weak presentational capacity and inappropriate attitudes to societal conventions," Mullivant continued.

"Hadn't thought of that," said Furniver. "I assumed it was because the little blighters usually haven't washed for years. Make other customers run a mile. Can't blame 'em. I meet most of my clients at Harrods."

"Harrods?"

"Local bar."

More note-taking accompanied the disclosure. Furniver soon noticed that everything he said was translated, as if he were speaking a foreign language. And as he entered words and phrases into his notebook he could hear Mullivant's muttered interpretation.

"It is not as if there is no money *(Liquidity is not a problem)*, the biggest snag is that they own bugger all *(No security)*. And another thing. I have yet to meet someone who does not want to do better. Work bloody hard, but keep their money under the mattress *(Excellent work ethic)*. So would I in their shoes. Who wants to put it in one of those banks on Uhuru Avenue? Takes them half an hour to get there; another half hour in the queue; then they have to risk thieves and pick-pockets on the way back home *(Technological and societal hurdles).* And at current rates of interest – they cannot keep pace with inflation."

Furniver paused while his visitor caught up.

"Conventional environment inappropriate . . ." he heard him muttering, *"link-up with informal institutions breaks traditional workplace convention."*

Furniver continued.

"So when I came here and looked around, I got in touch with a chap who runs an investment fund, Whiteney Management. Between us we raised the capital – about twenty-five thou – and off we went. Maximum loan is 100, minimum twenty-five."

"Below the commercial banks' ceiling, but still a significant resource flow . . . what rate of return on a hundred thou?"

"Steady on," said Furniver. "We have got bigger, more members, but 100 *ngwee* is still the maximum per individual. But if they make a joint application, it goes up to 500 *ngwee*. To borrow 1,000, need twenty members, and goes to committee. Anything less and it's up to me."

"Records?"

"No, thank God. No paperwork, or very little, thanks to the computer."

Furniver looked thoughtful, and added: "By the way, really should replace it. Already out of date when it was donated by a UK charity. Any chance you might know where I could lay my hands on one?"

Mullivant rustled in his briefcase, and came out with a lengthy form.

Furniver read it, and looked up.

"But all I want is a computer, preferably new. Questions on this form are hard to answer. Anticipated cash flow in year 5 . . ."

He broke off to pour the coffee.

"Got to play by the rules," said Mullivant.

He handed Furniver another document, this time an application for technical help.

"I don't think we need 'technical help' ", said Furniver, "unless that covers an office messenger."

His eyes lit up.

"We could certainly do with a messenger."

Mullivant laughed.

"Fortunately we have several UK-based computer experts. Now look, if you can sign this before I fly to Lesotho tomorrow night, it could well be cleared by April. Otherwise we miss the cut-off date for the programme budget. Real risk we'll underspend. May I use your computer and printer?"

He disappeared for a few minutes, and returned with a print-out, which he handed to Furniver.

"Just a suggestion: 'An international consulting firm should be entrusted with a twofold purpose: to assist in the system design; and to reinforce the credibility and legitimacy of the following enhanced economic objectives.' That should pull in decent response."

A series of questions were attached to the end of the print-out.

"For example: What proportion of your capital falls below the productive rate of return?" Mullivant asked. "And how do you handle it?"

"What we in the business call bad debts? About 1 per cent. Not in my hands. Committee calls them in, sorts it out. Which reminds me. Cephas Gulu. Did a runner owing 200 *ngwee*."

If he didn't leave now, he would be late for the airport.

"Must dash. Confirm his identity."

"I can give you a lift to the Outspan, got a taxi waiting . . ."

"Much obliged, but I am off in the other direction. Hospital."

He watched as Mullivant left the office and picked his way through the muck and the mire to a waiting taxi.

Furniver looked at his watch. He decided to take a chance on the traffic. There was time for a late breakfast. Kigali had anticipated him. Furniver sniffed the air appreciatively. Nothing like Kigali's mushrooms, fried potato and scrambled eggs.

Mullivant frowned. For the fourth time in a distance of 100 yards his taxi, bumper to bumper with four-wheel drives and *matatus*, came to a halt. The cars had just begun to move, slowly at first, before picking up pace, when there was a loud thump.

The appearance of the face of a small boy, pressed so hard against the window that its features were deformed, accompanied by a lolling tongue which left a slimy trace across the car window, coincided with a loud hammering of the door panels. A cupped hand emerged, supplicating yet threatening, and grubby fingers smeared a path across the dusty pane of glass, not thick enough to keep out the dreadful sounds of heart-rending distress. Unintelligible moans came from within the skinny frame of the creature that in any other society would surely have been kept in an institution.

With the passenger's attention focused on this pathetic sight, it was the work of an instant for a second boy to open the opposite door and make off with the bag that lay on the back seat.

The first lad gave a final demented shriek, and set off in the other direction, both boys waving bulging, foul-smelling plastic bags, the notorious "flying toilets" which provided a disposable method of relief for Kireba's residents.

The best bang-bang team in the business had struck.

Having seen Mullivant off, Furniver went downstairs, sat in front of his office computer and looked gloomily at the screen. He had intended to finish his annual report, but his heart was no longer in it. Breakfast would be ready soon, though.

Furniver wondered whether Charity would insist on a Christian marriage. He could live with that, provided the words used were not too specific, and they didn't burn things like incense, and water wasn't splashed around. But becoming a Lamb? Now that was another matter.

Goodness knows what they got up to at the circle. He had come to like and respect Kigali, and the prospect of Charity becoming a member of the Lambs had, until now, never bothered him.

First things first, he thought. He had yet to propose to her, although he thought he had made his position perfectly plain.

Their courtship had proceeded at a pace that almost satisfied Mildred Kigali's concern for convention. A kiss on the cheek had broken the ice after weeks of daily handshakes; an embrace was the next milestone; though what had really broken the ice was the episode of the *jipu*, that wretched fly.

For months, Furniver had been verging on making a formal proposal. Whether he had it in him, he was far from certain. He could hardly have been more forthright as he expressed admiration for the way Charity had tackled that grilled corncob, at supper, during their first chaste weekend on her *shamba*.

"Your teeth, Charity. White. Teeth, strong teeth."

The recollection of Charity ripping through the sweet ears of roasted maize on the *shamba* that weekend produced powerful emotions in Furniver's breast.

"Next time," he vowed, "next time." Provided, course, there was no nonsense with the Lambs.

"Breakfast, suh?"

Furniver looked at his watch. He had half an hour in which to do justice to his favourite meal.

18

Furniver pushed his breakfast plate aside, poured himself a second cup of coffee, resisted the temptation of a cigar from his supply of Davidoff No 2, and then changed his mind.

"What the hell," thought Furniver, and lit up.

With Kigali's breakfast under his belt, a decent cigar and two fine cups of coffee, he was ready to face the rest of the day. More importantly, to tackle the Lambs.

Breakfast was, by mutual consent, the time when Furniver and Kigali discussed the issues of the day, with each man giving careful consideration to the views of the other.

While they did so, both men got on with their business, the white man tucking in to his meal, washed down with a glass of orange juice and a cup of coffee, while Kigali polished the brass handles on the windows of the first-floor flat.

At first Furniver had found Kigali's close attention to his breakfast needs embarrassing and finally demeaning. He hardly had to think of butter or marmalade before Kigali would interrupt his polishing, and pounce, pushing them closer, or topping up his coffee.

A lifetime of domestic service had left its mark on Didymus Kigali. Physically it had produced a permanent deferential crouch in a man who would have had to struggle to reach five feet six inches even if he stood ramrod straight.

Psychologically it seemed to have left Kigali in a state of permanent servitude. But when Furniver attended a service of the Church of the Blessed Lamb he hardly recognised the confident, eloquent and persuasive speaker that kept a huge audience hanging on his every word.

His "cricketer's" outfit had been replaced by his Saturday best – smart blazer, grey slacks and a green tie that Mildred had bought him to mark his first Admonition.

But it had been before he had seen this unexpected side to his elderly steward that Furniver had complained to Charity.

"Just want him to let me get on with it . . ."

He had expected sympathy, but Charity rebuked him.

"Kigali is doing his job," she said firmly. "He is one of the best stewards in Kuwisha. You must respect that."

It did not take long for Furniver to accept her advice. The longer Kigali worked for him, the more Furniver appreciated his talent. Had he been given the chance, thought Furniver, Didymus Kigali would have managed an international hotel . . .

Furniver found these sessions engrossing – but they also gave rise to a secret suspicion that gnawed away at him. Until recently he had been prepared to marry Charity unconditionally. But the more he discussed with Kigali the doctrine of the Lambs, the more uncomfortable he felt at the prospect of Charity converting to the faith.

She seemed to be taking an unhealthy interest in the sect. And while he had not indicated his concerns to anyone, he was starting to wonder what Charity and her friend Mildred actually did at the circle's monthly meeting. Surely she was not really contemplating becoming a Lamb? If so, their relationship was surely heading for trouble.

The tenet that especially disturbed him, currently under discussion with Kigali, was fundamental to conversion to the Church of the Blessed Lamb: members of the sect were never to be naked. And clearly this was of considerable importance to Kigali, who seemed to be speaking in capital letters when he repeated the injunction, not once but twice:

"Never naked, suh. Never naked."

So it was that at breakfast that morning, Furniver had asked

Didymus Kigali to explain and defend this article of faith adopted by the Lambs from their fellow worshippers in the Congolese sect, the Kimbanguists.

"Right, Mr Kigali, fire away."

The steward intensified his dusting, and began by pointing out that Christ himself had retained what Kigali called his "smalls" during baptism and crucifixion.

Furniver nodded.

"With you so far . . ."

"Thank you," said Kigali. He put down his duster, and started clearing the breakfast table.

In the presence of God, he continued, it was vital to be decently dressed.

"And is not our blessed Lord ever present in our lives?"

Furniver nodded.

"And is He not all-seeing?" Kigali demanded, snapping his duster.

It was less of a question than an assertion, and Furniver grunted, a noise that could be taken for assent.

"Eh-heh," said Kigali.

Never was there any reference, none whatsoever, in the entire scriptures, to our Blessed Lord divesting himself of his smalls, maintained Kigali.

"Never."

Furniver had one question.

"Man and er, woman . . . Never naked . . . Even after, er, marriage?"

"Especially after marriage," said Kigali with all the certainty of an elder of the Church of the Blessed Lamb.

"Especially after marriage," he repeated firmly.

A true believer would never under any circumstances, undress completely, always taking care to retain their underwear, whether in bath, shower or bed.

Furniver's heart sank.

While he was as tolerant as the next man, a chap had to draw the line somewhere. And while Edward was a man who had not been favoured by any particular faith, he could not see himself living happily with a woman who made a solemn promise never, ever, to go naked . . .

19

"Since when," asked Edward Furniver, "did Ntoto want to be a pirate?"

It was after lunch and Charity, who had finished supervising preparations for the evening meal, looked astonished.

"A pirate? How can the boy know about pirates? That Ntoto, he is watching too much television."

"Well, that's what he told Mr Kigali this morning. Pretty clear he has set his heart on becoming a pirate."

Charity looked sceptical.

"Bang bang boy maybe. But pirate?" She shook her head. "Never."

"Well, I heard the boy myself."

"Tell me again, what happened?"

Patiently and methodically, Furniver went over the events of the past few hours. He had, he told her, risen earlier than usual. As she knew, it was that time of the year when he had to write the bank's annual report, and the deadline was more pressing than usual, for he had foolishly agreed to talk to a delegate to the World Bank donors' meeting.

"I was on my way to the kitchen to make myself a cup of coffee when who should I find, already hard at work, but Mr Kigali. He seemed a bit put out."

"You would have been cross, Furniver, if it had been round the other way, and he, Kigali, had come early into your office for dusting."

Furniver acknowledged that Charity had a point.

By his standards it had been very early that morning, intruding on a time that Kigali could usually be certain he had the flat to himself for half an hour.

And it was thirty minutes that he put to good use. It gave him a chance to read the newspapers before taking them to Furniver with a pot of tea; and from that pot he had already poured his own first cup of the day, into which he had put two spoons of condensed milk. The radio played in the background, a combination of news and music.

In the remaining ten minutes, before Furniver surfaced, he would complete small chores that would otherwise go undone, or at least be delayed, such as the odd bit of sewing. Only when these rituals were complete did Didymus Kigali, husband of Mildred, house steward to Edward Furniver, and elder in the Church of the Blessed Lamb, feel ready to start the day.

So Furniver's cheery greeting prompted an entirely understandable irritated cough of acknowledgement, which he was fairly confident that had it not been so uncharacteristically early, Furniver would have recognised.

"We spoke about this and that, for ten minutes or so. Then," said Furniver, "there was a knock on the door. And there was Ntoto . . ."

Charity interrupted.

"I had sent him with fresh corn-bread."

"Jolly good it is too," said Furniver, realising that he had been remiss in not thanking her immediately. "I left him and Mr Kigali to it, went up to the office. Pottered around, went back to the kitchen, and something had been going on with Ntoto . . ."

For Titus Ntoto, Kigali represented the values of pre-independence Kuwisha. The steward's very uniform angered the boy. The old man kept his outfit immaculate, his starched white shorts flapping above his wrinkled brown knees, white knee-length socks, and spotless plimsolls. Kigali even applied Blanco to the shoes last thing at night, placing them at the door of his house, like sentries.

Ntoto, of course, had only seen cricket on the small television Furniver had donated to Harrods, and even then very infrequently, for the sport had no appeal for him. It was Cyrus Rutere, keen of eye and sharp of tongue, who spotted the similarity of the outfits and described Kigali as looking like a cricketer.

And it was Rutere who popularised the term, invariably referring to Furniver's steward as "the cricketer"; and any Mboya Boy who evinced an interest in domestic service was contemptuously accused of wanting to be a "cricketer".

Meanwhile Ntoto had kept his eyes fastened on Kigali's plimsolls when the door opened.

"Mrs Charity sends this corn-bread for breakfast . . . maybe you want me to clean your plimsolls, suh?"

Mr Kigali gritted his teeth. He was starting to suspect Ntoto of cheek. If he had told the boy once, he had told him a dozen times.

He, Didymus Kigali, would entrust no-one – not even Mildred – with the task of cleaning his shoes. It was an act he found therapeutic, contemplating the ways of the world, last thing at night.

Ntoto knew this full well. But this boy was cunning. How could Kigali complain to Charity that the boy was "cheeky"? Because the boy offered to clean his shoes?

Ntoto then started to scratch, an act that he well knew worried Kigali, who dreaded an invasion of head lice.

But Didymus Kigali was a fair man. For all the boy's cheek, he had something, there was definitely a quality that could be channelled into great things. And he, Didymus Kigali, could open up a fine career for Ntoto.

"Show me your hands, boy."

After checking that Ntoto's hands were clean Kigali made his move.

"Come, come inside, Ntoto. I want to show you a very good kitchen . . ."

Kigali pointed to a spot where Ntoto should stand, and then set about opening the cream-coloured doors of the waist-high cupboards that ran the length of one wall. And as he opened them, he listed their contents, lined up in serried ranks, like toy soldiers.

"Polish."

"Brushes."

"Laundry."

"Drinks."

"Flies."

"Shoes."

"Cooking."

Tins of Brasso sat next to bottles of bleach, *stoep* polish was lined up with shoe polish, black and brown, Blanco sat alongside Jeyes Fluid, jars of sugar and salt lined up with tins of tea and coffee, while bottles of gin and whisky stood alongside crates of tonic and beer. Brushes and brooms stood to attention, and mops and cleaning rags lay in their allotted places.

Didymus Kigali beamed at Ntoto.

"Smell, Ntoto, just smell!"

Kigali sniffed an intoxicating mix, as enthusiastically as a daytripper making his first excursion along the beach. With immense pride, Kigali made a gesture that embraced every bottle and container, every spray and every abrasive as if he were a circus trainer who had established his mastery over the beasts parading in the ring.

And then with a solemnity that underlined what came next, he announced: "And a uniform . . . free! One day, Ntoto, all this could be yours, with gratuity after five year service, a pension, even, for ten year service . . ."

Didymus Kigali, his voice trembling with emotion, rested his case.

Only then did it dawn on Ntoto that Kigali was not just showing off. The terrible truth was coming home to the boy when Furniver had appeared at the kitchen door, wondering what had happened to his early morning tea.

"Just as I went into the kitchen," said Furniver, "Ntoto rushed out, blubbing away. Waterworks at full blast. And as he passed me I distinctly heard him say: 'I want to be a pirate. Not a cricket man.'

"I said to Kigali: 'What's the matter with the boy? Why on earth would he want to be a pirate? And what does he mean, a cricket man, Mr Kigali?' We were both stumped. Had not a clue."

Charity had to admit that she, too, was baffled.

Furniver fiddled with his watchstrap, and shook his head.

"Pirate . . . pirate . . . not a bloody clue."

20

Ferdinand Mlambo was in luck.

Just as he was saying farewell to Philimon Ogata, promising to come back later to discuss the offer of an apprenticeship in the funeral business, Ntoto and Rutere returned from their city trip. From behind the shelter provided by the Pass Port to Heaven Coffin Parlour, Mlambo watched as the boys reported back to Charity, and then disappeared into the bar, out of sight.

Mlambo stayed concealed, waiting and watching for his chance to slip in undetected. While he waited, the hubbub of Harrods washed over him.

"Tea with milk, corn-bread and relish."

"Dough ball and tea, extra sugar!"

"Two Tuskers, quick!"

"Sweet dough ball, six."

"Porridge and tea."

Thick and fast the orders came, from women with babies strapped to their backs, shift workers returning from work, *askaris* setting off to work, from loafers and louts, chancers and *tsotsis*, from clerks and teachers, nurses and mechanics, the halt and the lame, the quick and the nearly dead.

Duty Mboya Boys, hands scrubbed in accordance with Charity's instructions, ran back and forth with orders; others helped with the washing up, where unnecessary splashing was forbidden.

Finally there was a lull, and Mlambo moved smartly into the container that housed the bar, and rapped twice on the counter, just above the boys' den.

He rapped again.

No reply.

Then a muffled voice called out: "Go! We are resting . . . not on duty."

"It is me, Mlambo. I need urgent talk."

Rutere appeared.

"Mlambo! Why are you here?"

Mlambo's first and only prior visit to the den had been to press his claim that he did meet the residential qualifications for membership of the Mboya Boys' football team, successfully arguing that although they were born in Zimbabwe, his aunt and her husband had lived in Kireba for five years, only fleeing when they, along with other foreign minorities, had been the target of rioting organised by thugs and bully boys from the ruling party.

"I need helping," he said simply. "Helping, please . . ."

Construction of the den had been carefully monitored by Mildred Kigali. And when they installed the old paraffin can in which they made *changa*, she did not conceal her horror.

"*Changa* is evil," said Mildred.

It was true that illegal home brewers who used formaldehyde or battery acid to hasten the maturing killed hundreds of drinkers. This, Charity readily acknowledged, was a thoroughly bad thing.

"But what must I do?" Charity had responded, hands on hips. "Street boys drink. That is a fact. All I can do is to make sure they drink clean *changa*."

"In the Lambs . . ." Miriam began.

"In your church, no-one drinks. And how many street children are Lambs? Not one. Negative street boys are Lambs."

Mildred admitted that much. But she hit back.

"To give boys soft touches," said Mildred, "will not help on

120

the day we are all summoned for judgement at the feet of Our Lord."

"I am happy to leave judgement to God. And I, Charity Tangwenya Mupanga, will tell Him that my boys never, never made bad *changa*, which can kill their friends."

Just in case, however, when their den was complete, she gave them a stern warning: "If I catch you using battery acid when you make *changa*, I will stop your dough balls. That will be the first time. Second time, you will leave. Finish."

The boys had given her a blank stare.

To mark the opening of their den, Charity gave the boys a small suitcase Furniver was about to throw out. She had painted their initials on one side, in big letters, and on the other a single word: "SAFE". It was in this case that the boys stowed their possessions, including pictures or photos that had impressed them.

Rutere pulled back the retaining latch of the bar counter and ushered Mlambo through the entrance of the den, where a makeshift lamp – a length of string in a cola bottle – threw out a guttering, flickering flame, revealing Titus Ntoto, with heavy lidded eyes, pupils dilated from glue sniffing.

Past differences were set aside as Ntoto and Rutere listened to their companion outline his plan for revenge. There were still problems to resolve, but the more Mlambo considered his plan, the more feasible it seemed to him. There were only two possible snags. The prospect of State House security guards opening fire – and far more likely, of Chief Steward Mboga himself taking a pot shot – did not seriously bother the boy.

What did concern him, however, was the prospect of running through the city central park, his *butumba* there for all to see, and his *balubas* bouncing. Any self-respecting *mungiki* gang member would soon spot that the runner was not circumcised, and mark him down as a candidate for an initiation ceremony in which a jagged piece of glass and a rusty nail would be the instruments of choice.

It was Ntoto who asked three or four questions, all short and to the point.

Finally he nodded.

"We will talk more, on the roof, while we peel vegetables."

Just as Mlambo was backing out of the den, Ntoto called out: "Don't tell anyone about the oil lamp. Mrs Charity says it is banned, strict. Fire."

21

The boys left the den, and using the beer crates as a step, scrambled to the top of Harrods. They made themselves comfortable on a pile of old sacks taken from the bar, but just as Mlambo was about to begin, Ntoto asked him to wait.

The gang leader jumped down from the roof, disappeared into the kitchen and emerged back on the roof with a dough ball, which he presented to Mlambo, the gift carefully wrapped in a page of old newspaper.

"Extra sugar," said Ntoto, "I put extra sugar."

Mlambo almost wept with gratitude. He was about to cram the dough ball into his mouth, and then changed his mind.

"I will eat later."

They all sat cross-legged on the flat roof while Mlambo began the first part of his extraordinary tale. If Mlambo was a good storyteller, the boys were a good audience, making expressive noises, clicking their tongues and sucking their teeth at appropriate stages.

"Here is my story . . . and then I will tell you my plan."

He started with his account of how Lovemore Mboga had summoned him to the pantry and announced his punishment. Slowly, his audience captivated, he built up to the climax. "And then this Mboga, he reached to my ear, and began to pull, pull and as he pulled it hurt all the way, inside, terrible hurting."

The boys sat wide-eyed. "He had pulled out my name, Ferdinand Mlambo, and it struggled, but that Mboga, he is strong, and he put it in a box, which he has buried, and he said: 'You are Mlambo no more.'

"And Mboga told me that his dog would piss on the name Ferdinand Mlambo, and it would rot, and then he gave me a new name."

Mlambo could not bring himself to speak the new name, and to his dismay he felt tears well up, alongside fresh anger.

"Say it," urged Ntoto, "say your Mboga name."

Mlambo said something, but so quietly that neither Ntoto nor Rutere could hear it.

"What? What?" said Rutere, and then corrected himself: "Pardon?"

This time Mlambo made an enormous effort.

"He said I am called Fatboy, only Fatboy, forever Fatboy."

The revelation was greeted with sharp intakes of breath, and they passed a glue tube round, each taking a deep sniff. Shocked clicks then greeted his disclosure that he was expected to be an informer. "I must report to Mboga after the staff meeting this Friday morning," continued Mlambo, "or else he will beat me."

"That is true," said Rutere, with a shudder. "He will certainly beat you."

"There is more I must tell you," said Mlambo.

"About *mungiki*?" asked Rutere anxiously, but Mlambo had already risen to his feet, the better to act out the tale that followed.

"Yesterday just before sundown, I came here, to Harrods, very slowly," he walked on the spot, exaggeratedly lifting his knees and cautiously placing his feet, "and no-one could see me."

His hand shaded his eyes as he looked around.

"Soon I saw where I could hide."

The boy huddled his shoulders and seemed to shrink in size.

"I saw that between the gas for cooking and the empty beer crates, there was a place."

The boys looked over the edge of the container, and Mlambo pointed to the spot, a few feet from the bougainvillaea.

"For a time I was sleeping. And then I was digging, like a dog, so my hand could lift the bolt on the other side . . ."

"Why?"

"In case for stealing," said Mlambo simply, and it was a motive Rutere and Ntoto could well understand. It was the work of a few minutes to remove a loose rivet at eye level which gave him a view of what was happening within.

It was from this vantage point that Mlambo, fascinated and horrified in equal measure, forced himself to watch the extraordinary events that unfolded.

It was a natural break in his long story.

Mlambo carefully unfolded the paper in which Ntoto had wrapped the dough ball. "You cut for three and we choose."

Rutere dropped down, and returned with a sharp knife from the kitchen.

After examining the dough ball with all the concentration of a diamond cutter presented with a raw unpolished stone, Ntoto made his incisions, knowing, of course, that as the person who wielded the knife, he would be left with no choice.

One generous gesture deserved another.

"You have the sugar, Mlambo," said Ntoto, and Rutere nodded his agreement.

Mlambo funnelled the grains that had detached themselves from the dough ball into his mouth and licked his lips. And when satisfied that not a morsel remained, resumed his tale.

22

David Podmore, First Secretary (Aid) at the British High Commission, was longing for a smoke. What was the point of having your own office if you could not have the odd fag? His unlit cigarette dangled from his lips, placed there in the hope that someone would put their head round the door, spot it, and say in the priggish tone of the converted: "By the way, no smoking, old boy."

But nobody had, and his act of petty rebellion went unnoticed.

His telephone rang.

"Podmore," said Podmore.

There was a pause at the other end of the line.

"Podsman?"

How long had he been in Kuwisha? Three years . . . and the bugger still could not get his bloody name right.

"Dave Podmore here," he said, pretending he had not recognised the gravel voice of the president's press secretary. He lingered over his surname, stressing the last syllable.

"Ah, Podsman, my brother!"

The genial greeting immediately alerted the British diplomat, who halfway through his tour realised that tone and substance were seldom related when President Nduka's press secretary was doing business.

In a couple of sentences Punabantu passed on the unwelcome news. Podmore's face fell.

"Really? You're not, are you?"

He nevertheless tried to match Punabantu's jovial note.

"Letting him out! You're getting soft, you lot!"

Puna laughed.

"Goodbye, Podsman."

"Podmore," said Podmore, but Punabantu had rung off.

"Damn and blast."

He had to move fast.

The arrest of a British hack was an irritation; but the release of a British hack could prove far more problematic for the High Commission. Both events could do much damage, and neither was desirable.

Only that week, there had been good news: a UK company had been awarded the main contract for the Kireba project, and the last thing needed was anything that encouraged outside interest in a country that was renowned for corruption and a tender process that was less than transparent.

"Bugger!" said Podmore.

Fortunately, he had enjoyed a spell in the notorious Foreign Office news department in London, where British diplomats were sent to learn the art of dissembling. While there, one principle had been drummed into him.

In any crisis ask yourself, or better, ask somebody senior enough to carry the can if all went pear-shaped, the question: what are the interests of HMG? And the next step was to get your retaliation in first.

Podmore moved quickly. It was time to lay a few false trails.

He picked up the phone and dialled an agency bureau chief.

"You heard that Pearson has been released? Jolly good news . . . not that we expect any thanks . . . just doing our job . . . half the commission been working on his case. By the way, a word to the wise," said Podmore. "Stay clean on the forex front. We're told there's a crackdown. If you get caught, not a thing we can do to help. Not a sausage. Even though the *ngwee* is over-valued. Got to manage somehow. All we can do is to arrange consular access, that's all . . . anything to do with

Pearson's arrest? What? . . . Absolutely not. No idea . . . though I had heard . . . on the record? . . . no comment. Off the record . . . well, you know how the system works, as well as I do. Suggest you ask Pearson."

Podmore put the phone down.

That should do the trick.

23

Mlambo resumed his story.

"My head was heavy from smoking, so after I had made a hole, so I could look, I was sleeping. Then there was noise. Too much," he said disapprovingly. "Noise of women, singing and laughing inside Harrods."

"Was it a naming ceremony?" Rutere asked.

Naming ceremonies were important occasions in Kuwisha, and Mlambo crossed himself. When it came to Christian faith and local beliefs, he took no chances. At a naming ceremony, he would lead the chanting; at a christening he would uncap a vial of water taken from the nearest river, as he had been instructed by his gran. Before a football match he would burn a crow's feather in both goalmouths, and bow his head as reverentially as any of his team-mates, when they gathered in a huddle while the coach called on the Lord to bless them.

"Naming ceremony, maybe."

He continued: "This noise woke me, and I looked through the crack and watched, but my legs were already getting ready for running. There were many ladies, some with babies on their backs. Then I saw Mrs Mildred as the head of the dancing; and then she took the knitting needles from the wooden case made by Mr Ogata. And I saw, with these eyes that are my own, with my eyes I saw . . ."

He stopped, overcome it seemed, by the extraordinary nature of what followed.

"What? What did you see, Mlambo?"

Rutere was almost squeaking with anticipation, and Mlambo did not let him down.

"Mrs Mildred, she pushed each needle into two paw-paws on the counter. Next, Mrs Mildred called Mrs Charity to join her, and they danced and danced around the tables, and other ladies followed them, all dancing, dancing. It was, for sure, I think, the dance of the Lambs."

His audience were stunned. Like Edward Furniver, they had displayed little interest in the activities of the circle. But it was a very different matter if it involved the Lambs, for rumour had it that the sect was planning to enter a team in the under-15 league.

"Or . . ."

Mlambo held up his hand.

"We must not jump conclusions . . . it could also be that it was women's business."

Mlambo's knowledge of the rites and ceremonies of the Church of the Blessed Lamb was limited. But as he watched Mildred lead a conga round the bar's interior, brandishing the paw-paw capped needles, he knew he had witnessed an important dance.

"If it was women's business, what were they dancing?" asked Ntoto, though he could readily guess the answer.

Mlambo looked very uncomfortable.

"Women business."

All three boys were uneasy. Female initiation dances were not a proper subject of discussion.

"Phauw," exclaimed Rutere, wide-eyed.

Mlambo shifted from one comfortable buttock to another. Storytelling, he discovered, came naturally to him.

"With my eye, I looked and watched. Eh! What I saw! My gran . . ."

"What? What?" urged Rutere.

Mlambo appeared to fight an inner battle for control of powerful emotions, bit his lower lip, gathered himself, and continued, describing how he had seen Mildred Kigali dance with almost improper abandon, brandishing the paw-paw capped needles.

He had little doubt about the significance of what he saw.

"It was *muti*. Very strong *muti*. It was so strong, that the needles helped Mrs Mildred dance, like a young girl."

"How could you know if it was good *muti?*" asked Rutere, uneasily.

"If it had been bad, it would have been fighting Mrs Mildred, because Mr Kigali is a deacon of the Church of the Blessed Lamb," replied Mlambo confidently.

Rutere nodded. That made sense.

Mlambo continued his tale.

"When Mrs Mildred put the needles on the counter, she was so close I could have touched her arm. And when she went to start the meeting, I could see the needles."

"Next?"

"So I stretched my arm, and took the needles and the paw-paws. And then, when I pulled my arm back, I saw it – I saw the *tokolosh*."

He corrected himself.

"I heard this noise first, before seeing anything. A noise of great pain, in a language I do not understand. 'Omigah! Omigah!' I looked and saw this thing crying, crying, and . . ."

Mlambo paused for effect:

"It had a blue head. Then I knew I had to run for my life.

"*Tokolosh*!" I cried. "*Tokolosh*! And I ran."

His audience sat silent. Even Ntoto was convinced. They knew they had heard the truth.

"But first, before running, I had picked the needles, and the paw-paws," said Mlambo triumphantly. "And now, with this strong *muti*, I can make Mboga cry, and I can get my name back."

Ntoto, who had his doubts about *muti*, was nevertheless intrigued.

"How can needles help you, Mlambo?"

"If you come with me now, I will tell you my full plan for Mboga. But you must assist me."

Ntoto and Rutere were in no doubt. Mlambo deserved their help.

"First," said Ntoto, "we must do duty jobs for Mrs Charity. Then we will go to your place."

Mlambo clapped his hands with delight and relief.

"You will be welcome," he said, somewhat formally. "Very welcome. And I will show you the needles."

24

Edward Daniel Furniver, 50-something and battling to keep a developing paunch under control, had not intended to spend so long in Kuwisha. He had seen himself as no more than a well-intentioned stranger who was passing through, but to his surprise he had been in the country for more than four years.

If asked how it was that the son of a British diplomat, who had become a successful investment banker in the City of London, had ended up running a micro-lending bank in an African slum, he tended to reply: "Luck, pure luck, old boy!"

But if pressed, he would disclose that it had all begun with a failed marriage to a socially ambitious wife called Davina, who announced her intention to divorce him through a letter from her lawyer while she was on holiday in Antibes – with the lawyer, he later learnt. It triggered a bout of binge drinking and sober reflection, which culminated in early retirement and a decision to travel the world, beginning with Africa.

It was, he readily admitted, a somewhat irrational act of defiance, born of a perverse identification with a continent that had become synonymous with debt, disease and disaster.

And if pressed further, Furniver would say that he had succumbed to a temptation which afflicted many of those who were over 50 years old.

"It's a dangerous stage, when you want to do good. And when you reach my age, it is jolly nearly irresistible. And in Africa, the temptation is overwhelming."

To Furniver's surprise, and often to his dismay, the continent had taken him into its warm, generous and hospitable embrace, an experience marked by serendipity, a series of happy coincidences, including the pleasure of unplanned reunions with old friends in unlikely circumstances and in bizarre places. But Furniver soon came to appreciate that for most of the continent's people, life was fragile, cheap, dangerous and unpredictable.

After a few weeks in Lagos he flew to Cape Town, where he nearly succumbed to the opportunity to buy a share of a Sea Point restaurant; then he worked his way back north in stages: a few months in Johannesburg, the same in Gaberone, a spell in Lusaka, then on to Blantyre, and from Blantyre to Kuwisha.

There, in the slum of Kireba, he saw an opportunity to put into effect a plan he had been considering for years. He never forgot the day he had tagged on to a tour of the sprawling, lively shanty town, laid on by the then leader of the local street gang for a visiting British journalist.

Looking around as they trudged along muddy alleys he saw the residents working hard, in tough conditions, but with little hope of changing their world, for they had not the resources to do so. And without access to capital, they never would.

"Seemed as obvious as the sky was blue," Furniver had said.

The answer, he argued, was micro-banking – lending small amounts of money to people too poor to obtain commercial bank credit. This, he felt convinced, was part of the elusive solution to Africa's woes.

And so, with his stay now running into months, he decided that Kireba was as good a place as any to start putting these thoughts into practice. If the concept could work in a country drained by corruption and mismanagement, demoralised by failure, and let down by its leaders, it could work anywhere.

It did not take long for the Kireba People's Co-operative Bank to become a great success. Despite its impressive name, it performed a simple function, with results that were as evident as green shoots in a desert.

The intricate scale models of bicycles, lorries and cars made out of wire by street boys, for example, needed nothing but skill, imagination and a pair of pliers to construct. A small advance, sufficient to buy pliers and a bundle of wire could turn an unruly adolescent into a self-sufficient worker who could earn enough from tourists eager for an authentic local artefact to repay the society's low-interest loan in a few weeks.

Shoe-cleaners, watch repairers, tailors, vegetable vendors, coffin makers, hairdressers, corncob hawkers, model makers, curio sellers, all owed their start in commercial life to the bank's small loan.

From a base of 500 members and capital of 500,000 *ngwee*, provided by an obscure international charity that was in fact funded by Furniver himself, the society had steadily grown. There were now nearly 3,000 members of whom 500 were borrowers.

It showed, Furniver believed, that it was possible to transform a community with a limited amount of capital, spent in ways that were decided by the people who would be affected. With a hand-operated pump and a few thousand feet of plastic piping, women could be released from the daily, backbreaking burden of carrying water. Provide a loan that was enough for the purchase of a locally made, fuel-efficient stove, and hundreds of trees could be saved.

Within a few weeks of his first visit to Kireba, Furniver had commissioned the building of what would be the slum's first brick structure, with a modest flat above the office of the bank and the strong-room in which members could store their most valuable possessions.

It had not taken long to show that administration was straightforward and cheap, and that fears of the contrary were ill-founded. Put the details into a computer, and push a button every day, was all that was required – plus, of course, the peer pressure which often took a form that left Furniver uneasy.

In theory, it meant that the borrower's friends would express their disapproval should the borrower default. They, too, wanted a loan, or possibly were recipients of a loan already. Would-be borrowers would have to wait longer for money to become available; and those who had loans would have to pay a higher rate of interest.

In polite society, mere disapproval would serve as peer pressure. In Kireba, as Furniver soon discovered, the term had a more robust interpretation, and was usually a euphemism for a sound hiding administered by the members of the local committee. It was an approach, he had to admit, that worked very well. The effect of the rare beatings was so profound that the society's ratio of bad debts to loans outstanding was the envy of his commercial bank colleagues.

Furniver had no illusions: micro-lending would not change Africa overnight, but at least the lives of many could be transformed – and the people of Kireba would happily bear witness to that encouraging fact.

25

Geoffrey Japer's flight from London was running late, and Furniver whiled away the time inspecting the new airport's facilities.

First he popped into the Gents for a pee, and as he stood in the stall, was struck by the fact that no graffiti were to be found. Not on the wall in front of him, nor to the left or the right of where he stood.

Curious, he investigated the toilet cubicles, and noted an extraordinary phenomenon. There were graffiti all right, but the word seemed inappropriate for what he found. The handwriting was neat and mature, as if from a school exercise book. This was surprising enough. But the contents were quite remarkable. Slogans and exhortations were exclusively political, with not a swear word in sight.

"Nduka is a thief" was the general theme, with elaborations that were almost polite. Thus "No amnesty for Nduka" was alongside "Nduka must face justice".

It was, thought Furniver, oddly heartening. He returned to the lounge, and watched and listened as intending passengers buttonholed airport officials, as friendly as they were vague. Yes, their flight would take off; but it was, alas, delayed, until further notice. In the meantime, the incoming flight had not yet landed.

Bad sign, thought Furniver.

He kept a close eye on Reconciliation Point A, alongside Customer Service Point A. Both desks were deserted, as indeed were Reconciliation Point B and Customer Service Point B.

Sitting in the middle of the cream-tiled, white pillared departure hall were two amiable ladies, one perched on a first-aid box.

Some chairs, white, plastic, were in great demand, but in short supply. Passengers eyed them, as they would an unattended suitcase at Heathrow, but covetously rather than fearfully.

He continued to scrutinise the hall's neat blue signs, and went in search of the Restaurant, the Shops, the Post Office, and the Bank, only to discover that they did not exist.

They were no more than promises, well-meant indication: a metaphor, thought Furniver, for Africa's good intentions, from the African Union to the Lagos Plan of Action.

Every few minutes he made a foray for news. Old airport hands, used to delays, sought out the baggage handlers, best informed and most co-operative of workers, and pooled information; shared the confused dispatches from far-off battlefronts. A plane had been sighted in Dar es Salaam, or possibly Entebbe. Whatever, wherever, it was on its way!

The good news was relayed to the two friendly ladies. After all, they were in charge of the blue-signed Information Desk.

Furniver was now being closely followed by an earnest young man.

"Where are you flying to? I can help."

"I don't deal with ticket touts."

The man pushed his spectacles back onto his nose.

"Suh, I am not a tout." He gave Furniver a pained, dignified look: "I am a travel adviser."

Furniver regretted his pompous reply.

After all, his credentials for the job were probably as good as any expatriate in Africa. Consultant, adviser, con man, tout. There are a lot of us around, thought Furniver.

We experts from Europe, we communicate silently with each other, a raised eyebrow, a shrug – but loudly and effusively and insincerely with our African partners.

We bump into each other at the hotel bars and at the business centres, invariably staffed by ladies debilitated by bilharzia, malaria, or other ghastly parasites.

We swap horror stories, of hotel rooms without minibars, and "lazy" locals, and complain about those business centres that charge $15 an hour for use of the internet, and airlines that demand more for a journey within Africa than a return flight from Kuwisha to London.

And we watch as Africa's best and brightest leave. Each year they flee, by the scores of thousands: doctors and dentists, bankers and accountants, writers and athletes, footballers and musicians; they desert the continent for Europe and the US . . . and expatriates come in droves to take their places.

What the OM had talked about started to make sense.

"Brain drain and capital flight. Killing the continent. The best bugger off, taking their money with them," the OM had complained at their last session at the Thumaiga Club. "And in return we send in second raters, and the donors tell Western investors to put their money here. Beats me. Odd business . . ."

Furniver's ruminations were interrupted.

"Trust me," said an airport official. "Your plane will arrive soon."

The scuffle over Japer's bag had been embarrassing.

"How was I to know that the chap was a customs officer?"

Furniver stayed silent.

"These people . . . no wonder . . ." said Japer, shaking his head. He described his passage through immigration.

"Tourist? They asked me. I said I was in Kuwisha to help them.

"From Eng-land. Ambassador. Children and rhinos . . . The immigration bod gave me a filthy look. And then the penny dropped. I handed over my passport, with a $10 bill folded inside. The foreign editor was right."

"Place is absolutely riddled with corruption," he had warned. "But don't offer a penny over $10. You'll just spoil things for the rest of us."

Japer and Furniver walked through the dozens of taxi drivers soliciting for fares.

"I gather that NoseAid want a picture of me and a baby on my lap, and as close to the rhino as we can get."

"So I gather," said Furniver.

"Don't want to do it," said Japer.

"It won't be as bad as you think," Furniver replied. "It's not going to bite you."

"But they tend to piss on you," said Japer truculently.

Furniver was no expert on the characteristics of large African herbivorous creatures, but he felt that he could say with confidence that the prospect of Japer getting pissed on by a rhino was remote.

Lucy had warned him that Japer, scourge of the British establishment, had a notoriously short temper, invariably ignited should someone disagree with him. So it was with some diffidence that Furniver ventured an opinion, with what for him was unusual eloquence. It was a measure of his essential naïvety that he had failed to recognise that Japer was not referring to the big, horned beast.

"I think you will find, Geoffrey, that although it is a remote possibility, given the precautions that are taken at the rhino refuge, and that your contract also stipulates that guards equipped with dart guns should be on hand, you just might be gored. Most unlikely, given that the rhino will have been sedated, and confined to a stout wooden enclosure."

He looked thoughtful: "Though if you were determined to be gored, and threw yourself at the rhino's feet, grabbed its testicles, and squeezed them vigorously, it would in all probability gore you.

"But while I am not an expert in these matters, I think that the prospect that you will be peed on by the rhino, under those or any other circumstances, is so remote as to be ruled out. I have discovered that elephants have been known to piss on their victim after trampling on them. But rhinos? Before or after they've done their goring? Never happened," he said, "never been reported. Never, ever, happened."

He braced himself for an explosion.

But the prospect of what lay ahead, and its attendant risk of getting peed on, appeared to have filled Japer with such gloom and foreboding that even his effervescent temper had been dampened.

He looked at Furniver miserably. "Babies, Edward, not rhinos. Babies. I have to hold a baby. They tend to pee on you. I know. My sister's got one."

Once again, Furniver was lucky with the traffic, and the airport taxi dropped Japer at the Outspan, where Lucy, clipboard in hand, took over.

Japer checked in, left his bag with the porter, and climbed into Lucy's car.

Twenty minutes later they parked, and walked the last few hundred yards to the railway track, from where they looked across a plastic and corrugated iron mass of huts and hovels.

Kireba, which had replaced Johannesburg's Soweto as the slum that was *de rigueur* to have seen at first hand, never let itself down. No self-respecting visitor left it off their itinerary. From US students seeking to enhance their CVs, to visiting politicians and heavyweights of the aid industry; none could leave Kuwisha without having done their bit in Kireba, which provided both a photo-opportunity and the chance to earn curriculum vitae entry: Worked with Aids sufferers in Kireba, Kenya.

That was worth a good twenty points on the informal rating of the benefit of a gap year spent abroad. Africa itself was worth ten points; any thing to do with public health was worth fifteen points; assisting with an Aids programme was worth double that;

and if you could claim that management skills had been honed by helping with the running of the Kireba clinic, or promoting a literacy campaign, and furthermore argue that all this "impacted" on "gender issues", you were close to the 100-point maximum.

A visit to Kireba, then, was the East African aid industry equivalent of a tourist notching up one of the game parks' big five; along with Kireba as an essential stop on the compassionate visitors' itinerary was an Aids orphanage, a tree planting, a visit to Lokio, and a look-in on a local clinic.

Japer was suitably appalled at what he saw.

"To be honest," said Lucy, as they surveyed Kireba, "there are worse spots – Lagos or Luanda are easily as bad – but the hotels are lousy."

"Hotels? Slums? Don't get you," said Japer, unable to conceal his surprise.

But rather than correct him, she continued to rattle off statistics of life in Kireba: 600,000 people, one clinic, and more than 40 per cent of over-16s had Aids.

"Stand a bit to the left, so we can get in the corner of the State House grounds as background," said Lucy, aiming her camera. "Smile! Now a serious look . . . thanks. That's Kireba done," she said briskly. "No time for the clinic. Got to get back for the start of the conference."

On the return journey, Japer said little, but Lucy had no doubt that her visitor had been suitably moved.

"The donors' conference starts in fifteen minutes," said Lucy. "Ask for Newman Kibwana. I'll be back after the opening session to take you to Wilson – that's the domestic airport. I'll see you here; got to collect my briefing notes for your trip to Lokio. Oh, and look out for Cecil Pearson, *Financial News*. He should be inside . . ."

26

Corruption in Kuwisha was a tangible presence, like a flatulent dog in a small room on a hot day, and the people battled to overcome the noxious stench that permeated their lives. Nothing and nobody could escape it.

You could certainly smell it in the mounds of uncollected rubbish that grew larger by the day, piling up on the street corners, monuments to the venal incompetence of the city council and Mayor Guchu. Goodness knows where the city taxes ended up. Not in providing salaries for honest workers. No wonder many of the city wards were refusing to pay their rates, and were instead spending residents' rates directly on local matters, such as filling the potholes in the area roads.

You could always read about corruption: there were stories in the papers every day, revealing kickbacks to ministers, cuts on contracts, and letters from parents who complained that teachers were demanding money or sexual favours from their pupils, as a condition of passing their exams.

And you could experience it at first hand on every journey in a *matatu* when you encountered a police road block. Either you gave what they asked for, "a little present", or they would discover that a headlamp was defective, or the tyre tread too worn, or seat belts were unfastened.

Sleaze permeated life, eroded values, all around, every day, day after day.

The road project, backed by UNDP and a group of non-government aid agencies led by the Oxford-based WorldFeed, would be an acid test of the government's commitment to probity.

In theory it would be part of what planners called "an integrated development project" – which would include low-cost housing, a primary school and a clinic.

It seemed a fine scheme, and tenders were coming in from construction companies in Europe, South Africa and Kuwisha itself.

But many residents suspected it was a way of driving them from their homes in the name of "slum clearance". Once out, they feared they would never be allowed to come back, and the new flats and houses would be sold to middle-class supporters of President Nduka and the ruling party.

When completed, the highway would cut through the slum, effectively dividing it in two. The road itself would be as effective as the Berlin Wall, with six-foot ramparts on either side and with no provision for pedestrian crossing.

"Stop the Kireba ring road!" and other slogans were appearing more frequently on the sides of the shanties that lay in its path.

And who could explain the mysterious stand-pipe business? For the first time in its history, Kireba had sources of clean water in the form of stand-pipes.

With much fanfare and jubilating, the first six taps had been turned on by Mayor Willifred Guchu, who thanked UNDP "for acting like fathers" in the course of his unctuous speech. But within weeks water was emerging at a trickle from the taps in eastern Kireba, the section which was to become the area for the promised 'low-cost' housing, yet the water flowed powerfully from the taps located in western Kireba.

Charity would eat her hat if this was a coincidence.

She should not have let Lucy, articulate, persuasive and ambitious, a veteran of the aid business though still in her early thirties, overcome the reservations Charity had voiced from the start.

"Why punish the people for the faults of the politicians?" Lucy had said, with a passion that infused her and infected anyone who listened to her. "We know the government people all chop, but that's no reason to stop helping the *wananchi* to help themselves."

And so Charity had allowed herself to be persuaded. True, she did not actively support the project, even though there were promises to build cheap but decent homes, and provide water and electricity. That would have been too much. But she had agreed not to oppose it.

Clean water, decent toilets and lessons in basic hygiene would do wonders for Kireba, yet somehow these simple needs were not big enough for the foreign non-government agencies that had proliferated in Kuwisha.

Charity went into the bar's kitchen and turned up the gas flame under the vat of water, already close to boiling, and set to work preparing the avocado soup.

There had been few takers for the full breakfast that day. On most mornings she could go through as many as ten tins of condensed milk as orders came in for sweet tea and a dough ball.

But times were getting harder. Fewer and fewer people could afford a decent breakfast, not even *ugali* and relish, the cheapest way to fill a hungry stomach. For some, times were so hard that they were lucky if they could afford one meal a day, not even a slice of corn-bread and a cup of tea. These were the customers that Charity feared for. And every now and then, she would pop into the kitchen and emerge with an oily brown paper packet in which she had wrapped a couple of fried chicken necks, left over from the night before, or a maize meal bun, hot from the oven. She stuffed the food into the coat-pockets of the young, or the sick, or the elderly, and those with child, and do it so efficiently and swiftly that few of her customers noticed, while the recipients of her decency were never embarrassed.

Most days Charity was on hand, behaving like a cross between a maître d' and a grandmother, patting backs here, shooing there, admiring one man's outfit and frowning at another's, backslapping encouragement to all. Stick together. Life out there in the city was tough, really tough. If you fell by the way, there was no-one to pick you up – unless a fellow resident of Kireba took pity on you.

With the help of the duty Mboya Boys, preparations of food for that day's lunch had gone well. There was time for Charity to consider a kernel of unease, gnawing away somewhere in the pit of her stomach, as if she had eaten one of her dough balls too quickly, and it had not been properly digested.

She could no longer avoid a confrontation with her dear English. For nearly a month Edward Furniver had been behaving oddly. He would find a reason to disappear for a few minutes, always taking his briefcase. A few minutes later he would reappear, looking a bit dishevelled, distinctly pink, and with a faint smell she could not quite place.

Unlike many of her friends, Charity had no time for astrology; but she seldom missed the agony aunt column in Kuwisha's leading daily newspaper. The subject raised that very day was so pertinent, and the advice so blunt, that she cut it out.

Aunt Mary, of 'Ask Aunt Mary' fame, had posed three questions:

Does your man regularly slip away for few minutes without explanation?

Does he return very talkative?

Can you smell drink on him?

If the answers are yes, said Aunt Mary, run for your life! He is a secret drinker, and one day, sooner or later, he will surely beat you.

Charity had started to notice that when Furniver did this disappearing act, he nearly always had his briefcase with him. The prospect of going through his briefcase made her feel deeply uncomfortable. Never in a thousand years would she have intruded on his privacy for any other reason. That would have been dishonourable.

But this matter, it involved his health, and ultimately her health. She had seen the consequences of too many drunken marital conflicts to doubt that.

She had tried checking with Didymus Kigali, but had made no progress on that front. Kigali's loyalties were to Furniver. That was fair enough. Standards may have fallen with the new generation of stewards, but Kigali treated any information he might gain from working for Furniver like a priest respects the confessional.

Yes, Boniface Rugiru, the bar steward at the Thumaiga Club, was probably her best source, and he had reported that Furniver had gone into the Gents the other night, and emerged smelling "like aftershave".

Indeed that very morning Furniver had turned up as usual for a cup of coffee and true to form, after a few minutes he went away; and once again, when he returned he was looking a little bit crumpled . . . Charity could not quite put her finger on the subtle change in his appearance.

It was time to investigate.

His briefcase lay temptingly close, on a nearby table, and was not locked.

"Furniver," she had said, in between cleaning her teeth with the chewed end of a *mopani* stick that served as a toothbrush, "I cannot get the gas cooker working properly. Is it leaking?"

"I'll take a dekko," he replied, and ambled to the kitchen, and out of sight.

Feeling ashamed of herself, Charity had looked inside the case. Her stomach churned as she encountered a bottle, the size of half a litre of gin, filled with a colourless liquid.

Hearing him returning, she replaced it. But not before a sniff had confirmed her worst fears. She would demand an explanation later. It was a prospect she dreaded . . .

27

Like schoolboys returning from summer holidays, delegates from the international aid community were gathering in Kuwisha for the World Bank conference, many having arrived on the same flight as Japer. They greeted each other with easy familiarity as they lined up at the conference registration desk in the lobby of the Outspan Hotel.

A cynic would have seen the venue as appropriate to the event, likened by a local newspaper columnist to a meeting of neo-colonialists in a hotel as old as colonial rule itself, built around an oasis of green lawns and flowerbeds, an implicit challenge to an independent Kuwisha.

Ghosts of long-departed settlers patrolled the wooden-floored corridors, decked out with the same Christmas decorations, brought out by the same staff, year after year. Yellowing framed photographs of the colony's first farmers lined the walls. They sat in stiff poses, a Remington rifle by their side, dogs lolling at their feet, and servants on hand, in front of thatched homesteads named after the British counties from which they and their families had come.

A dapper, well-spoken government delegate, wearing a plastic accreditation card marked "Official" was holding court in the hotel's lounge.

"First, your people came with the Bible. When they arrived, we had land. We started reading the Bible. A very, very good book indeed. But when our forefathers looked up from reading, the settlers had occupied their land."

His audience of half a dozen or so delegates listened respectfully.

"Then we fought for our independence. But you people had not forgotten your magic. You gave us independence. And when we looked up from our celebrations, we found that we had debt to your banks. Forty years after independence you give us what you call debt relief. Too late! You call it commerce, I call it exploitation."

The speaker smiled.

"In fact, it is what the Good Book calls usury. You people from the World Bank and from Europe, you see yourselves as our benefactors. But we see you" – he prodded a delegate from Sweden who was nodding approvingly – "as members of the new generation of colonisers."

With that salvo, Newman Kibwana, lawyer and former opposition leader turned senior civil servant, bellowed with laughter, slapped his thighs, and got up. "See you at the conference."

Before he could leave, however, the UKAID minister had a question for him.

"How are things at Lokio?"

The aid base in northern Kuwisha was Africa's biggest such centre.

"Fine! Keeps me busy, too busy to make trouble," grinned Kibwana, before striding away with a retinue of officials, supplicants and kinsmen, escorting him to the hotel entrance like tugs around an ocean liner.

The UKAID minister could not contain his enthusiasm.

"Impressive. Bloody impressive."

His colleagues rumbled their assent.

"Do you know," he asked the group, "that Kibwana flies to Lokio every weekend? Back and forth to that godforsaken place. Week in, week out, he monitors the UK aid shipments. No picnic, I assure you . . . Looks certain he's going to get a cabinet job. And we will really miss him."

Just then their order arrived, and Noraid, who was about to ask a question about stakeholders and ownership, was distracted.

"Bloody starving," he said apologetically, tucking into a toasted cheese sandwich.

UKAID continued: "We'll really miss him. Pay his air fare to Lokio, plus a per diem. And by golly, we insist on receipts – and to be absolutely frank, he comes up with them at the end of every month, like clockwork. Everything from petrol for his Land Rover to the weekly flight."

Most of the listeners agreed. Newman Kibwana set a good example. And sharp though his comments were about the role of the donors, he had a good case. Even the Germans and the Japanese were prepared to concede that there was much in what he said.

While their visits to Kuwisha would last a mere three days – less in the case of those who had to get to Maputo for the opening of the UN preliminary conference on climate change – the decisions they took had an impact on the lives of the people of Kuwisha that would be as far reaching as those taken by their colonial predecessors.

In the meantime there was much to be done.

Wearing expressions of harassed concern, the delegates lined up for their identity badges, signed for their per diems, enrolled in workshops and seminars and breakaway sessions, and slung over their shoulders the conference bags packed with learned papers, engraved pens, key-rings, and a T-shirt which declared: "Kuwisha, Home of Hope".

"Any spare T-shirts?" asked the representative from DANIDA.

"No," firmly replied the young lady from Kuwisha who was responsible for their distribution.

DANIDA gave her a sceptical look. He was about to say something to her when an angry exchange at the hotel reception caught his attention.

A delegate from UKAID was complaining that the hotel's email system had collapsed, and that the business centre was to close at eight o'clock that evening, despite assurances that it would be staying open until ten o'clock.

"Typical, bloody typical," he was saying.

"I don't believe it! It can't be . . ." exclaimed DANIDA.

Adrian Mullivant looked up.

"Yes, yes . . ." said DANIDA. It all came back to him now. "It was at Naivasha, that conference, what was it called? . . . 'Managing good governance in post-authoritarian transition'."

Mullivant's irritation about the emails lifted from his features as he matched memory with the enthusiastic face in front of him.

"Good Lord! Surely not! Noraid?" He looked surreptitiously at the identity card which hung around his greeter's neck. "DANIDA, yes of course, DANIDA . . . was it at Lake Naiva? Or Nairobi? Yes, Nairobi . . . 'Conflicting paradigms in multi-ethnic communities'."

The two men embraced, foot soldiers in an endless battle against poverty.

"You're right, absolutely right," said DANIDA. "It was Nairobi. But wasn't it 'Transparency and good governance – the challenges for Africa'?"

"Didn't you chair the breakaway group?"

"The workshop, actually. Called 'Monitoring resources . . .'"

". . . without conditionalities'." UKAID completed the sentence, adding: "Bloody marvellous it was, too. Great presentation."

"Someone had to say it," said DANIDA modestly.

"Gather you got a bit of stick when you got home?"

DANIDA nodded.

"The usual suspects. The NGOs . . . Gave me a hard time. Local rep. of CCA said I was patronising . . ."

His voice trailed off. Christians Concerned for Africa was one of the heavyweights in the aid business and any government agency that took them on had to be sure of their ground.

"Claimed that I had failed to adapt to a stakeholder agenda. Sods! What about ownership, I asked . . . they just ignored that."

Mullivant sucked in air through his teeth, and wished he had not raised the subject.

"The old stakeholder line, eh? Must have hurt."

DANIDA nodded again. "We do so much for them. Pour funds down their throat. Without our support, where would they be? Half their programme is paid by us. And do we get any thanks?"

Mullivant slapped his colleague on the back. "Won't seem so bad after a gin and tonic, old boy," and he marched DANIDA off to the bar where they were joined by two delegates from Scanaid, who were ending a grim account of their money-changing experience at the airport.

". . . so instead of selling *ngwee* at whatever it is to the pound, he was selling at the euro rate, and pocketing the difference."

The others murmured commiserations.

"Place is full of scams," said Mullivant. "Getting as bad as Lagos. Take what happened to me this morning."

Colleagues around the table looked expectantly at Mullivant.

"I was sitting in the back of this taxi, just this morning, on my way here, from Kireba."

The very word Kireba was enough to move the listeners. To have actually gone there . . . there was a satisfying murmur of respect for a man who had braved the horrors of the notorious slum.

"I was reading a rather good paper on the role of women in semi-arid areas. We were stuck in a traffic jam, crawling along, when there was a thump, and the face of a young lad was pressed against the right-hand window.

"Seems that a retarded boy had deliberately fallen under the wheel, a common ploy, it appeared, and his companion had threatened to call the police. You know what that means?"

His audience had not a clue, but nodded nevertheless.

"Under Kuwisha law, anyone who witnesses a vehicle accident is obliged to go to the police station and report it. My taxi driver was terrified. Kept saying how terrible the police were. One of us had to go. Meanwhile my briefcase had disappeared, presumably lifted when my head was turned. Then the driver said he had to go to the cops, and I got pretty concerned. He warned me, pathetic really. Said he had no choice. Had to go, because the boys had his taxi registration number. 'Please, suh, don't come with me. You are a friend of Kuwisha who helps us with aid. But these police, they are always chopping . . . They will want you to give them presents. Let me go' . . . So off he went, poor sod; he'll be lucky if the police don't hold him. Anyway, I gave him $100 for his trouble . . . the police may leave him with half that. D'you think I paid too much? Would hate to be taken for a ride."

"Cheap at the price," said DANIDA.

"Lucky escape – would have done the same thing," said Scanaid. "Bastards."

They broke up, but not before a brief and inconclusive exchange about the difference between the per diems provided by the World Bank, the UN and their respective employers.

Mullivant looked at his watch.

"I'm off. Want to get a seat for the opening. Gather Hardwicke is in good form. Apparently his speech will shake up things in our business. Not before time . . ."

The hot water system at the Hotel Milimani was not working.

The room steward summoned by Pearson shrugged his shoulders.

"It is World Bank, suh."

Much of Kuwisha, it seemed, was "World Bank", thought Pearson.

So why should the hot water system at the Milimani work when the state-owned electricity company operated well below capacity, and the railways did not run on time, and the primary schools overflowed with pupils? They were all "World Bank", the term that in Kuwisha had become synonymous with non-performance or inefficiency.

He had a shave, did not spend long under the cold shower, welcome though it was to wash away the traces of prison, and decided he would walk to the office.

The journey from the hotel to the *Financial News* office at Cambridge House took little more than fifteen minutes, and was safe enough during the day. Nevertheless, Pearson took off his watch, and put it in his briefcase, along with his wallet, and set off.

It was a journey he enjoyed.

Halfway down the hill, he bought a cob of sweet young maize, roasted over a charcoal brazier, and read the papers while having his shoes polished; and he fended off the good-natured efforts of the curio vendor to get him to buy one of the animal carvings on display.

As he made his way along the boulevard into the city centre he felt that something had changed in the way he saw Africa. He had been held by the police for a short time, yet somehow the experience had both brought him closer to the country, and created a sense of detachment.

No, "detachment" was not the right word. Perspective? That was it. He had acquired a sense of perspective. He was still thinking about this when he rounded the corner of Kaunda Street and went through the lobby of Cambridge House, the press centre for foreign hacks.

Pearson had to remind himself that he had been away from his office – his former office – barely three days, yet Africa already seemed to be reclaiming its urban territory.

The lobby was being retiled; a restaurant had just opened up on the floor above his office; and the drab grey building was getting its first coat of paint for years.

The lift took him up to the third floor. Although the Gents toilet on the press-centre corridor was a good thirty yards away, the sweet-sour whiff from the combination of Jeyes Fluid and male urine climbed up his nostrils like a homing pigeon into its roost.

For the first time, he took a close interest in the notice-board on the right as he went in. It had been something he had taken for granted before his arrest, seeing it as no more than a source of second-hand Land Rovers and other four-wheel drive vehicles, of radios and CD players, flat screen televisions, iPods and DVD players, all for sale by departing expatriates.

Now Pearson read the ads differently, looked at them in a new light, paying more attention to accompanying notes, handwritten and typed, that were sprinkled between photos of TVs for sale, or houses for rent.

The notes seemed like *haikus* on themes of loyalty and service. There was Anna, "a first rate nanny, loves children, references from BBC and VoA"; and Shilling, "a brilliant cook, loves catering, great references"; and "Blessing, hard working maid"; and Loveday, "excellent driver and first class mechanic"; not to mention a dozen "superb" gardeners and "reliable" *askaris*.

For all of these citizens of Kuwisha, the departure of their employers was a cataclysmic event. Not even the promise – which often would be kept, at least for the first year and sometimes even longer – of help with school fees, or a parcel of old clothes, or settlement of medical bills, would ease their anxiety.

But for the owners of the goods on sale, however, their departure was a financial bonanza, thanks to the sale of their stereos or their four-wheel drives, or TVs, at the market rate.

As workers for foreign non-government organisations they were allowed to import their possessions, free of tax. And when the goods were sold, when the owners left Kuwisha, they were entitled to remit the proceeds, through the account of the aid organisation that employed them, at the official rate of exchange.

It was a financial bonus, and in the views of the recipients, well deserved recognition of their commitment and dedication to the welfare of the people of Kuwisha.

Pearson continued on his way down the passage to his office. Apart from the hardworking and conscientious correspondent for the Japanese news agency, no-one else was in.

Some things didn't change.

28

Podmore continued with his efforts to light a cigarette, hoping against hope that someone would come into his office in the drab barrack-like building that was the British High Commission.

It took four matches. The first spluttered and then died before a flame could appear. The second broke off at the head. The third lit immediately, but the top of the match spun across his desk onto the office carpet, already pockmarked with tiny brown indentations.

The fourth attempt was successful, though someone initiated in the behaviour of Kuwisha's matches might have been fooled into flicking it away as another dud. An old hand like Podmore wasn't deceived. The half second of apparent inactivity was accompanied by a barely audible fizzing and the match head burst into life.

But it had been a damn close-run thing.

Podmore reached into the desk drawer, and pulled out a well-used blue notebook marked "Political risk".

The correlation between an African country's political and economic health, and the quality of its matches, had not struck him until he had attended a meeting of regional aid secretaries in Johannesburg. During his stay he noticed that the locally manufactured match lit first time, nine times out of ten. Comparing notes with colleagues from across the region, Podmore realised that he had stumbled across one of Africa's laws: the worse shape a country was in, the more matches were needed to light a cigarette.

Only South Africa met the one matchstick test. If two matchsticks were needed, there were grounds for concern; three indicated that decline was under way; while if it took four attempts, matters were perilous. Five matchsticks and you were living in a failing state; six matchsticks, and the state of collapse was so advanced that locally made matches were unavailable and all matches were imported.

Ever since that epiphanic insight, Podmore had kept a record of the outcome of attempts by him and by other smokers to light their cigarettes using local matches, which he meticulously inscribed in the notebook.

He checked his entries. For the third successive month, Kuwisha had been a four-matchstick country. "So much for those who think this country is turning the corner," he muttered.

Podmore's spirits rose. He would present his findings at the next session of the European Union delegation's economic appraisal unit.

He returned the notebook to the drawer.

It was not, he told himself, that he disliked Pearson. Or at least, he claimed to dislike him no more than he disliked any hack. But when pressed hard by colleagues he would confess a particular animus against the *FN*'s Africa correspondent. "He is a bloody know-all, and cynical to boot, one of those buggers who turn native – and don't realise that the natives cannot stand them."

And there was a personal element in Podmore's relations with Pearson. The "little shit", as he now called him, had jotted down Podmore's rules of Africa, ten in all, which had been pinned to the notice-board in his office. And then – "Can you believe it?" Podmore had asked his wife, "He turned them into a piece for the *Weekend FN*. The little shit!"

He took a long pull of his cigarette, and lifted the UK press summary for the last twenty-four hours from his in-tray. The *Clarion*'s story had been highlighted by his secretary, with the word "Visa" scribbled opposite the paper's announcement that it would sponsor a street boy from Kireba. He was about to ring the consular section when the new First Secretary (Political) put his head round the door.

"High Commissioner is asking you to look in – she wants to be brought up to speed on the *Clarion* story . . ."

His nostrils flared as he sniffed the air.

Here it comes, thought Podmore, here it comes.

"Thought there was a no-smoking policy . . ."

Gotcha! Podmore looked at his colleague with barely concealed smugness. He pulled the notebook out of the drawer and waved it triumphantly in the air.

"Research, old boy, research."

The door closed.

"Tosser," said Podmore.

The day was looking up.

"Off to Harrods," he called out to his secretary. "If Pearson rings, tell him I'm tied up, meetings, all day. And give Lazarus Mpofu in foreign affairs a call – remind him I need a travel document for a 14-year-old Kuwishan . . . chop chop."

29

World Bank president Hardwick Hardwicke was a great believer in making promises, even though experience had shown him there were usually more good reasons to break them than to keep them. But on his last visit to Kuwisha, he had made a promise to himself that he was determined to keep.

Never again would he allow himself to be in a position where he could be managed and manipulated by President Nduka. Were it not for his own shrewd understanding of what made the country tick, of its strengths and weaknesses, its promise and potential, his first visit could have been an embarrassing failure.

In his original schedule, the leader of the world's most important development agency had been due to call in at Kuwisha for a second visit, en route to Washington after a three-day visit to Ethiopia. And when the invitation had come to make the opening address at the annual meeting of aid donors, it had been accepted with enthusiasm.

It was his spin doctor, Jim "Fingers" Adams, who had come up with a suggestion that was simple and effective.

"You're not getting any younger," Fingers had said. "Everyone knows you have a dicky ticker. So let's put out the story that you had a nasty spell in Addis, and the quack told you to go straight home, rather than return via Kuwisha.

"The rest is easy. We'll put you in a wheel chair, to convince any doubters. I'll do a decent speech; you can deliver it live on a video link, and Bob's your uncle."

★

Pearson, who had arrived just in time for the official opening, sat along with local reporters, most of whom were taking the chance to have a square meal at somebody else's expense.

He looked around for other foreign journalists but there were none to be seen. Pearson felt disappointed. He had decided that the best line to take on his troubles should be dominated by a magnanimous and modest response, in which he appeared to dislike publicity.

He had gone so far as to scribble a few lines in his notebook. Just in case . . . Meanwhile he looked forward to writing a story which would certainly appeal to the *Financial News*.

Lights in the conference hall dimmed, and a single beam focused on a huge screen which dominated the stage. From his Washington office, President Hardwick Hardwicke was about to address the delegates. The video link established, the camera homed in on the wheel chair, opening up to show Hardwicke, clenching his teeth to accentuate his jaw line, as Fingers had suggested.

Delegates gave a low murmur of sympathy, which was the cue for Hardwicke to start.

He began by saying how sorry he was not to be there in the flesh; and how much he missed the opportunity to learn from President Nduka, the Ngwazi, whose experience of the highest office never broke his contact with the people.

Pearson smirked. The coded reference to corruption would be missed by most. But by World Bank standards, Hardwicke was being pretty outspoken.

Pearson particularly liked the "never broke his contract with the people" – a Fingers line if ever there was one. He translated it silently: "The president has his finger in every commercial pie there, and never misses a chance to milk the country."

Then, as Hardwicke got into his address, Pearson began taking notes: "Being in this contraption," Hardwicke was saying, "gives a bloke time to think. But I did not need much time to realise that when my mates see me sitting in it, they feel sorry for me. I tell them why I am in this wheel chair, and were it not for this dicky heart I'd be with you in Kuwisha."

He paused, giving the assembled delegates time to applaud.

"The problem about the chair . . . it seems to attract more comment than my heart. As I say, when my mates at home saw me sitting in the chair, they could not take their eyes off it. Yeah, they said all the right things – sorry as hell, and so on – but they kept looking at this bloody wheel chair. Distracted by it. Got me thinking. About words, and aid and wheel chairs. And then I realised the mistake. Why call this a wheel chair?"

He took a sip from the glass of water Fingers had provided. "I ask you. Seriously. Why call it a wheel chair? Very demoralising word is wheel chair, got a defeatist ring to it, if you ask me."

Delegates shuffled their feet. What was he on about? A rumour that Hardwicke had suffered a stroke which was far more serious than he had let on, and which had left him more damaged than he cared to admit, began to seem all too credible.

"All this talk of wheel chairs," he continued, "it did my morale no good. So I sat thinking. Why call it a wheel chair? And I answered my own question. I do not sit in a wheel chair. No sir! I do not sit in a wheel chair. No sir!"

He spun the chair round in a pirouette which he had been practising for the best part of the morning, and faced the audience again, 16,000 miles away from the bank's headquarters in Washington.

With voice lowered to a near whisper, he said again: "I – do – not – sit – in – a – wheel chair."

Delegates looked at their feet. Had the poor man completely lost it?

Hardwicke paused, and then, with a voice so loud it made several delegates jump, he declared: "That is defeatist talk. The fact is, I enjoy enhanced mobility in a seated position! Enhanced mobility in a seated position."

Delegates stood as one to applaud the man and his indomitable spirit.

Hardwicke raised and lowered his hands unconsciously mimicking the gesture President Nduka used to restore order at party rallies, when gratitude for his leadership threatened to get out of hand.

The applause subsided.

"The point I want to make," said Hardwicke, "is that words shape our reality. And some words distort it."

In a few succinct sentences Hardwicke went to the core of the issue that, he argued, had limited the effectiveness of the World Bank in Africa.

Aid itself – or rather, the use of the word 'aid', he had come to realise, was at the heart of the problem.

"Language shapes reality, and reality shapes our language," Hardwicke told the conference. "Poverty in Africa," he went on, "does not give us the right to impose Western solutions. Poverty is a problem that can be solved. We should consider the implications of the language we use. 'Poverty alleviation' and 'the poor' are terms that are loaded with meaning and heavy with historical baggage."

Representatives from the twenty United Nations agencies based in East Africa listened intently, together with the leaders of the heavyweight private agencies – WorldFeed, Oxfam, Christians Concerned for Africa, Save the Children, and AidConcern. Even the all-powerful state-funded donors – UKAID, Noraid, and USAID – had sent some of their most senior executives, having been warned that Hardwicke was going to deliver what Fingers called "a corker".

"Let me give you an example of what I mean." He wiped his brow, and continued. "Words can cripple as well as liberate.

Words and phrases like 'structural adjustment'; 'enhanced con-
cessionary lending facilities'; 'low interest loans'; 'conditionality';
and the word '*aid*' itself."

His voice took on a tone of evangelistic fervour.

"Aid – a simple word, made up of three letters. Sometimes I
think 'A' stands for Africa; 'I' is for Indigent, and 'D' for
Dependent."

A ripple of amusement ran through the audience, and there
was a brief outbreak of clapping from where the Scandinavians
were sitting.

"'*Aid*' – a word that above all other has distorted our thinking;
'*aid*', the word that has distorted and contorted our relation-
ships."

For years, he reminded his rapt and attentive audience, non-
governmental organisations, civil society, lobbyists, pressure
groups, pop stars and economists, all had called for faster, more
radical, quick-delivered support to countries in Africa that had
failed to realise their potential.

"There are many explanations as to why aid has not transformed Africa, recipient of billions of dollars. But we have
overlooked the most obvious explanation, my friends.

"There is a word that has become the development millstone of
our time. That word is 'aid'!

"To use the word 'aid' is patronising," said Hardwicke, "for it
divides the world into givers and receivers, into lenders and
borrowers.

"'Aid'" – he shook his head – "We at the bank must take our
share of the blame. We used that word, 'aid', without consulta-
tion with stakeholders.

"*Mea* bloody *culpa*, my friends, *mea culpa*."

This time the applause was prolonged, and the Scandinavians
were on their feet, hooting their approval.

"Ownership of the concept of 'aid'," he continued, "has been entirely in the hands of the Western agencies. Consequently," said Hardwicke, wiping his now perspiring brow, "the word inhibits the reappraisal that is long overdue.

"I urge you to reject this word if you believe, as I do, that it cripples the efforts to redress the biggest development deficit of our time," he declared.

"And I urge you to make a mark at this conference and find an alternative word or phrase to replace that ugly word 'aid'.

"So, friends and colleagues, let me set the linguistic ball rolling. How about this? Instead of using the word 'aid' let us vow to find a new value free word like 'instep' – 'international support to encourage potential'.

" 'International' represents the world community; 'support' is a word that is constructive, without any patronising associations; 'encourage' does not imply any agenda which has been foisted on the recipient; and 'potential' is a word which indicates that there are no limitations as to what can be achieved."

Hardwicke was on a roll.

"Momentum," he said, "must be sustained; poverty must be reduced; the region moved forward; the path must be one of sustainable development; argument must be persuasive; more must be done."

His peroration this time brought the whole audience to its feet.

"Additional resources . . ." said Hardwicke.

"Must be freed up," came the response, uncertain at first, then gathering in intensity.

"Challenges . . ."

". . . must be overcome," his audience replied.

"Developments . . ."

". . . are highly encouraging."

Louder and louder came the exchange, and Hardwicke fell into a liturgical cadence.

"Strong economic performance . . ."

". . . must be sustained," the audience roared back.

"Regional policy makers' resolve . . ."

". . . must be strong."

"And the tough challenges of development . . ."

". . . must be tackled."

"And so, my friends, let us apply ourselves afresh, 'instep' with each other and above all, 'instep' with Africa."

During the debate that followed, the Germans tried to change "international support" to "interest free", backed by Japan, on the grounds that it left open the possibility of interest rates; the Scandinavians were uneasy about "encourage potential", which was prescriptive, they argued, while "enable potential" allowed for choice, so important if the concept of policy ownership was to have any meaning.

Such was the enthusiastic response, and so intense was the discussion that delegates overran the scheduled time for the coffee break by a good fifteen minutes.

One intervention, however, threatened to turn this excellent start into disaster. A nattily dressed delegate, a member of the Kuwisha official delegation, stood up.

"I object," said Newman Kibwana. "The word 'encourage' smacks of the worst of colonial rule. It is the language of the *sjambok*!"

And he reminded delegates of a notorious case from Kuwisha's colonial past, when a white settler accused of flogging his "house boy" behind the *kia*, or servants' quarters, had been acquitted.

"He said the *sjambok* was only there to 'encourage' his boy to talk."

When the murmur of shock had died down, Kibwana continued in much the same vein, condemning corruption, but at the same time making a vigorous attack on the IMF and the World Bank – "our economic masters whom we cannot vote out of office; whose own development failures are buried in an elephants' graveyard; and who send us their child-graduates to become men at Africa's expense."

Thanks to the intervention of the World Bank resident representative, Kibwana withdrew his objection. But he had made his point.

"Damned impressive," said Norway's aid minister.

It was the turn of his counterpart at UKAID to speak. He did not pull any punches in a speech which Mullivant had helped draft.

"Britain leads the way in support of 'instep'. We have a long-term commitment to Kuwisha and its people. And the support we provide has only one condition – it must be used effectively and efficiently.

"We will not abandon the poorest in your community. Together, Kuwisha and Britain will stay 'instep' as we pledge international support to encourage potential."

Seldom had there been a clearer example of Britain's long-term commitment to Kuwisha and the applause he received could not have been warmer.

The conference press statement summed up the outcome: "'Change the language of support: ownership by stakeholders vital,' says bank chief."

30

It was only fitting that, immediately after the coffee break, Newman Kibwana would have the honour of introducing Geoffrey to the conference.

Newman was at his best on occasions like this.

In the opinion of many of those present, including Western diplomats, he personified the future of Kuwisha. Plucked from the private sector, along with seven more of the country's brightest and best, he was part of the "dream team" of technocrats appointed by President Nduka to steer the country through the minefield of economic reform urged on Kuwisha by the International Monetary Fund and the World Bank.

Articulate, well-educated, the 30-something lawyer turned senior civil servant was one of the leading members of the post-independence "born free" generation.

The parents of Kibwana and his contemporaries had first ensured their own material welfare through an economic system that functioned in the interests of the Kibwana family, their sons and daughters, and their peers.

If you failed, or fell out of favour, whether in business or as a top party official or civil servant, there was always a place for you as the chief executive officer of the government steel plant that was fundamental to genuine economic independence, or one of the other state-owned outfits, with company car, and company house, and a non-contributory pension scheme, and medical insurance for you and your family – not to mention unlimited travel to international conferences that discussed the future of whatever it was your company was involved in, with generous per diems.

Forty years after independence, this safety net for the elite of Kuwisha still worked, and when the cabinet was reshuffled, or top military brass were purged, there would be a job or – to be exact – a title to be found that would cushion bruised egos and sustain lifestyles, whether as chairman or board member of a state-owned company.

Those who suggested that Kuwisha did not have the iron ore to sustain a steel plant, or the supply of electrical power needed to run it, were no better than defeatists, who lacked vision and ambition.

Who better to overhaul this system and to bring Kuwisha into the modern age than the iconoclastic figure of Newman Kap-wepwe Kibwana?

And none better to set out the details of the debt-for-rhino proposal, whose approval seemed all but certain. All the delegates had received a summary of the plan, initially derided when raised in a World Bank study, but now gaining credibility after a favourable appraisal by Martin Fox, leading columnist in the *Financial News*.

"Before I introduce our distinguished guest," said Newman, I want to draw your attention to a document that was distributed earlier. You will see that it is marked Strictly Confidential, Limited Circulation . . ."

He paused, and added with great timing and a straight face, ". . . in the hope that this might encourage the press to take an interest in the subject it covers."

He winked at Pearson, who had looked up from his notebook.

After the laughter had died down, Kibwana went on to explain how the scheme would work: "The country's total external debt will be divided by the total number of rhinos still existing in our game reserves – say 100 rhinos. If, as in the case of Kuwisha, the country's total debt was $6bn, each rhino is worth $60,000,000.

Should the stock of rhinos fall below 100, the government pays what would be called a 'rhino' – i.e. $60,000,000 – into an escrow account. But if the stock rises above 100, the donors contribute a 'rhino' by reducing the external debt by $120,000,000. Payment by the government would be guaranteed, for it would have to put 10 per cent of tourism earnings into the same escrow account. The government can draw on the money – provided the rhino stock has been maintained at the agreed level, and provided that any money drawn will be spent subject to the donors' agreement about the specific use to which it will be put, although it would be spent in the interest of conservation.

"In short," concluded Kibwana, "the more rhinos, the better off is Kuwisha, and of course the more rhinos, the more tourists; and the more tourists, the more foreign exchange is earned.

"And the more forex, the better off Kuwisha's economy, which in turn would improve the country's capacity to deal with street children, by providing jobs."

"Very impressive," said Noraid. "Very impressive indeed."

Led by Kibwana, all Japer had to do was to raise his hands aloft, one grasping the document, one grasping Newman's hand: "Please welcome one of NoseAid's most passionate international ambassadors, friend of our children, defender of our rhinos . . . the well-known British newsreader, Mr Geoffrey Jaaaaper!"

Newman led the applause that followed.

"Save the fooking rhino," cried Japer, imitating an Irish accent, "wipe out the fooking debt! Just be sure we get it the right way round!"

"Very impressive," said Mullivant as he joined fellow delegates in a queue for Japer's autograph. "Very impressive indeed."

31

It had taken Podmore several attempts and the best part of a long day, by the time he got through to Lazarus Mpofu who had not returned the High Commission calls.

"Impossible. Not enough time, and there is a backlog of special cases," said Mpofu.

Podmore was in no mood to be told that he would have to be patient.

"Come on, Lazarus. We will choose a 14-year-old street boy, offered a once-in-a-lifetime opportunity, and I will accompany whoever is chosen to London. This is an exceptional case – as deserving of help as the father who wants to attend his son's degree ceremony."

Since the dad in question happened to be Lazarus's local MP, it was a telling point.

"As I was saying," Mpofu continued after a pause, "a passport is not possible. But we can issue a travel document to minors – 15 years and younger. It needs the same information, and the usual passport photos of course, valid only for a specified journey, must be surrendered on return, is valid for four weeks, and the bearer must be accompanied by a responsible adult."

So far so good, thought Podmore, and waited for the catch.

"Who must be approved by the minister, or a designated official."

Mpofu had indicated that he would be the designated official, and would repay the favour that Podmore would do in dealing promptly with the MP's application.

"Done," said Podmore. "I'm sure the visa will come through tomorrow; end of the week at the latest."

Lazarus chuckled.

"The forms are on their way to you. Return them, and the travel document will be with you twenty-four hours later."

A more sensitive man would have realised that his welcome at Harrods was less than wholehearted even under the best of circumstances. On this occasion he interrupted what, over the past couple of years, had become something of a ritual: the gathering of a group of regulars at the bar, over coffee or tea or, on an especially hot day, one of the fruit drinks.

Charity would preside, and Mildred would be there to lend a helping hand; Philimon Ogata had started to attend regularly as had Clarence Mudenge; Furniver, of course, turned out, and so did Lucy and Pearson; while Ntoto and Rutere would make themselves useful, and listen to the exchanges across the table, in slack-jawed concentration as they battled the impact of *changa* or glue. And there would often be various other aid workers, the odd diplomat and the usual run of disaster tourists and celebrities.

This time they had been joined by a middle-aged Brit, a shock of thick fair hair flopping to one side, with a bottom that said more about his mood than his eyes, or any other part of his anatomy for that matter. When he was depressed, the bottom seemed to all but disappear; when he was in a good mood, it was like a dog's tail, wagging from side to side.

"Hiya," said Podmore.

"Hiya," replied Lucy, while the others mumbled their greetings with mixed degrees of enthusiasm.

"Hello, Podsman," offered Furniver.

"Podmore," said Podmore.

He outlined the *Clarion*'s fund-raising plans, and the paper's intention to fly a street child from Kireba to London, for an appearance on the NoseAid evening.

"Wondered if one of your lot would be interested?" he asked. "I'll sort out the visa, and the lucky chap will have me as an escort. I'm going back for a spot of home leave anyway."

Charity shrugged.

"Ask the boys."

Podmore could not remember the names of the two street children who hung around Harrods.

"Do you want to visit Lon-don?" he asked, enunciating the words slowly and loudly. "Chance to visit Buck-ing-ham Palace for the lucky boy . . ."

Rutere, who had been running his finger around his left nostril, stopped in mid-circuit, and Ntoto, who until then had been examining his feet for jiggers, looked up.

"We are not boys," said Rutere.

"If you are not boys, then what are you?" said Podmore, speaking normally now.

"We are youths," said Rutere. "We are not your servants."

Podmore gave an exasperated sigh.

The cheeky little bugger deserved a clip over the ear-hole.

He looked in vain to Charity for assistance but she was preoccupied in the kitchen.

"How much money?" asked Rutere.

"It will be free," said Podmore.

Ntoto intervened.

"He is asking how much the man who goes to London will be paid."

"How much what? Money?"

Rutere exchanged glances with Ntoto.

What else did Podmore think they were referring to?

"How does money come into it?" said the diplomat, clearly shocked.

He turned to Charity, back from the kitchen with corn-bread. As he had expected, she disapproved of the *Clarion*'s plan.

174

"Foolish," she sniffed.

"But if one wants to go, he can go."

She went to attend to a customer, and Podmore turned to Furniver.

"Why on earth should the boy be paid? The lucky blighter is getting the trip of a lifetime, and you ask what he will be paid," he said, now looking at Rutere. "Don't know what things are coming to when street boys expect to be paid for going to Rondon."

It was said in a jocular tone, but the underlying irritation was clear.

"London," said Rutere. "It is London."

Nose-picking little creep, Podmore thought. He said to Furniver:

"The *Clarion* will cover a return ticket, meals and bed for five days. My problem is that we need to move pretty sharpish, Eddie. We need to apply for a travel document for the boy. Whoever is sent over, I will travel with them," promised Podmore, "as long as I don't have to sit next to them." He laughed.

The duo looked at Podmore through glazed eyes, their pupils dilated, and Rutere deliberately and slowly thrust his forefinger into his right nostril.

"Want pay," said Ntoto.

"Give me present," Rutere demanded. "Where is my present?"

"Bugger off, you two," said Furniver.

He apologised to Podmore. "Blighters act up, seem worse than they are. Go on, bugger off you two, haven't you got work to do?"

The boys reluctantly went into the kitchen, and climbed onto the container roof, where they usually prepared the vegetables.

From that secure vantage point they looked down at Podmore.

"Give us presents," said Rutere, finger again buried in his left nostril.

Charity emerged from the kitchen with a plate of dough balls, which she plonked down on the table, and looked up.

"Rutere . . ."

"I washed my hands, before touching the vegetables," he protested, holding them out as if for inspection.

"Don't be rude to visitor . . ."

It was time to intervene, thought Furniver. He shrugged and looked apologetic. "Boy has a point," he began, but this comment simply poured fuel on Podmore's fury.

"Greedy sods. Bloody typical."

Furniver let Podmore's wrath run its course.

"If you get the application form, Charity and I will pick one of the boys. Let me have it, asap."

Why did he bother, Podmore asked himself. One tries to help, and is it appreciated? Is it hell.

"Have a dough ball, Mr Podman," said Charity.

"Podmore," said Podmore. "Thanks, but must dash."

As he made his way back to his car, stepping carefully as he navigated piles of refuse, he was surrounded by a group of Mboya Boys who had appeared from nowhere.

"Give me *ngwee*. "

"Boss, give me *ngwee*."

"Fuck off!" he hissed, trying to ensure that his voice did not carry back to Harrods.

"You are shit," said a child, who could not have been more than 10 years old.

Podmore brushed away their entreaties.

Safe in the sanctuary of his Range Rover, he turned the ignition key and was about to drive off when he noticed the brown streaks that had appeared on the windscreen.

"Little bastards!"

The awful pong outlasted a cigarette, and Podmore lit a second and sat back in his seat.

"You do so much for these people, and how do they repay you? By shitting on your car!"

Conversation at Harrods resumed. When Mildred returned from her nap, there would be more discussion of the *tokolosh*. In the meantime, Lucy was on her mobile, negotiating the release of a consignment of cooking oil for delivery to the drought-stricken north-east.

"Our food aid reaches parts of Kuwisha where no-one used to live before independence," she boasted to whoever it was at the other end. Whatever she had been saying had achieved its purpose, and Lucy finished the call.

"Couldn't help hearing what you were saying," said Furniver diffidently. "Perhaps that is why . . ."

Lucy interrupted him. "Absolutely. Were it not for the work of WorldFeed, scores of thousands would have died of hunger."

Furniver considered pursuing the matter, but decided to move on.

"Did you see this, Lucy," he asked, nodding at the newspaper. "I know I'm starting to sound like the Oldest Member, but things like this really make you think . . . Did you know that Kuwisha is staging the First Session of the Conference of African Ministers of Culture, and that the outcome will be presented to the Special Session of the Assembly of Heads of State and Government?"

He read on: " 'I hope,' says the African Union Commission chairperson, 'the conference will take the interface between education and culture seriously and explore the possibility of maximizing the contribution of each to the other.' What are we expected to make of that?"

"Per diems," said Lucy, "it's all about per diems."

"All I know," said Furniver, "is that these conferences seem an awful waste of time."

Lucy sighed with exasperation. Sometimes she wondered whether Furniver lived in the real world – a world in which black market and official exchange rates, expenses, per diems and travel extras provided a significant source of income.

"Waste of time?" Lucy brushed a wisp of her blonde hair aside. "It's a waste of money, more like. All these delegates will be saving their per diems and fiddling their ex's. They're as bad as the hacks," she said contemptuously. "I remember when Pearson and I were in Zaire a couple of years ago. There was nearly a fight between the *Times* and the *Mail* at that rather good restaurant in Kinshasa . . . the one that serves salads made from five varieties of lettuce, all flown in from abroad." A wistful look came into her eyes. "They were pissed as I recall. Both wanted a seat on the WorldFeed charter to Kigali."

She snorted. "Neither of them gave a monkey's about the story. Both rewrote the wires as usual. The truth is they were fighting over the receipt for the ticket."

Furniver started to look interested.

"You know why, Ed?"

He could guess, but he shook his head.

"They sold their dollars on the black market. Let's say they got fifty krotniks to the dollar. Official rate was five krotniks. You work it out. You claim your ex's at the official rate, in the local currency – and you buy the krotniks with which you pay the ex's at the market rate. Beauty of the scam is that head office in London or New York can hardly complain, can they? Can't ask their staff to use the market, and then moan about corruption."

"So the more money you spend on expenses . . ." said Furniver, ". . . the more you make."

"Precisely," said Lucy, "precisely."

32

The reaction of Ntoto and Rutere to the news of Pearson's imminent arrival at Harrods was far from welcoming.

From their perch atop the bar, where they were preparing vegetables for the next meal, they began to chant: "Cheat, cheat, cheat . . ."

"Stop that nonsense," ordered Charity.

"He cheated in the game," said Ntoto, "you yourself saw it."

Charity nodded. It was perfectly true.

The boys undeniably had the moral high ground and they knew it. Pearson had indeed been late in giving the obligatory warning the last time they had played Ack-Ack, and she had witnessed his disgraceful behaviour.

"Cheat, cheat, cheat," continued the boys, who were not prepared to forget that Pearson had broken the most important rule in a game which they had devised. According to this rule, anyone who was seated at Harrods was open to aerial attack by any registered street boy; but the target was entitled to try and trip any approaching "aircraft", subject to two conditions.

The person or persons under attack had to simulate the sound of anti-aircraft fire; and they had to do so *before* extending their leg, crying out as they did so: "Ack-ack-ack!"

It was a rule about which the boys felt strongly, and understandably so. Successful raids could produce a satisfying cry of alarm as the target responded to a careening street boy. Failure, on the other hand, could prove painful, and a successful trip-up could lead to a skinned knee.

Pearson was due any minute now. Ntoto and Rutere kept an

eye on the comings and goings of customers, the one boy peeling carrots, the other scrubbing potatoes. Sitting on the roof of the steel containers, concealed by the sign of the bar, they could look out without being spotted themselves.

Beneath them and beyond them spread Kireba, tough, hard-working and ambitious, the size of a small city where all but the truly destitute and the utterly hopeless nursed dreams.

Some dreamt of becoming a lawyer or teacher or doctor; others worked for seven days a week, labouring for the extra *ngwee* needed if they were to extend a one-roomed shack.

But ambitions went far beyond these dreams. Some did indeed become a doctor; but if this proved out of reach, you tried to become a nurse; if you failed to become a nurse, you could become a health clinic assistant; and failing that, a messenger who worked at a clinic. And if that proved impossible, then a friend of a messenger. Who knows? Life was full of opportunities, and the people who lived in Kireba were nothing if not ambitious.

What is more, they took pride in being ordinary – ordinary in the sense that they lived in a community that had as many saints as sinners, or at least the same ratio of saints to sinners as any other town or city. Or, for that matter, the same ratio of Samaritans who would lend a hand to strangers to others who would walk on by; the same ratio of honest folk to rotten thieves; or of good citizens anxious about the school fees they could not afford to bad citizens who cared for nothing.

Kireba was as honest or as rotten, good or bad, and had heroes and villains, just as any city of similar size, with one difference: there were none of the comforts of modern life, there was no clean running water, there was no electricity.

Systematically the boys worked their way through their re-spective chores, Ntoto peeling carrots, and chopping cabbage. Rutere was equally absorbed in his task, and after the potatoes were scrubbed, he began picking greenfly out of cauliflower heads, driven by the deal he had struck with Charity: if she could not find a single greenfly in a sample of her selection, Rutere would qualify for three dough balls. Thereafter he would lose a dough ball for every three that she found, with the appalling prospect that he could end in deficit – actually owing Charity.

Ntoto chatted away, sharing with Rutere his thoughts, and occasionally inviting his friend's comments.

On that afternoon, when the sun beat down and their bellies were full of corn-bread and pumpkin soup, and they had managed to grab a spoonful of condensed milk, without Charity catching them, they played one of the word games they had devised to pass the time.

The game itself was simple – a question was asked in the form of a riddle, and if it got the answer that the questioner had in mind, you scored full points. But beyond that simple rule were qualifying rules and sub-rules, and extra rules, all of such fiendish complexity that the boys themselves would be unable to finish a game.

That day was an exception, however.

"If Kuwisha was an animal," said Ntoto, "what would it be, Rutere?"

It was a tough question but there was plenty of time to answer it.

The answer had to begin with the letter of the current month.

"A dog," said Rutere, "tied with a piece of string and always hungry, and always barking and only stopping when kicked."

"Phauw," said Ntoto – it was a good answer, though not the answer he had in mind.

Rutere gave a little whoop of self-congratulation, nothing to do with Ntoto's question, but the discovery of a nit on his head, which he deftly decapitated between thumbnail and forefinger.

"Wash your hands," said Ntoto.

Rutere made a great show of doing just that in a pail of water Charity had provided for the purpose.

The boys continued their work, lost in their thoughts.

"Or a donkey," said Rutere. "If Kuwisha were an animal, rather than a country, it would be a donkey. Better than dog," he continued, and looked up to see if, by the rules of the game, he had got it right.

"Explain," said Ntoto.

"The donkey works very hard, is not treated well, but has a big heart. The politicians are the man that beats his donkey, to get the donkey to work harder, but feeds him badly. We are like donkeys, working harder but not doing well."

Ntoto clapped his hands. There was no doubt about it, Rutere was clever. He dealt with the last carrot, and turned to help Rutere, as friendship required.

"Shssh," hissed Rutere suddenly, "someone is coming."

Pearson surveyed the 300 yards between the *matatu* stop, where he had been dropped, and Harrods. The direct route had more hazards, and he had to assume that he could clear the foul black stream in a single leap. On the other hand, while the alternative route was as much as twice the length, the lean-to toilet, which was within striking distance of Harrods, provided secure cover.

He opted for the long way round.

He knew that his plan was childish, and certainly no way for an adult to behave at Harrods. But what the hell – the sanctimonious little bastards deserved to be taken down a peg or two. Pearson was pretty sure that Ntoto had sold the tape recorder he had lent him, and made up that cock and bull story about being mugged.

He reached the toilet, fairly certain that he had not been detected. Pearson was close enough to hear snatches of exchanges between Charity and Furniver, and greetings as Lucy arrived, earlier than he had expected, and the chatter in Swahili between Ntoto and Rutere.

It was a perfect moment to launch his attack.

Pearson burst onto the group, wheeling and diving like one of the aeroplanes the street children became, arms outstretched and crying:

"No mercy, Ntoto, ACK-ACK-ACK . . . no mercy, Rutere, no . . ."

To say the response was disappointing was an understatement.

"Aren't you a bit old for that sort of wheeze?" said Furniver mildly.

"I thought . . . there you are . . . thought I heard Ntoto and Rutere . . ."

Pearson stuttered to an embarrassed end.

His targets sat atop the bar, legs dangling over the edge.

"We don't play ack-ack with cheats," said Ntoto.

Rutere sniggered, and started a further chorus of "Cheat! Cheat! Cheat!" pointing his finger at the journalist in time to the chant, just like the supporters of English football teams, which he watched on the black and white television in the bar.

"Bloody childish, Pearson," said Lucy dismissively, who had emerged from the bar with a tray of drinks.

Pearson tried to recover his dignity, but he did feel foolish.

"A crash landing, I assume?" said Furniver, and guffawed.

"Childish!" said Lucy.

"Give me present," demanded Rutere, sniggering.

It was not exactly a hero's welcome.

33

"Rum place, Kuwisha," thought Furniver, as he sipped an ice-cold Tusker. Here he was, sitting at a bar in the middle of Africa, reading news about Manchester United in the local papers, chatting with a young English journalist, arguing with an aid worker, falling for the bar's owner, and discussing the appearance of a thing called a *tokolosh*.

And carols. Christmas bloody carols, couldn't escape them, banging on about sleighs and snow. Couldn't escape them.

Furniver waited until the radio news headlines had been listened to and absorbed.

Most of the Harrods' regulars were there. Mildred Kigali was about to meet Didymus, Charity was pottering around, rattling the occasional saucepan, issuing instructions to a couple of Mboya Boys, with Ntoto and Rutere keeping an eye on the new recruits. At last, hoped Furniver, there was a chance of piecing together the events of the night before, and this time, God willing, there would be no interruptions.

"Time to get to the bottom of this *tokolosh* business," said Furniver.

"Charity says that you saw it," said Mildred.

"True," said Furniver, "absolutely true."

His audience looked at him expectantly.

It was now his turn to complete his version of events.

"Not much more, really," he told the listeners at Harrods. "I went to my office to make notes for my speech at around four. No, probably closer to five o'clock. I was supposed to be on parade at seven o'clock. But given that I knew my subject, inflation and so on, I had bags of time . . ."

Bags of time . . . Edward Furniver looked out of his office window, beyond the shacks that were crammed together until his gaze rested on the eucalyptus trees that formed a section of the border which marked the start of the city.

The crows were returning to their roosts, and Furniver followed their flight, fascinated.

When he looked at his watch again, no less than thirteen minutes had passed. A further few minutes were spent checking the pace of the second hand on the clock in the kitchen. He was halfway back to his desk when he spotted the almost-empty packet of biscuits, and nibbled at the last one. For the life of him, he could not remember eating four? Or was it five?

He tapped the title of his talk onto the screen, and wondered whether it should be presented as: By Edward Furniver, MA Oxon.

Or would it be more . . . what was the word Lucy used so often . . . accessible . . . if he called himself Eddie Furniver?

"OK, OK," he said, rubbing the palms of his hands together, "Here we go . . ."

He took a quick peek at his watch. Not quite six, but definitely gin-and-tonic time. He poured a generous tot, drank half of it on the spot, topped it up, and went back to his desk.

"This should be a doddle," he said, and recalled advice that one should always start with a decent joke . . .

But no sooner had Furniver pulled up his office chair, settled in front of the computer, and started to gather his thoughts, than he realised that his preparations for the task were incomplete.

He got up, went to the kitchen, read the sports pages of the *Standard* while waiting for the water to boil for a cup of coffee, and returned to the desk.

"Damn!" he said, getting up again, and returning to the kitchen to collect a chocolate-coated biscuit from the packet he kept in the fridge.

He checked his watch. Still bags of time.

He poured another gin and tonic . . .

An hour later, Furniver just had time to press the print button, grab the pages, and set off for Harrods. He must have nodded off . . .

Once outside, he came within an ace of slipping on what certainly was not mud, if the smell was anything to go by. Furniver reached into his jacket pocket and took out his key-ring. It included an "everlasting" torch, the size of a credit card though slightly thicker, which emitted a blue beam.

"Can see it a mile away," said the assistant at the Tottenham Court Road store.

The noise from within Harrods was growing, and the sound of ululating was becoming positively unnerving. He decided on one last circuit around the bar, and would use the torch to read through the pages of his talk.

Furniver's head had begun to ache. The inspiration from the emergency gin and tonics was evaporating, and his talk no longer seemed as perceptive and witty as it had when he read it on the computer screen.

He stumbled along the path that took him to Ogata, past "Results" Mudenge's clinic, and as Harrods loomed into sight, Furniver held up the pages and focused the tiny torch on the text, trying to make sense of what he saw.

"Start with a decent joke," it said.

The joke was passable. But what followed made little sense . . .

Phrases about the cost of living based on a basket of consumer goods were mixed with attempts to explain the relationship between the price of bananas and the *matatu* fare from Kireba to the city centre. And at intervals throughout the gibberish were variations of his name, from Ted Furniver to Ed Furniver.

Someone – he did not remember doing it himself, though no-one else had been around – had made a diagram of inflation and money supply.

"Oh my God, oh my God, oh my God," he moaned.

Humiliation awaited him.

"Furniver!"

Charity's voice broke through his reverie.

"Are you sleeping? You were telling us what happened last night . . ."

Furniver jerked to attention.

"Where was I . . . oh yes. Bags of time. And so I was reading and checking my speech, just before going into Harrods. Just as I passed the beer crates, you know, behind the kitchen, nearly tripped over this dwarf thing. It let out a hell of a scream. Made the hairs on the back of my neck stand up. I was terrified, don't mind admitting."

His audience made sympathetic noises. Even Charity, ever sceptical about the existence of a *tokolosh*, had no doubt that she had heard an honest account of an extraordinary event.

Like everything else they had heard that day, it had the ring of truth.

"Your turn, Mrs Kigali," said Furniver.

Quite who started the dancing was a moot point, and Mildred was reluctant to take the credit. She was far from sure if that would have been appropriate for someone of her advanced years. To have subtly emerged as the leader of the dancers was another matter, she felt.

One thing had led to another.

"It was the paw-paws," Mildred began, somewhat hesitantly. "Yes, it was the paw-paws," she said, confidently this time.

"Gladwell Sibanda brought two paw-paws, quite small but very sweet, for her membership fee. That we accepted after talking to Charity. Then I went with Sibanda to sign the membership book, which is kept next to the needles of the circle. Sibanda signed."

Mildred nodded her head.

"Yes, Sibanda signed. I will show you . . ."

Mildred was about to get up and collect the membership book, but Charity interrupted.

"Paw-paws, tell us about the paw-paws."

"I have not forgotten the paw-paw business," Mildred said sternly. The new generation, Charity included, was far too impatient. If someone had a good story to tell, it should not be hurried. If a story is worth telling, it is worth telling well. On second thoughts, perhaps she should move on and discuss the paw-paws, for there was a look in Charity's eyes that suggested this was not the time to argue for the values of traditional storytelling.

"Paw-paw business . . ."

A faraway look came over Mildred's face.

"I was remembering the dance in my village, when I was a girl . . ."

There was a warning cough from Charity. For someone of her advancing years, Mildred continued to display an unusually close interest in the initiation rites of adolescents, and unless headed off could discuss them in embarrassing detail.

That, at least, was Charity's view. Mildred, on the other hand, felt that the decline in the practice of initiation and the rise of immorality were connected. She was about to say as much but again there was something in Charity's eyes that told her she would not get very far.

"It reminded me of the initiation dance," she continued. "The needle entered the paw-paw and . . ."

It was Furniver's turn to interrupt.

"Thank you, Mrs Kigali," he said firmly. "We get the picture."

Mildred ignored him.

"And so I was captured by my memories," she said, and looked at Furniver as if defying him to contradict her, "and just as I did as a young girl, I began to dance. Like this . . ."

Mildred got up from the bench where she was sitting, and hitched up her skirt.

She took a turn round the table, moving as easily as a teenager, in a shuffling version of the conga.

She beckoned Charity, and her friend joined in, placing her hands on Mildred's hips and moving behind her in a subtle counter-rhythm.

"And that was how it started," explained Mildred. "We had danced maybe three times around Harrods. Some ladies ululated. It is a very exciting dance," she explained. "Then just as I was finished what in my young days we called the paw-paw dance, there was a cry that was horrible to hear.

"*Tokolosh*!"

The shrill shriek had cut through the hubbub. The dancing ladies had stopped mid-step.

"*Tokolosh*!"

The terror in the cry had been palpable.

34

It was the sheer scale of activity at Kuwisha's nondescript Wilson airport that impressed Japer as he waited while Lucy Gomball completed her briefing for the hacks who would be on the same WorldFeed flight to Lokio.

The airport itself, long supplanted by the international airport built soon after independence, had a cast-off appearance, rather like a World War Two airfield in Britain, with prefabricated huts and a lonely control tower.

Even a coat of paint would have transformed the grubby departure hall, hardly more than a shack, where Japer stood and looked around.

To say that business was booming would have been regarded as bad taste. Nevertheless, the twin pillars of Kuwisha's economy were certainly thriving.

Tourists heading for game parks or the Indian Ocean clambered into small planes that could have been swallowed whole by the huge lumbering giants with UN marked on their sides, attended by an army of workers, and which operated out of the farther away of the two runways.

Land Rovers and mechanical loaders went back and forth between a collection of hangars and huge planes with gaping bellies, as if feeding a gargantuan appetite for sacks of rice, or dried milk powder, or containers of cooking oil marked "Gift from the people of the USA".

Across from the hangars were the offices of the many safari companies that catered for the dreams of an Africa that was exclusive to visitors from abroad.

Japer moved closer, close enough to overhear Lucy's account of the state of the civil war in the neighbouring country that had left hundreds of thousands of civilians dependent on organisations like WorldFeed for shipments of essentials.

As he listened to her briefing, Japer felt he was being seduced by a vast continent, and life in London seemed humdrum by comparison, trivial and inconsequential.

Wild animals and children, Lucy explained, were the innocent victims of the conflict; a conflict that inevitably spilled over into Kuwisha. She described the world of journalists and aid workers, a world in which the sun was African and invariably blazing, the horizon endless, and the rivers infested, usually with crocodiles.

As she warmed to her task the catchphrases and the clichés beloved of the press corps flowed off her tongue. In the world in which they lived and breathed, the players in the stories they filed occupied a region that invariably was hostile, where battles that were distant were fought in towns that were remote. On streets that were dusty, dogs that were mangy chewed on scraps that had been abandoned.

She pulled no punches as she described a civil war that was bitter and brutal and bloody, which cost the lives of hundreds of thousands of civilians who always were innocent.

Lucy described lines that were unending, of refugees who were pitiful, living in scenes that were biblical, carrying possessions that were pathetic, and who were fleeing warlords who were ruthless.

And the cost of the war that created these horrors, the BBC asked?

"About a million dollars a day," said Lucy. "It's time to go."

Japer was about to follow her, when he heard raised voices.

He edged closer to the source. There was little doubt that something not far short of a scuffle had broken out between the correspondent for *The Guardian* and the *Telegraph*'s Africa editor.

The two of them were at the head of the queue for tickets on the flight to Lokio, which this morning was operated by Christians Concerned for Africa.

"It is my turn to buy," said *The Guardian.*

"Absolutely not," said the *Telegraph.* "You bought the tickets when we went on the charter to Kisangani."

Japer listened in, astonished, as back and forth went what seemed to be an exchange about a matter that to an outsider seemed unimportant, yet one that aroused such passion it required the intervention of a *Times* colleague to resolve.

Lucy ushered Japer onto the waiting chartered plane. As soon as he was seated, he took out his notebook from one of the jacket pockets of his safari suit, and started scribbling.

He had heard about the calibre of the Africa correspondents, but what he had seen cast a new light on this particular group.

"In the cut-throat business of journalism, the Africa corps operates like the front-line elite," he wrote. "The quarrels and tensions are kept within their close-knit ranks – women, drinks, personality clashes; and it is hard for an outsider to win their confidence, impossible to persuade them to talk about the stress of reporting on the continent's horrors. But when it comes to paying their way, they are scrupulous to a fault."

In his crumpled cream linen suit and Panama hat, David Podmore cut a figure of some elegance as he stepped out of the High Commission car which had drawn up at the entrance to the departure hall at Wilson airport.

Briefcase in hand, he made straight for Lucy.

"Wish I was going to Lokio, but the High Commissioner needs me here . . . pity, would have loved to have gone." His voice trailed off.

During his three years in Kuwisha, Podmore admitted, he had enjoyed few opportunities to get out from behind his desk, but when he did he relished it. And here, at Wilson, he felt close to the front line in the unending battle against disease and disaster, war and famine waged by the international community.

Unlike some cynics, he was not inclined to bash the foreign aid agencies. By and large, he felt, they did a jolly good job. All things considered. Given the challenges they faced; and the environment in which they worked.

True, some were what he called "a waste of rations". Most, however, did a hard job very well, like the Irish charity he supported, encouraging his many visitors to follow suit. On his office notice-board was pinned a photo of a goat he had sponsored, yellow-eyed, wispy bearded, jaws caught in mid-grind, giving the creature's face a lopsided look.

"No ordinary goat, but an Irish goat," he explained, one of 200 flown to Kuwisha by the charity, and distributed to needy families.

Pearson's response to the suggestion that he paid out the £10 needed to sponsor one of the creatures had been "typical, bloody typical" of the man: "Talk about coals to Newcastle. Africa needs goats from Ireland about as badly as the Sahara needs sand from Darfur."

The diplomat had responded with vigour.

"You think you are so bloody smart. Whoever came up with the idea deserves a medal. Simple, affordable and makes a difference. Makes a hell of a difference, in fact.

"I tell you," he continued, "the look of sheer delight on the faces of African families. With the greatest respect, Pearson, if only your cynicism could be matched by their optimism we would all be better off."

He looked around the departure hall but couldn't spot Pearson. Pity. He would have liked to have seen his reaction to the press release prepared earlier at the High Commission.

Lucy would do instead.

"Nice to have a good news story for a change. All the horrors can get one down." He allowed a look of pain to cross his face, and put on an expression that suggested he had witnessed horrors no man should ever see. "How's it going in Kisangani?"

Ever since Podmore had briefed a British aid minister on a visit to a WorldFeed project in the eastern Zaire town, he presented himself as something of an expert on the trials and tribulations of that part of the world. "If the ceasefire hadn't held . . . Kisangani," he would say, an expression of pain crossing his face, "Kisangani."

"I've got some good news," said Podmore now. "Bit of a scoop," he added.

He gave Lucy a copy of the press release he had prepared.

"Britain will lead the way in a campaign to show the link between saving Kuwisha's endangered rhino and tackling the country's homeless youth. Aid minister Hilary Bland will announce in London today that £5m will be committed to an on-going programme in support of education and conservation.

"Note to editors: Britain will provide a total of £40m through UK and European development initiatives."

"Not exactly generous, is it?" said Lucy, knowing that she was breaking the golden NGO rule about the inadvisability of biting the hand that funded you.

"Five million quid may not seem much to you, Lucy, but it could do a lot on the ground."

"Five million, if they ever got it, would be marvellous, but you're up to your old tricks," said Lucy, wagging a mocking, admonitory finger at Podmore. "It's the old double counting device. You announce a country programme at the start of the aid year, worth forty million in the case of Kuwisha. Then when something crops up, like a famine, or an education appeal, or assisting street kids, or supporting an Aids campaign, you dish out five million here, ten million there – but it is not what we call 'new money'."

Lucy was getting into her stride.

"Result is you get three public relations bangs for your buck. First, when you announce the forty mil programme. Then you get another pat on the back when you support a famine appeal or education project, 'cos most of us, including just about every hack, assume it is in addition to the forty mil the UK originally committed. And then we learn that you've included money from the European Development Fund. All very naughty indeed."

Taken aback by this onslaught, Podmore did his best.

"Strictly off the record . . ."

"Sorry, Dave, I've got to dash," said Lucy.

Although it was a bum-numbing, bone-shaking fifteen-hour journey to Lokio by road, it was a mere thirty-minute hop by plane.

From the air, as the airstrip loomed closer, the camp, with its rondavels around the decent sized swimming pool and a double tennis court alongside, could easily be mistaken for an up-market tourist lodge in the middle of one of Kuwisha's famed animal reserves.

Japer's plane bounced along the grass airstrip and rumbled to a halt next to one of half a dozen warehouses, fenced and patrolled by security guards.

As Japer stepped out of the plane he was greeted with a snappy salute from the driver of a waiting Land Rover.

"Good day to you, suh. I am Isaac."

"And I am Wilberforce, your guide," said a young man smartly dressed in the uniform of the National Park Service. "I can answer your questions."

Both men smiled broadly.

Japer returned the salute, and shook hands with both men.

After coffee and biscuits by the pool next to the office buildings, they set off for the rhino sanctuary.

Now this was really living, Japer decided. Africa was starting to work its magic. There was, after all, something worthwhile in this ambassador for children business – provided, of course, the appointment at the rhino sanctuary, a short drive away, did not turn out to be the ordeal he feared.

35

The Land Rover carrying Japer and Wilberforce was waved to a halt yet again. If the number of police check-points on the road from the landing strip to the rhino sanctuary were any indicator, the vehicles of Kuwisha must surely be among the most frequently checked in the world, Japer thought to himself.

In the space of sixty kilometres there must have been no fewer than three roadblocks. At each one, a well-turned-out policeman circled the car, barking out questions in Swahili to which Isaac, the driver, gave monosyllabic responses. Tyres, brakes, headlamps, rear-view mirror, all came under scrutiny.

Each time Japer went through his routine, explaining that he had come from London, to help the people of Kuwisha.

"The Queen greets you," he said when one inspection seemed unnecessarily rigorous. "I am ambassador for NoseAid," he added.

And each time, after checking the papers for the car and an exchange with Isaac, the police waved them on.

"It's the end of the month," said Isaac.

"Ah," said Japer, "I get it. Car. Licence. Expires. Checking."

"No, no," said Wilberforce. "End of the month. They are hungry . . ."

"Good Lord," said Japer, impressed by the example of hungry policemen who nevertheless gave road safety such a high priority.

Soon they turned off the potholed main road, onto a rutted track.

The Land Rover lurched from side to side, and only Japer's seatbelt prevented his head from hitting the roof.

Potholes and punctures permitting, Wilberforce assured Japer, they would reach the camp, which was home to the rhino the readers of the *Clarion* had adopted, in twenty minutes.

"I assume," said Japer, "that the road is like this because of the poachers?"

"Excuse?" said Isaac.

"The worse the road, the more difficult to get access," Japer suggested. "In this way you can keep the location of the rhino a secret . . ."

Isaac swerved to avoid another pothole.

Wilberforce intervened.

"Politicians," he said, "always chopping, always eating." His hand conveyed invisible food to his mouth, in the ubiquitous gesture that across Africa accompanied the phrase. "Eating," he repeated, "always eating."

"Good God!" said Japer, shocked. "Disgraceful."

Wilberforce pointed to a group of giraffe, and Isaac concentrated on the track ahead. No further words from them seemed necessary. Though they were surprised that their passenger had reacted so strongly to the disclosure of what was common knowledge.

Surely everyone knew that Kuwisha's Department of Parks and Wildlife was rife with sleaze, and notorious for crooked deals in which money intended for road maintenance went on inflated or non-existent contracts, into the pockets of the politicians?

Roads were bad because money was "diverted", as the World Bank would put it. Simple as that. Deliberate neglect of a route in an effort to make sensitive areas of the national parks inaccessible in the hope of protecting vulnerable or endangered species, had nothing to do with it.

Isaac negotiated another pothole.

Just to make sure that he hadn't been misunderstood, Wilberforce repeated both the feeding gesture and the words: "Politicians. Always eating."

He glanced at Japer, who seemed satisfied.

"Absolutely," said Japer. He searched for a pen and notepad in one of his many useful pockets. "Like where I come from. Except they eat cows, not rhinos."

"Like Kuwisha?" said Wilberforce, somewhat uncertainly.

Japer gave a cry of triumph. The notebook and ballpoint pen had been located in a handy pouch, sewn onto his trouser legs. This particular pocket was just above his knee.

"Now tell me about the Masaai," said Japer, pen in hand, notebook open. "At least they don't eat rhino," he chuckled.

Isaac and Wilberforce laughed politely. The man must be mad. Best humour him.

"Can I see Masaai in town?"

"Plenty, plenty," said Wilberforce.

A thought suddenly struck Japer.

"How many rhinos do you have in Kuwisha?"

Wilberforce gave the question careful consideration for some time.

"Many."

Japer made a note.

"So how many is many? Approximately?"

Although Wilberforce had a fair idea, he kept the figure to himself. Depending on the motive of the questioner, the correct answer could be "very few" or "too many". It had to be pitched just right – few enough to keep up a shuttle of concerned visitors from far-off countries who used his services, and not so many that the shuttle would cease as international attention was focused on another African state. True, there was talk of a wave of poaching, not only of rhinos. According to the minister for the Department of Parks and Wildlife, there were at least fifty of the beasts – though the minister of finance thought this estimate was generous. Wherever the truth lay, Wilberforce was determined to keep his head down.

More than his job was worth.

"Plenty," he said.

Had the Land Rover not hit a particularly deep pothole at that moment, Japer would have pursued the matter. As it was, the combination of the jolt, and the answer to his earlier question – the matter-of-fact assertion that politicians as well as poachers were responsible for the plight of Kuwisha's rhinos – distracted him.

They stopped for a coffee break, and Japer took the opportunity to jot down a few ideas.

It was not his job, strictly speaking, to prepare a script for the NoseAid presentation of his visit to Kuwisha, but the excursion into the countryside had emboldened, informed and inspired him. Anyway, the notes could always be used for one of his columns in the *Clarion*.

He started writing: "Deep in the East African bush, reached after a bone-shaking journey along a potholed track, stands one of Kuwisha's magnificent rhinos . . . protected from the predations of poachers and politicians alike.

"Its sheer inaccessibility is a first line of defence against the notorious armed poachers and their cruel search for what they call 'white gold', the beast's fabled horn – in fact a compressed mat of hair.

"But these extraordinary creatures come under attack from a less well-known source . . . Kuwisha's corrupt politicians!

"They love to eat the surprisingly succulent flesh of these ponderous pachyderms . . . beasts that pair for life, and remain attached to their offspring."

He knew he should have checked on the last two facts, but what the heck? It would work wonders with the public, and anything that got them digging deeper into their pockets was surely worthwhile.

The track ran out in a clearing, where there was a wooden palisade, behind which stood a rhino, representative of Kuwisha's endangered population.

All involved played their parts competently. A director commissioned by NoseAid, a young man who had made the award-winning TV ad for Crunchy Peanut Butter and was donating his services free, took charge of proceedings.

Neither beast misbehaved. The rhino had been sedated, the tiny orphan kept his bladder under control, and Japer was not peed on. Japer had taken one look at the infant chosen to represent Kuwisha's new generation and refused point blank to have it on his lap.

Far from causing offence, his refusal to handle the toddler was easily turned to the big-hearted columnist's advantage. The guest from England, it was explained to onlookers, had, the day before his departure from London, been visiting his local children's hospital. He had been warned shortly before his departure for Kuwisha that one of the toddlers he had embraced was displaying the symptoms of measles. It would be safer, the doctor in London had advised, if Japer had no direct contact with children for the next fortnight.

The explanation was greeted by murmurs of appreciation. And when Japer suggested that the massive syringe used on the rhino also be applied to the wide-eyed child he had been expected to cradle in his arms, a sympathetic audience laughed heartily.

The director himself sat with the little boy on his knee. A second photo was taken, this time of Japer looking fondly down on a small sack of coffee beans that he was cradling in his lap. Using computer wizardry it would be a simple matter to transpose the images.

Now it was just a matter of the last lines, and Japer delivered with a passion that surprised him: "So thanks to this partnership, this unique alliance between NoseAid, the *Clarion* – the paper with a heart as big as Africa – the people of Kuwisha, and the World Bank, we can help a child, save a rhino."

"Or help a rhino, save a child," continued Japer. "Or help a rhino save a child." Japer threw his canvas hat on the ground in mock anger.

"Who fooking cares?" he exclaimed, doing a passable imitation of an Irish accent. "Together we can make Kuwisha a better place, for animals and people alike."

It was a wrap.

36

There was an awkward moment when the boys arrived at Mlambo's shelter. He felt obliged to offer his guests something to eat or drink, but the days of sneaking titbits out of the State House kitchen were over. Then he remembered he had a *stompie* under the mattress.

"Would you like to smoke?"

Mlambo lifted his mattress, and retrieved the cigarette stub he had found on the State House drive the day before. He examined it carefully, and taking a razor blade from the same place, trimmed the end, removing the ash and the burnt fibres. He felt under the mattress again and took out a box of matches, made in South Africa. There was one left, and he carefully scraped it against the side.

It flared into life.

He applied it to the *stompie*, made sure the butt was burning and handed it to his guests.

There was enough tobacco for each boy to have a deep drag, sucking the smoke into their lungs, to hold it there for a few seconds, and then slowly exhale.

The ceremony over, Mlambo got down to business.

First, he lifted the mattress once more, took out two silver needles, and pushed them carefully into two small paw-paws on each side of the mattress.

He positioned himself between them, and cleared his throat. His friends sat cross-legged in front of him, and when Rutere had stopped searching for head lice and Ntoto had taken a quick look outside to make sure that no-one was in sight, Mlambo began.

"This is my plan . . ."

Ntoto and Rutere listened intently.

Five minutes later he had finished: ". . . and then, when it is over, I will run to hide at Harrods, if you will help me."

It was a masterful performance. Ntoto and Rutere had been won over. But there was still work to be done, and critical calculations to be made, on which the success the plan depended. It was not yet nightfall, and there was time for a quick recce of the route to the dam.

Mlambo led the way, and pushed aside the branch that concealed a hole in the State House fence. He looked around. The coast was clear. The boys climbed through, examined the stepping stones laid by Mlambo, and then returned to his den, inspecting the surface of the overgrown path.

Laid in the days of British colonial rule, when it was used to get access to what was now little more than a stagnant patch of weed and water, it had survived years of neglect. Mlambo's plan was straightforward, but putting it into practice required split second timing and a clear run.

Mboga, Mlambo told the boys, was due to address the State House staff the next day. This, he stressed, was a regular event. Attendance was compulsory. And it was to be on this occasion that he would be subjected to public humiliation at the hands of Mboga.

"In front of staff," said Mlambo solemnly, "I will be given the name I do not want to say, because it hurts me, and I will lose my family name and no longer be Ferdinand Mhango Mlambo."

"What if he is not there; what if he is with the president?" asked Rutere.

Mlambo shrugged.

"Never has Mboga missed this meeting. But if he cancels, then we try again, next week."

The boys looked again at the distance from the portable

podium – assuming it was placed in the usual position when used by Mboga – to the hedge behind which Mlambo would be hiding. It was thirty-three paces. This was the critical measurement. From the hedge to the edge of a copse, beyond Mlambo's shelter, it was around seventy paces. At this point the overgrown path to the abandoned boathouse started.

A further hundred paces and one emerged from the trees, and it was another fifty paces to the carefully concealed hole in the State House fence, made by Mlambo.

Once through that, there was a curving run that went through the city park, and past the parking lot used by university workers. From there the route followed the road that ran past the Outspan, where the lobby opened onto the pavement.

All three agreed on the distances. Now Ntoto and Rutere needed to know what Mlambo would say to his adversary. What jibes would be used to lure the State House steward? They had to be as tempting to Mboga as a fly to a trout.

Mlambo had given this much thought. And as he recited his script of abuse, Ntoto and Rutere made suggestions which Mlambo promised to consider.

"If Mboga does not chase, he is not a man," said Ntoto, and Rutere nodded in agreement.

Ntoto still needed a question answered.

"What if the security men shoot you?"

Mlambo could not deny this was a risk. But if there was shooting to be done, Mboga would want to do it himself; and if he was really cross, said Mlambo, he would want to break the *toto* with his own hands.

Anyway, only for the first ten paces would the security people have a clear shot – after that trees and buildings would come between them and their target, not to mention onlookers. There was nothing a Kuwisha crowd enjoyed more than watching a cheeky street boy get a good hiding.

Finally Rutere, who had been bottling up the obvious question, gathered the resolve to ask it: "What is to be your new name?"

Mlambo thought carefully, and beckoned Rutere closer. It was a risk, but a risk worth taking. Premature disclosure of a desired new name could prejudice its chances.

He whispered in his friend's ear, who in turn whispered it to Ntoto.

The response could not have been more pleasing.

"Phauw," said Ntoto, echoed by Rutere.

"That is a very fine name, very fine indeed."

Already, it seemed to Mlambo, they looked at him with more respect, and his resolve hardened.

For the last time they explored the path to the outer fence. Rutere, who had been counting the paces aloud, looked worried.

"It will be touching go."

Ntoto nodded.

"Very close. But Mboga is not stupid. If he is not touching go, he will not chase. He must be able to smell Mlambo."

Had the circumstances been less serious, it would have been a signal for ribald exchanges. But such was the gravity of Mlambo's situation that the boys did not smile. Instead Ntoto and Rutere took it in turns to stand downwind of Mlambo, beginning at twenty paces and moving closer, a step at a time, nostrils flared.

They settled on eight paces. As Rutere had rightly noted, it was going to be touch and go.

Before they broke up, Ntoto drew attention to a serious hazard.

"When people see you running" – Ntoto ran on the spot, arms flailing, looking over his shoulder, panting heavily – "people will see a street boy running like a thief. And they will lynch you," he said matter-of-factly.

Mlambo had already thought of this.

The distance across Uhuru Park to the entrance of the Outspan was just less than two hundred paces. And if onlookers took it into their heads to intervene?

"Flying toilets," Mlambo said simply. Rutere could have kicked himself. It was obvious.

There was, however, one more element in Mlambo's plan that concerned both Rutere and Mlambo, and which they had raised earlier with Ntoto.

"You won't forget the . . ."

Mlambo tailed off. It was a matter of some delicacy.

"I will get them," promised Ntoto. "Tomorrow morning. For sure."

"Certain?" asked Mlambo anxiously. The more he thought about exposing himself to the general public, the more uneasy he felt.

"Certain sure, certain sure," replied Ntoto, and with that promise Mlambo had to be satisfied.

Dusk was now falling. There was time for a final check of the first stages of the route from State House to the Outspan Hotel. Mlambo had a last practice run, sliding through the hole he had cut. There was no reason for Ntoto and Rutere to hang around.

Mlambo exchanged the street-boy salutation, making a fist, punching his heart, and meeting the reciprocated gesture in mid-space, first with Rutere and then with Ntoto.

"Don't forget the flying toilets," said Mlambo.

Back in his den, Mlambo whiled away the time, talking to his gran and caressing the needles, their points newly sharpened. He practised throwing them, and discovered that up to five paces he could control their flight, provided he had attached tiny wings of plastic, cut from an abandoned Coke bottle. Any greater distance and there was no guarantee that the needles would hit the target.

After an hour or so of practice, Mlambo covered himself with his blanket, curled up on the mattress and was asleep in minutes.

It was too late for Ntoto and Rutere to make the journey all the way back to Harrods. But they were fortunate. They found a refuse container, full to the brim with rubbish. They climbed in, burrowed halfway down, where the heat generated by the rotting contents helped send them to sleep. Ntoto looked up at the sky, spread like a warm blanket over the city.

"Look, Rutere, look! A star for Christmas! It is good luck, Rutere."

But Cyrus was already lost to the world, his mouth open, and snoring. Within a couple of minutes Ntoto had followed suit.

37

An early morning mist still hung over the dam as Titus Ntoto and Cyrus Rutere set off and made their way via Furniver's flat, where Ntoto returned a packet of sugar Charity had borrowed.

Rutere waited outside, picking a scab on his knee, until Ntoto reappeared, and the boys continued on their way to Mlambo's den, over the stepping stones and through the hole in the fence.

By mid-morning the sun was blazing. Charity looked at the cloudless sky. It looked like it would be one of those hot and breathless Kuwisha days.

"More water, more juice," she ordered the duty Mboya Boys, just as Edward Furniver ambled up with the day's newspapers.

"Don't want to make a thing of it," he said to Charity, "but um, ah, a pair of my, er, smalls, um, underpants is missing," he said. "Do you think . . . ?"

She interrupted him.

"Furniver, if you think that Mr Kigali . . ."

"Absolutely not. Trust the man with my life, let alone my thingies. It was Mr Kigali who told me that one lot was missing. Keeps a sharp eye on the things. Counts them out, counts them in. Ever since that *jipu* business.

"One pair's definitely missing. And the only visitors to the flat have been Ntoto and this chap Mullivant from London. Certainly there when Ntoto came by this morning. Saw them myself. Mr Kigali put them out on the kitchen table."

Charity gave him one of her looks, which struck fear into the heart of the toughest of street boys.

"So, Furniver. You think that Ntoto is a boy who steals underpants."

She raised her eyebrows and waited for him to respond.

"Well, it's either Ntoto or Mullivant. You tell me which one is more likely to be guilty? It's got to be one or the other," said Furniver.

Charity was silent. He was right.

"Say again, Furniver, what happened?"

Patiently and methodically, Furniver went over the events of the past few hours. There was no doubt that there had been only two visitors to the flat. Ntoto, who according to Kigali had been twice, once when Furniver had seen him sobbing, and saying something about wanting to be a pirate, and then early that day, when he returned some sugar.

"That is right," said Charity.

"Well, when I came down this morning to collect the laundry that Mr Kigali had ironed, I noticed that a pair of my, er, smalls was missing. So I asked Mr Kigali . . ."

"My um, smalls, seem to be one short."

He anticipated Kigali's concern.

"Ironed properly . . . Absolutely first rate. No problems there."

Kigali went to the kitchen table, where the freshly ironed shirts, sheets, skirts and trousers were neatly piled. In a separate pile were Furniver's underpants. He counted them.

"Six. Suh."

"There should be seven of the blighters."

"Suh."

Kigali did a weekly wash in the kitchen where he also did the ironing. Furniver would collect the neatly arranged shirts, trousers and socks, together with the underpants, kept in an adjacent pile.

Kigali double checked.

"Six. Suh."

The two men looked at each other. Neither Ntoto nor Mullivant seemed deserving of suspicion.

"The bird that cleans the crocodile's teeth does not defecate in the crocodile's mouth," observed Kigali.

That seemed to rule out Ntoto.

But surely it could not be Mullivant? It seemed unlikely that the UKAID expert might have an unhealthy interest in another chap's underwear.

Kigali kept his counsel. Any dispute between white men was not one that should involve a steward in any way, and woe betide the steward that did not heed this wisdom. After nearly fifty years of domestic service, Didymus Kigali had observed the spectrum of human behaviour, and had encountered many deviations and aberrations. But the thought that a *mzungu* might have an irresistible urge to steal a pair of underpants was somewhat far-fetched.

It was a mystery. The two men had exchanged looks.

"At least they were ironed."

"Suh," said Kigali.

Podmore had been true to his word.

The application form for a minor's travel certificate, valid for only one journey but quicker to obtain than a passport, arrived the day after his conversation with his contact in the Kuwisha Ministry of Foreign Affairs.

Ntoto and Rutere sat down at a table at Harrods, and with Furniver's help, began filling in the form.

"So which of you is going to London? Who is the lucky blighter?"

"Rutere goes," said Ntoto.

"Right . . . when were you born, Rutere?"

Rutere was prepared.

"Four years after the wet season of the great flood, in the month of the first rains, on the day before Ngwazi's return from exile," he replied.

Charity looked up.

"That is foolish, Cyrus Rutere, very foolish. I have taught you your birthday. Now tell Furniver . . ."

"December 23, 1991."

That Rutere, he was a sharp boy, thought Charity. Between them, Ntoto and Rutere were capable of outwitting most adults. Something was afoot. She could not put her finger on it, but something definitely was going on.

Furniver moved on to the next question:

"Now, schools attended – easy enough. None."

Rutere interrupted.

"St Joseph Primary School."

"Rutere, that is simply not so," Charity scolded him. "I know you didn't go to school because your father could not afford the uniform."

"The St Joseph Primary School for Boys," repeated Rutere.

"Really, Rutere? First I heard of it," said Furniver.

St Joseph's was the only state primary school of any merit, and its list of distinguished former pupils was a long one.

"Just when were you there?" asked Furniver.

Rutere fell silent, and Ntoto said nothing.

"You have to tell the truth, you know," said Furniver.

Rutere asked: "Am I stupid, Mr Furniver?"

"Good God, Rutere, certainly not. You're as sharp as a tack."

"Would I have failed at St Joseph?"

"Jolly sure you would have made a good fist of it."

"My father had no money," said Rutere. "But I am a sharp tack with a good fist. So would I have gone to St Joseph if my father had the money?"

"St Joseph it is," Furniver conceded.

A few minutes later all that remained was for the boys to get a passport-size photo of Rutere, clip it to the form, and return it to Podmore. That could be done easily enough at one of the several photo booths in Kireba, and Furniver handed over the *ngwee* required.

Arms folded, Charity said nothing. But those boys were up to some sort of mischief . . .

38

"Mboga!"

The call began in the heart of the overgrown kitchen garden and travelled between the neglected cabbage and carrot beds, crossed the path that led to the disused boathouse, and over the hedge that was the last obstacle before the lawn that led to the French windows of State House.

"Mboga!"

The weekly staff meeting was coming to an end.

Lovemore Mboga gave no sign that he had heard the interruption.

"Mbooogaaa!"

The voice, quavering with tension, came from a young throat, whose owner was concealed behind the hedge.

To address the senior State House steward in this fashion was disrespectful in itself. All but a handful of the assembled staff knew him only as "Senior Steward, suh", and woe betide the forgetful few who left off the "suh". The rest called him "Mr Mboga, suh", and only President Nduka called him "Mr Mboga".

The senior steward continued to read out the final instructions for the week, from the provision of fresh flowers – something the president set great store by – to warning that the consumption of sugar was far in excess of demand. Someone was stealing State House sugar. It had to stop, warned Mboga.

"Mbogaaa!"

The call came once again, gathering in confidence, and this time with an obscenity attached, so crude that the men in the

214

group looked at their feet and the women let out little gasps of dismay.

Even Ntoto and Rutere, who had returned at dawn and had concealed themselves in a mango tree at the point where the path to the old boathouse forked, could not help feeling shocked to hear Mlambo's challenge take to the air.

Beneath their defiance was a respect for authority, and to hear a man who personified that authority treated in this way made their stomachs tense, and left them unsure whether or not to giggle.

"What do you see, Ntoto?" hissed Rutere, perched on one of the branches below his friend.

Ntoto peeked cautiously through the leaves, and described the scene.

"Mlambo is behind the hedge . . . now he is getting close to the gap in the hedge . . ."

"Security," hissed Rutere. "What are security people doing . . ."

"Watching, just watching . . . Mboga is looking, but cannot see . . . oh yes, yes, he is looking now, at Mlambo, who is standing in the opening of the hedge . . ."

The steward had put down his file, left the podium, and walked through the ranks of the assembled staff.

"I see you, Fatboy. I see you."

He turned to the staff. Like a conductor, he orchestrated a chant of "Fatboy! Fatboy! Fatboy!"

As the staff did his bidding, he moved closer to Mlambo.

"Fatboy, you are sick in the head."

"Don't Fatboy me, Mboga," said Mlambo quietly.

He took a step forward, and his bare feet encountered the lawn.

"Are you afraid, Mboga? Do you need your security people? Why are you frightened, Mboga, of a sick *toto* who has Aids?"

Mboga's cruel response sealed his fate.

"You have Aids, Fatboy, because you sleep with your mother and your sisters."

"Mboga, you are just a piece of dog nothing."

Blast! Despite the rehearsal of the night before, he had not got the abuse quite right. Nevertheless, the message was clearly getting through to the State House steward.

Mboga's offensive response overcame any doubts Mlambo had about delivering his final insult, so disgusting that until then he had been far from certain that he could bring himself to employ it.

The steward unbuckled his leather belt, and slapping it against his palm, advanced slowly on Mlambo.

"I see you, Fatboy," he said again, his voice filled with menace. "Fatboy, forever Fatboy."

Mboga repeated the phrase, with various tones of loathing and contempt.

Mlambo stood his ground.

Rutere was beside himself.

"Mlambo must run, very soon! Tell him to run . . ."

The *toto*, trembling, took half a pace forward.

The security staff, who until then had guffawed and taken no action, began to get nervous and started to advance on the boy.

Mlambo had reckoned on this – and he had also reckoned that Mboga would not want to be physically humiliated in front of his underlings.

"Are you afraid, Mboga? Afraid, so you send your security people?"

Mboga started to chatter with rage, and Fatboy knew then that he could get his man.

"Mboga. Don't Fatboy me, never. I can forgive you Mboga, and spare you, only if you give me my name back and call me, in front of every people present, my name – Mzilikazi, which is my new name, Mzilikazi Ferdinand Mhango Mlambo."

"Fatboy, Fatboy, Fatboy," sneered the steward.

Flecks of spittle appeared at the corners of Mboga's mouth.

"Don't Fatboy me, Mboga. Remember, I have thin disease."

The steward continued to slap his belt against the palm of his hand, chanting "Fatboy, Fatboy" as he did so.

Barely the length of a cricket pitch separated the two. Mboga continued to advance. Still Fatboy stood his ground.

"What is happening?" demanded Rutere, his view of events blocked by the intervening hedge.

"Get ready," said Ntoto, "Mboga is close to smelling Mlambo."

He dropped from the tree to the ground, and he and Rutere waited for the shout from Mlambo that would set them running.

Fatboy and Mboga faced each other, both motionless.

Suddenly Mlambo, in one movement, stepped out of his shorts, turned around, touched his toes, and looking at Mboga from between his splayed legs, shouted the obscenity which was to seal the fate of the steward:

"Kiss my arse, Mbogaaaaaa."

A split second later, letting out a shrill scream of terror, Mlambo emerged from the gap in the hedge. His arms and legs pumping, he ran for his life.

Mboga led the pursuing, whooping crowd, belt still in hand.

"Run, run," shrieked Ntoto and Rutere, now alongside their panting friend, but their urging was not needed.

39

Like police motorbike outriders, Ntoto and Rutere ran a few
paces ahead of Mlambo, pursued by a furious Mboga, trailed by
a dozen overweight security staff, and followed by a hollering
and hooting throng of State House domestic staff.

When they reached the State House perimeter fence, Ntoto and
Rutere each pinned back a flap of the wire, leaving a gap through
which Mlambo scrambled a few seconds later, pausing only to
slip on the pair of Furniver's blue underpants many sizes too big
for him.

Ntoto had reduced the waist by knotting one side, and to the
boys' relief, they now fitted Mlambo.

Rutere had been adamant.

"I myself cannot let my friend Mlambo not run across Uhuru
Park to Outspan with his *butumba* showing and his *balubas*
bouncing. Never! Neeever!"

Such public exposure would be so humiliating that neither he
nor Mlambo would be able to commune with their respective
grandmothers again. And what was more, any *mungiki* lurking in
the park would have the opportunity to see whether an Mboya
boy had been circumcised.

"Well done, Ntoto, well done, Mlambo!" shouted Rutere.

So far, so good.

Across the park, past the monument and the water fountain,
they ran, all the way monitored by strategically placed street
boys, equipped with flying toilets. There was less than a hundred
paces to go to the exit when Mlambo let out a wail, and hopping
on one foot, as if he had stood on a thorn, came to a halt.

Mboga redoubled his efforts as the distance between the two shrank.

As Mlambo set off again, Ntoto hugged himself with delight and relief.

The ruse had worked.

"Say what you like," said Japer to no-one in particular, "I know it's a cliché, but they really do have an amazing sense of rhythm."

The return journey from Lokio had been uneventful, and in the few hours to spare before leaving for the airport to catch the overnight flight back to London, he had joined up with a group of delegates and gone shopping in the city market.

About fifty Mboya Boys, several clutching plastic bags, were assembled in the flower section, their reputation and numbers a guarantee that none of the stallholders would dare try to eject them. But there seemed no reason to be alarmed. The boys appeared both drugged and disciplined.

They had entered the market, less than a block from the Outspan Hotel, doing the *toyi-toyi*, the South African protest dance, running on the spot yet inching forward, knees raised as high as their bones and sinews allowed, all the while grunting, deep sounds that came from the solar plexus.

The delegates were thrilled.

As they followed in the boys' wake, heading for the Outspan, cameras popping and videos whirring, Japer provided a running commentary on what they were watching and just who was performing. Some delegates thought it might be a Masaai cattle dance; others suggested they were Samburu performing a fertility ritual.

What was later to be universally and tactfully referred to as "the event" reached its conclusion when the procession reached the hotel lobby. Japer displayed an extraordinarily cool and calm demeanour. Perhaps with good reason, for he had every right to consider himself an old hand. He had, after all, read most of the *Rugged Guide to Kuwisha*, he had seen Kireba for himself, had made the trip to Lokio and survived an encounter with a rhino.

"You really are jolly lucky. We may have bumped into a gang of *moran*, young Masaai warriors, practising one of their ritual dances. Most people go a lifetime without seeing it . . ."

The delegates were impressed, and Japaid hissed in appreciation, saying, "Please wait for camera."

The leader of the delegates bowed to the receptionist, was given his room key, and returned with a tiny digital camera. For the next ten minutes, he and his colleagues filmed enthusiastically, delighted to have the chance to capture raw, untamed Africa in such an incongruous setting.

"I say, be careful with that thing, you could do yourself an injury," exclaimed a delegate, backing away as one of the youths appeared with a needle which he plunged into a paw-paw, time and time again.

At this point, cutting through the hubbub came Japer's cool, measured tones, like a young David Attenborough.

"Samburu – fertility dance," said Japer confidently. He was beginning to enjoy himself. He smirked.

"I think you can guess the significance. The needle represents the thingy, and the paw-paw the wotsit . . ."

But when members of the group tried to leave the lobby, the boys contrived to make it impossible.

Adrian Mullivant turned to Japer and asked him if he would take a picture of him standing next to a "Masaai".

"My turn next," said Japer.

He was now delivering a running commentary.

"Ritual scarring – usually follows the jigjig business.

"Don't leave now," he cautioned DANIDA. "Would be bloody rude. We should feel privileged."

"This," said Mullivant, "is the real Africa – and we are seeing it in the middle of a city!"

Bearing the two knitting needles sticking out of the paws-paws, the dancers circled the tourists, most of whom were beaming with pleasure at their good fortune to have encountered – indeed, almost to be part of – this remarkable ceremony.

One of the boys barked an order. With timing that the president's brigade of guards would have been proud of, the needles were removed from the paw-paws. The boys formed a line, and at that moment it seemed that the dart-like needles had vanished . . .

40

The run that led through Uhuru Park was the stretch that was the easiest for the street boys to protect. The difficult section began when Mlambo emerged from the park, puffing heavily. Just five blocks on the edge of the city centre lay between him and the final showdown with Mboga at the Outspan Hotel.

The traffic hazard was easily resolved. A well-aimed stone from a catapult shattered the traffic lights that regulated cars travelling along Uhuru Highway to the airport. At the end of the road on which the Outspan stood, a *matatu* was hastily abandoned by driver and passengers after a flying toilet had been emptied inside. Within a few moments, a long queue of cars had formed behind it.

At the university opposite the hotel, students needed no encouragement to abandon lecture halls, and gather in the car park, and the police responded in the only way they knew how, cracking the ring leaders over the head with their batons and firing tear gas before retreating under a hail of stones.

There was a further diversion which nearly cost the life of a curious onlooker, when a street boy yelled "Thief! Thief!" and what had been a passive crowd turned into an angry lynch mob.

In the bedlam that ensued, the way was left clear for Mlambo, as he ran through the seedy town centre.

A city that had once had sufficient appeal to claim a day in the schedule of the foreign visitors who visited Kuwisha in their hundreds of thousands each year, had become a place to avoid, and only the ignorant and the foolhardy left the sanctuary of their hotels.

"Never by foot" was the watchword. Instead wise travellers ventured out in taxis, in search of spoils that would provide evidence on return to Europe that they had been to Africa, whether it be a dozen mangoes, with orange-pink flesh that had the consistency of a peach, a soapstone elephant, a carved walking stick, or a woven basket.

On Mlambo ran, past the *dukas*, small family shops whose contents were dominated by tat – plastic wall clocks, nylon socks, cheap watches, calculators made in Taiwan, combs and hand-kerchiefs, Vaseline and other balms, Chinese-made bric-a-brac, rough blankets, hair pomade, and the tinniest of radios – staffed by father, sitting in one gloomy corner, assisted by son who checked the stock, and employing a single black man who in between serving the customers and keeping a sharp look-out for shop-lifters, made tea and collected the post and raised and lowered the steel grille or roll-up shutters at the start and the end of the day.

Outside the hotel, as the noise of the chase got louder, sounding like angry bees, a crowd of the curious formed: taxi drivers, messengers, bar stewards and table waiters. The expatriate hotel manager moved through their ranks. Time to move them on.

From inside, the belly grunts of the dancing children took on a hypnotic note, and one by one the delegates joined in, over-coming any initial unease, grunting in counter-rhythm, arms around the shoulders of the teenagers.

There was a sudden shout, a shrill sound that came from Ntoto, as he and Rutere peeled away from the fast approaching bunch of runners, allowing Mlambo to keep sprinting through the onlookers, into the hotel lobby, and into the protective circle of *toyi-toyi*-ing street boys.

Although this scene had not appeared in the guidebook, Japer kept his nerve.

"Obviously, enacting a hunt," he explained, and any nervous delegates felt reassured.

"Little bastards," said the manager. "Clear off, show finished, thank you, very good."

Someone in hotel security would pay for this.

Casually, deliberately, an Mboya Boy thrust his hand into one of the plastic bags, withdrew it, and flicked something at him. It landed just above the pocket of his jacket. The manager brushed it off, and then raised his fingers to his nose. He recoiled.

Japer looked around desperately for Adrian Mullivant. Spotting him, he gestured across the room and indicated that he was ready to have his photo taken. A big lad seemed to have taken over the proceedings.

As planned, the confrontation between Mboga and Mlambo took place in the hotel lobby.

It did not take long. The dancing boys continued to grunt. The steward, panting with anger and exhaustion, seemed barely aware of his surroundings. He gasped over the heads of the stomping children.

"Fatboy, Fatboy, Fatboy!"

Saliva began to drool from the corners of his mouth, and his eyes were glazed in fury.

"Don't Fatboy me, Mboga," said Mlambo breathing heavily. "What is my name?"

"Fatboy!" screamed the steward. "Always, forever, Fatboy!"

Mlambo held out his hands, like a surgeon in an operating theatre, and kept his eyes on Mboga. Ntoto and Rutere each slapped a sharpened knitting needle, with the dart-like fins which had been attached the night before, onto his open palms.

With a high-pitched wail, and right hand to left, left hand to right, Mlambo plunged the needles into his bare chest. Blood spurted out.

The street boys moved aside, leaving the boy with a clear shot.

Before Mboga could react, or grasp the nature of his danger, Mlambo threw the first needle at the State House steward.

"Hold on a mo! I want my photo . . ."

Japer's intervention undoubtedly saved Mboga from the first needle. It missed the steward by inches, just as Japer grasped Mboga's arm with one hand while trying to attract the attention of Mullivant and his camera with the other.

"Now, take it now," he cried, just before the needle sank into his upper right arm.

Mlambo coolly took fresh aim, and let fly with the second, which found its mark, like a dart in a bull, in Mboga's chest.

"Run, Mlambo, run," shouted Ntoto and Rutere as the ranks of onlooking street boys parted and closed behind the former kitchen *toto*. Their urging was not needed, and Mlambo made his getaway without obstruction. No-one was prepared to risk being hit with the contents of those plastic bags; and no-one wanted to risk the plague called HIV-Aids.

The trio had agreed to meet on the roof of Harrods. Ntoto was the first to arrive, followed by Rutere, and a few minutes later Mlambo, still panting.

"You are an outlaw," said Rutere.

Mlambo shrugged.

Ntoto reappeared, clutching a brown paper bag, a half-full bottle of Coke, a twist of *mbang*, a half litre of *changa*, and three fried chicken necks. And for the next thirty minutes they ate and drank and sniffed glue, and laughed as Mlambo retold his tale.

Smoke drifted across the rubbish dump, and a dog scavenged nearby. Below them customers crammed inside, discussing the matters of the day – the rising cost of school fees, the cost of living. Every now and then came a mention of the *tokolosh*, but the story was rapidly losing its appeal. The ring road was more important . . .

Drunk with triumph as much as with *changa*, the trio began to dance, arms interlocked. Silhouetted against a moon that was close to full, they shouted their defiance of the world outside Kireba, and chanted: "Kiss the arse, Mboga, kiss the arse of Mzilikazi Ferdinand Mhango Mlambo."

41

Lucy felt feverish, a bout of malaria perhaps, and she took to her bed, grateful for Pearson's concerned presence. They had the house to themselves. The Nomads had left on the evening flight to London and the Pastoralists, who were off to Lokio at dawn the next day, were already abed and asleep.

The *FN*'s foreign desk had rung Pearson on his mobile. They were asking for an analysis of recent events in Kuwisha in 500 words, from Hardwicke's dramatic speech to rhino aid and the unfortunate fracas involving street boys and the NoseAid ambassador.

Pearson had brought his laptop into Lucy's room, and had drafted the story at her desk. The computerised filing facility didn't seem to be working, no doubt because of rain, and he was now put through to the *FN*'s last remaining copytaker to dictate the copy.

Before he started, they exchanged observations about the weather in Kuwisha and London, and when these courtesies were done, Pearson got down to business.

As Lucy drifted in and out of sleep, phrases from his dictation floated into her consciousness, and periods of lucidity were interspersed with her own fever-driven imaginings.

"Geoffrey Japer . . . Agonising time . . . brings home . . . millions dead, modern plague . . . street boys victims . . . corruption a cancer . . . NoseAid . . . rhino relief . . .

"Land of contrasts . . . hungry majority . . . cavorting Kuwisha cowboys snort cocaine . . . rolling acres, tea, coffee, as eye can see Green lawns Outspan Hotel, Thumaiga Club, shrubs, hibiscus, fresh flowers, leather armchairs, deferential servants, silence please, gin and tonics, make a fortune, market rates, old buffers dying breed . . . sunset Africa glorious, Rift Valley, *White Mischief*, Happy Valley, ancient hunger, yearning, loins swelling, heat, rains, red earth steaming, did she do it, are you married or do you live in Kuwisha . . . noble spear-propped Masaai guards, blah blah blah, cowboys languid, arrogant yah, perched high four-wheel drive yah, flicks hair, cripples begging . . . Girlfriends blonde, tanned yah, back at carnivore lion's liver, yum, sniffing coke, taking dope yah, Mombasa Gold and golden beaches, blah blah blah

"Third generation Kuwisha now, upper classes, trips abroad, lotus-eating artists' colony, beads, south coast, north coast, beach, white sand, blah blah, exhibitions, divorces, street boys sniffing glue, potholes, raining, sewers overflowing, President Nduka, blah, corruption, elephants' ivory, white tribe, time warp, gin, cocaine, once more, again.

"Blah!

"Read that last sentence back, please," said Pearson, and after a further exchange about the weather, ended the call.

"Get in," said Lucy.

"No," said Pearson. "It's the malaria talking."

"Love you," she mumbled.

"How much?" asked Pearson.

But Lucy was already asleep.

It had been a quiet meal, not the silence of companionship but the silence of a couple under strain. Finally Charity could stand it no longer – though the consequence of confirmation would break her heart. She reached into her apron pocket, pulled out the bottle which she had found in his briefcase, and said simply: "Furniver, why!" Open and frank, Furniver had decided, that was the best policy. He looked her in the eye, and made a clean breast of things.

"Every bloody morning, front of the mirror, less and less, each day."

Charity was baffled. What on earth was the man on about? Surely he couldn't be talking about another *jipu?*

"Finally I went and had a word with 'Results' Mudenge."

Furniver gestured towards the half-full bottle.

"Followed instructions. To the letter. Rubbed it in, massaged the old scalp, whenever I could. Been using it regularly. Notice any, um, difference?" he asked hopefully.

Charity could have wept with relief. Instead she hugged him.

"You don't mind?"

His heart leapt when he heard her say: "Make me a happy woman, Furniver . . ."

And then sank, as she continued: "Let me get your money back from that skellum, Mr Clarence 'Results' Mudenge. Results indeed! There is nothing wrong with your hair."

She ran her hand over his thinning locks.

"Anyway," she chuckled, "it is longer than mine, even."

Furniver blushed.

"Furniver," she declared, "please, I am sorry for not trusting you . . ."

"Potholes," said Furniver, "just potholes, not a road-block, old thing."

For a moment, Charity was baffled.

"What? What? Beg pardon?"

And then she remembered.

It was a reference to a prayer, written by her late husband, intended for the street children as well as parishioners, which she had once read to Furniver.

To her surprise, he took her hands in his, and began:

"When you rise, each day at dawn,
Praise the Lord for this fresh morn.
And keep in mind these lessons few,
This way you will your soul renew:
Look both ways crossing street . . .

The lines, banal though they were, always made her eyes prick with tears. She joined in, and together they recited the last few couplets:

"Or else you could your Maker meet!
Don't overtake on corners blind,
Keep sharp lookout for who's behind!
Wear your seatbelt, check your tyres;
Tell the truth, for God shuns liars.
And on the potholed road of life,
Respect the vows of man and wife!
Now clean your teeth, wash your face!
May you stay safe in our Lord's embrace."

Charity hooted with laughter when Furniver, screwing up his courage, had told her about his own fears.

"Never naked! Really, Furniver! Yes, I say no steamies, never before marriage. Never! But after?"

She winked, hugely and lewdly, and Furniver blushed to the very roots of his thinning hair.

As Ntoto was quick to acknowledge, Rutere had been absolutely spot on in his suggestion as to how the airport departure should be handled.

Needless to say, neither boy had any experience of airport departure formalities, or flying. For Ntoto this was all the more reason for turning up early, even if it meant waiting. But Rutere did not agree.

"We must arrive nearly late," he insisted. "Otherwise there is too much time for checking. You must think like an exchange boy. Don't give the customer time to check. You say quick, quick, police are coming!"

Both Charity and Furniver had wanted to come out to the airport to wave farewell, but when the boys had looked so uncomfortable at the prospect they settled for a hug and a handshake which left Rutere mightily embarrassed.

At the airport on the evening of the departure, Rutere and Ntoto and Mlambo peeked through the glass wall opposite the BA check-in. The boys could see Podmore was waiting at the counter, as promised, looking increasingly anxious.

As the check-in line grew shorter, and the last call for the flight to London came over the public address system, his agitation became more apparent.

He walked nervously back and forth, looking at his watch, clutching documents with one hand, an overnight bag in the other.

Rutere, who had grown quiet as Podmore became more agitated, said quietly: "It is time to go."

The three boys huddled together.

Good luck wishes were exchanged.

"Don't forget to be a geography boy," said Ntoto.

"Let me test you quickly," he said, playing the part of the foreign tourist: 'My sister, she is a student in Manchester.'"

"'Welcome to Kuwisha, suh. Phauw! In Manchester? My brother lives in Manchester. If you lend me 100 *ngwee*, he can repay you.'"

"'I will be in Manchester and I will visit her.'"

Despite the tension, the boys laughed.

Ntoto watched through the window. His friend was dressed in jeans and shirt, with shoes, all new, donated by the British newspaper. His heart beat faster.

Podmore gestured angrily as the Mboya Boy, who had decided to carry his shoes, approached. A BA steward came up and pointed to his watch. Podmore took his ward to the check-in desk, still gesturing. Then to the onlookers' enormous relief, together they went through the gate to the departure lounge.

It had gone just as Cyrus Rutere had predicted.

That Rutere, thought Ntoto, as two exhausted boys fell asleep in an abandoned waste container, that Rutere was certainly very intelligent.

42

The NoseAid Fundfest was, as always, a great success. Several careers were saved, many were extended, revived or – as in the case of Geoffrey Japer – enhanced. His plea, made live at peak time on national television, had been eloquent and persuasive.

If he had seemed subdued, or preoccupied, it was put down to his heavy workload and his newly discovered passion for the welfare of Africa, and the burden of responsibility for its recovery he and other like-minded celebrities now carried.

Above all, he awaited the outcome of an Aids test following what the *Clarion* called "a brush with death".

Japer had become something of a national hero, thanks to a photo that had taken up most of the paper's front page. It showed his hand tugging Mboga out of the path of a dart-like needle, a split second after he had shouted a warning, and just before he interposed his body between the man whom the paper identified as the Outspan's head waiter, and a gang of street children who had been rehearsing a Masaai initiation ceremony that had got out of hand.

On the night of the marathon Fundfest, the hit of the evening was a street boy from Kuwisha. Introduced as Pius Makuru, the lad's face seemed vaguely familiar to Japer.

"Haven't I seen you before?"

"My brother, suh. Works as kitchen *toto* at Outspan, suh. He greets you, suh," replied Pius.

Podmore's walk-on part, given in appreciation of his help, was a well-deserved reward. Getting the travel document ready in time had, he told the audience, been a damn close thing. The photo of Pius Makuru had arrived at the last minute. Were it not for the diplomat's good offices and the personal guarantee of the *Clarion*'s editor, the document would have been ready too late . . .

As Podmore left the stage, he raised a clenched fist in the air: "Save a rhino, save a child . . ."

Japer himself had a decent voice, in fact a pleasing baritone, and together the NoseAid ambassador and the boy from Kireba sang their hearts out.

Led by Pius, his angelic face caught in a single spotlight, and joined after the opening couplet by Japer, looking uncharacteristically solemn, the duo moved the heart of the nation; and the entire cast of pop stars, celebs, wannabes, has-beens and newsreaders, joined in a rousing finale to the evening:

> "Together, together we stand
> United, all children demand.
> Together, under one sky
> United, we join in this cry –
> Help children like me,
> Let rhinos range free,
> Forgive debt that we owe
> So we all can grow;
> And each builds a home
> And let rhinos roam
> Together, united we plead
> Together, help meet our need."

Overnight their song became a best-seller and NoseAid's national anthem.

Did Japer really rescue an innocent head waiter from "a crazed Masaai mob", as the *Clarion*'s story claimed? Who cares?

The readers of the *Clarion* will never know, nor does it matter. The brash tabloid, voted newspaper of the year, has launched a new appeal – Toys for African Tots. And there is a new competition, in which the winner is the entrant who gets closest to answering the question: How many stamps were originally stuck to Phoebe's delightful frame?

Japer's relief at the outcome of the Aids test was overwhelming.

"Such a little prick," he said, "I hardly felt it."

His doctor tried to make a joke of it:

"That's what all the girls say."

"And if I haven't got it, nor has that Boga chap?"

"If he has, he didn't get it from the needle."

"And the boy? The one who threw it?"

"Can't be sure."

The doctor, who together with his young family had watched NoseNight, walked Japer to the door.

"What an evening," said the doctor, "what an evening. As for Pius, that boy really can sing."

"Big lad, isn't he?" said Japer. "Wants to be a footballer. Told me after the show. We got talking about this and that, about our families and so on. I told him about my sister, who lives in Dulwich.

"Turned out that young Pius has a cousin who's a student at some technical college nearby. Apparently this cousin is having difficulties raising the fees, so I gave Pius a few quid to pass on. Amazing thing, you know, Africa and the extended family business. But what a coincidence!"

This time the postcard arrived within days: "Greetings from London", it read, and was signed simply: "Ferdinand".

It was time to celebrate their stunning victory over Mboga with a few cups from their latest batch of *changa*.

"It is fresh," said Rutere proudly, "fresh, like Mrs Charity's food."

Altogether it was enough to make the boys light-headed.

The establishment would pursue them, of course, but the forces of law and order would enter the maze that was Kireba at their peril.

"To Mlambo," said Ntoto, taking a swig from the plastic container which he then passed to Rutere.

"Mlambo," said Rutere, and gulped down the remaining mouthfuls.

The persistent ring-ring of the old telephone in the hall of Lucy's bungalow forced Pearson awake, and he stumbled down the corridor, bath towel wrapped around his waist.

He picked up the receiver.

"Good morning, Pearson."

The cheery tones of the president's press secretary turned Cecil's bowels to water.

Early morning calls seldom brought good news in Kuwisha.

"Have you seen the papers?" asked Punabantu.

"Hold on a mo," said Pearson, "they should have arrived . . ."

"Just read them, Pearson, read them carefully. When do you go back to London?"

"Tomorrow night."

"Good," said Puna, "very good."

"I'll ring back as soon as I have had a look . . ."

Punabantu interrupted him.

"No need. Just read."

He rang off.

The stone floor of the kitchen was cold under his bare feet as Cecil unlocked the back door and picked up the day's newspapers from the box in which the security guard placed them every morning.

Just then, Lucy's steward came in to prepare tea, and Pearson took the papers into the living room.

Ill-health and old age were taking their toll on the Ngwazi, who had already indicated that he would step down before his term was complete. But he continued to circle above the Kuwisha political arena, like a hawk eyeing chickens on the ground, occasionally swooping on an unsuspecting bird.

"Crack-down on Forex Deals", read the headline in the *Daily Times*. "President Promises Currency Probe". "NGOs and Ex-pats to be Quizzed".

Pearson read on. Newman Kibwana, "high-flying permsec" who was still in London after his appearance on the NoseAid Fundfest, had been recalled for "urgent consultations", said the papers.

Across town at Harrods International Bar (and Nightspot) Charity Mupanga took a sip of her early morning tea, and read extracts from the newspaper to a distressed Mildred Kigali, dwelling on one story in particular: "Kireba newtown given OK".

She remembered Furniver's quip after President Nduka had reshuffled his cabinet: "What do you get when you shake a can of worms?".

"Dizzy worms," muttered Charity, "dizzy worms."

At least the new toilet, designed in Zimbabwe, was working.

43

News travelled fast in Kireba, and word of Mlambo's arrival in London had already reached Charity. At first her reaction was one of outrage. The boys had cheated, as far as she was concerned. Perhaps Mildred had been right. They should have been given up to the Lambs, after a sound talking-to behind the *kia*.

Furniver, however, had taken a different view.

"Smart little buggers," he said. "The next thing we'll hear is that Mlambo has been signed up by Arsenal."

Charity said nothing.

"We have got to be realistic, my dear. And you have to save your anger for the big issues – such as the Kireba housing scheme. Get Ntoto on your side on that one, and there is a chance of stopping it."

Her hopes that Ntoto and Rutere would go to school were a pipe dream. "A waste of hot air," as Mildred had said. Charity reluctantly agreed.

On the far side of the slum, well beyond Ogata's funeral parlour, a boy emerged. Even at a distance, Charity identified him.

She watched as Ntoto made his way to Harrods, across the sludge, hands in his pockets, glue apparatus dangling from his neck. She knew he would now be courted by politicians, for it was within an area boy's power to deliver the Kireba vote.

He looked up, spotted her, and for a split second his face was creased with a smile, a beam that warmed her heart.

Once he reached the bar, however, he became taciturn. Ntoto disappeared behind the counter, and crawled into the space that he and Rutere had created for themselves.

Charity had made a point of treating it as their private den, and had never looked inside; and when Mildred had tried to do so, she had been defeated by the ripe, rich odour of street boy.

Mildred had banged her head on the bar counter when she recoiled in disgust, and had been quite cross when Charity said it was her own fault for parking her nose where it was not wanted.

Ntoto was there longer than Charity had expected, and she was reluctant to intrude. But she assumed he had gone to the suitcase she had given him and Rutere.

The rustle of paper suggested that he was sorting through his possessions.

She knew, because he had once shown them to her, that they included birthday cards sent to him by Charity and Furniver, pictures of Nelson Mandela, Desmond Tutu, Tom Mboya, the Kenyan trade unionist who was assassinated, and a photo of Robert Mugabe, all cut out from local papers.

She left him to it, and busied herself in the kitchen.

Then he called out.

It was time to talk.

"Thank you to Furniver."

"I will say you thanked him," she said. Furniver had offered to pay the school fees of Ntoto and Rutere, but the offer was turned down. No jobs, said Ntoto, and who could deny it?

"Furniver will be here soon," Charity added.

Ntoto looked down at his bare feet.

He muttered something, and Charity moved closer, and asked him to repeat it.

"Beg pardon," she said.

His face seemed more mature, gave less away, and Charity realised it was becoming a hard face.

Ntoto looked at his feet.

"I have decided," he said. "I am to be the area boy," a mix of defiance, pride and resignation in his voice.

She winced.

"I know. The truth is, Ntoto . . ." Charity began, and then abruptly stopped. Who could say what was the truth of this matter?

Stick to the facts. She could hear her late husband, as clearly as if he were by her side. Bishop David Mupanga had always distinguished between the two, between facts and truth. Facts were essential to truth, but truth? Often truth could be more than the sum of the facts.

She would stick to the facts. So she stood silent, saying nothing. Once again she felt she was living in a dream, a dream without noise. So many of the people around her in Kireba seemed always to be sleeping, or dozing; and moved with agonising slowness. At first she thought it was bilharzia, or malaria. Then she had realised it was worse. It was Aids, and it was sapping the vitality of Africa, draining the life from a continent that already was getting poorer while the rest of the world was getting richer.

Charity delved under the counter, and produced a cardboard box.

She handed it to Ntoto.

"Dough balls?"

She was about to respond, indignantly, when she realised he was joking.

He unwrapped the package, and took out the contents.

"Phauw!"

A pair of shoes. New! Well, as good as new, anyway. The cobbler had guaranteed that the replaced soles would outlast the rest of the shoe leather, and Didymus Kigali himself had spent the best part of half an hour, polishing, shining and buffing until they gleamed like the feathers of a crow that had just preened itself.

Ntoto looked at his feet.

"I am now a proper area boy."

He did not smile.

Charity wanted to weep. Her vision blurred. She intended to pat the boy on the head, and found herself patting his shoulder. He had grown . . .

They formally shook hands. If there had been a demonstrative gesture of affection, Charity knew she would have cried.

"Good luck, Ntoto."

Ntoto tried the shoes on, nodded, and took them off.

He tied the laces together, and slung them around his neck.

Just then a breathless Furniver turned up, and handed over a manila envelope. Not only was a membership card for the Kireba People's Co-operative Bank enclosed ("Refundable deposit 500 *ngwee*"), complete with a photo of Ntoto, but the card registered a credit of 5,000 *ngwee*.

Furniver launched into an explanation of short- and long-term interest rates, which Charity felt obliged to interrupt.

Ntoto turned away abruptly, and set off down the track that led to the railway line.

Charity called after him:

"Bye-bye, Ntoto . . ."

No response.

Again: "Bye-bye . . ."

Still no response.

Suddenly, spontaneously, she called out: "Ack-ack!"

Still he kept walking.

She called out again, for the last time. He would soon be out of earshot: "Ack-ack!"

"Good luck, Ntoto!" cried Furniver.

They watched, as Ntoto, a teenager who had never known youth, set off on his way to the *matatu* stop, about a hundred yards distant.

Suddenly the boy stopped, and bent down.

She saw that he was putting on the shoes.

At first she thought he was dancing, doing the *toyi-toyi*. It was Furniver who was the first to realise just what Ntoto was doing.

"An aeroplane . . . the boy is an aeroplane."

Then Ntoto extended his arms, one hand closed into a fist. No, no, he was wrong. It was not a fist, but a microphone. Captain Ntoto was reporting to base, awaiting clearance from traffic control.

"Of course! He's a pilot! The boy wants to be a pilot. And here I am, thinking that he wanted to be a pirate . . ."

Charity took his hand.

Ntoto pranced like a young gazelle, along the muddy track that was parallel to the railway line that formed the western border of Kireba.

Then he stopped.

For half a minute, his knees rising, higher and higher, he built up power, containing the thrust of the Rolls-Royce engines that would propel him through the sky. The noise reached a crescendo, and with the perfect timing born of years of training, he gave the plane its head. His words carried in the breeze that came up most afternoons, and they could hear the boy, a teenager for the last time, announce: "Welcome on your flight to Rondon, England. This is your pilot speaking, Captain Odhiambo Titus Ntoto. With Vice-Captain Cyrus Rutere, Senior Engineer Ferdinand Mlambo and Chief Steward Bright Khumalo . . ." And as he spoke, Captain Ntoto pulled back on the joystick, and the great silver machine soared into the sky and waggled its wings in salute as it cut ties with Earth.

EPILOGUE

The Oldest Member's car pulled up. Furniver's chats with the OM over a couple of gin and tonics had become a regular part of his life, and each time the OM drove Furniver back to Kireba, stopping as close to Harrods as he could get. From here on Furniver would have to walk. The OM had done most of the talking during the twenty minute drive. The lights from Harrods shone out, like an oasis of light in a sea of darkness.

A duty Mboya Boy, summoned to escort Furniver via the bar's mobile phone, loomed out of the shadows.

"The *matatu*, it is waiting and ready, suh."

Furniver unlocked the passenger door, climbed out, and shook the OM's hand through the open window.

"Africa. Don't get so worried, young man. Relax. It will work out. A hundred years, and you won't recognise the place."

He reversed the car.

"But then I am an optimist," he added.

Furniver looked closely but the light from the car's dashboard was faint, and it was impossible to see if the OM was joking.

The evening flight to London flew overhead.

Charity was waiting for him, standing patiently beside the *matatu* that would take them to the *shamba*.

She gave him a welcoming hug, but there was something that she wanted to do before they set off.

Clarence Mudenge deserved a piece of her mind.

Furniver trailed reluctantly behind her. When she was in this mood, there was no stopping her. The beam from his spare torch guided them across the filthy rivulet, as they stepped on stones laid by a team of Mboya Boys, and followed the muddy path to the Klean Blood Klinic.

An oil lamp was burning, and "Results" Mudenge, who seldom went to bed before midnight, was reading yesterday's paper.

He stood up as they approached.

"Welcome."

"Good evening, Mr Mudenge," said Charity. "I am here, with my friend Furniver. He has had business with you."

Mudenge gave Furniver a friendly nod.

"Furniver," she ordered, "show Mr Mudenge your head."

"Do we have to do this now, my dear?" he asked plaintively.

His protests were in vain.

Clarence Mudenge examined Furniver's scalp, and carefully parted the banker's hair.

"I cannot see head lice, but I have *muti* . . ."

Charity interrupted with a bark of triumph.

"You are too clever, Mr Mudenge. His hair! What about his hair!"

Mudenge frowned.

A man's hair was a private matter.

"Is his hair growing?" Charity demanded. "Is it longer, Mr Mudenge, or shorter? Is there more, or is there less?"

He whispered in her ear.

"Furniver, I think he is going bald . . ."

"Ehehe!"

Triumphantly, Charity held out her hand.

"So, Mr Clarence Mudenge," and pointed at the sign above the shack.

"Clarence Mudenge: Proprietor, Klean Blood Klinic. Results or Money Back", she read out.

"Haugh!" she barked scornfully. "No results for Furniver! So money back!"

Furniver did not know where to look.

"Return Furniver's *ngwee*, Clarence Mudenge."

Mudenge pulled out a handful of grubby notes.

"Before I give you this money, I have one question," he said, and turned to Furniver: "Are you happy, Mr Edward?"

Furniver looked at Charity . . . those teeth! That smile!

The truth was that he was happier than he had ever been.

He squeezed her hand.

"Absolutely, er, happy, yes. Definitely."

"And are you happy, Mrs Charity Mupanga?"

She was about to insist on the money, but the question made her think again, and take stock. And as she did so, she realised that she was in danger of forgetting the very blessings she counted so assiduously each day.

Furniver kept her hand in his, and she felt his forefinger curl around hers. And with a rush that made her chest tight, she remembered what it was about him that appealed to her, and won her heart. Many things about him she enjoyed, but there was one thing in particular.

He had faith in the future. They both believed that tomorrow would surely be better than today.

"Yes, Clarence Mudenge, I am happy."

Clarence Mudenge returned the *ngwee* to his wallet as his visitors made their way back to their waiting car.

They slammed the boot, now packed with weekend provisions, and squeezed into the *matatu*.

Charity broke the silence with a chuckle that made her body shake.

"That Clarence Mudenge, he is too clever."

Furniver kissed her on the cheek.

"Results, my dear. He gets results."

MICHAEL HOLMAN

Africa has been his life. Brought up in Rhodesia (now Zimbabwe), his opposition to minority rule led to his arrest in 1967 and a one-year restriction order. Allowed to take up a postgraduate place at Edinburgh University, he returned to Rhodesia in 1971, where he worked as a journalist, and left illegally in 1976 after refusing to do military service. From 1977 to 1984 he was based in Lusaka, Zambia, reporting on Africa for the *Financial Times*, before moving to London in 1984 to take up the position of the newspaper's Africa editor.

In 2002 he took early retirement to write books. His first novel, *Last Orders at Harrods*, was published in 2005, and was republished by Abacus in Spring 2007. He now lives in London, and continues to travel frequently to Africa, in particular to east Africa, where his novels are set.